Praise for *Sex and Sunsets*

"A jolly book."
—Edward Abbey

"Kelly is full-tilt gonzo crazy. But crazy people can make good protagonists, particularly when they narrate in their own uniquely whacked-out voice."
—*The Atlanta Journal-Constitution*

"I loved Kelly, someone who is obsessed with something and willing to go to any lengths to accomplish this goal."
—W. P. Kinsella

"Compelling . . . Sandlin tells his story with a poker-player's shrewdness and a cattle-roper's dexterity, catching readers between their sympathy for Palamino and a suspicion that he is one cowboy who's definitely had a tad too much loco weed."
—*The Oregonian*

"Sandlin is a powerful writer . . . *Sex and Sunsets* is a funny book."
—*The Pittsburgh Press*

"Mr. Sandlin brilliantly and knowingly captures the spirit of the Wyoming wilderness." —*New York Times Book Review*

"A celebration of tenacious spirits . . . about running into the sun and keeping on, with humor, passion, and faith."
—*Los Angeles Times Book Review*

"Tim Sandlin writes about crazy people. Not scary crazies, but the kind of interesting, funny eccentrics with whom the reader would like to spend an evening drinking beer . . . *Western Swing* is funny, wise and a bubbling joy to read."
—*Kansas City Star*

"Tim Sandlin never forgets that he is a storyteller, and an exceptionally entertaining one. He writes with humor and a cheerful energy that keeps the narrative going at breakneck speed . . . *Western Swing* is a spirited novel of love and loss, and Loren and Lana Sue are genuine modern-day folk heroes."
—*The Toronto Globe & Mail*

"Droll and high-spirited . . . Two vividly sympathetic characters whose adventures have something of the grit and pathos of a funky country-and-western ballad." —*Publishers Weekly*

"Ongoing life is what this book is all about. . . . Sandlin's voice is a wry mix of cynicism and innocence. Add to that a well-developed sense of the bizarre, and you have a book that's fun to read, brimming with high-spirited zaniness."
—*St. Louis Post-Dispatch*

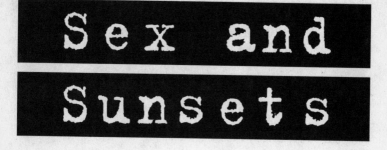

Sex and Sunsets

TiM SANDLiN

Riverhead Books,
New York

Babe Stovall was a blues singer in New Orleans in the late 1960s and early 1970s. Everyone else in this book came straight from my imagination. The characters are in no way connected to anyone who is or has ever been real. To think otherwise would be impolite.

Riverhead Books
Published by The Berkley Publishing Group
200 Madison Avenue
New York, New York 10016, a member of Penguin Putnam Inc.

Copyright © 1987 by Tim Sandlin
Cover design by Marc Cohen
Cover photograph of man and daisy: Tom Rafalovich, Winston West

Reprinted by arrangement with Henry Holt & Company, Inc.
Henry Holt & Company edition published in 1987
First Riverhead trade paperback edition: September 1997

The Putnam Berkley World Wide Web site address is
http://www.berkley.com

Library of Congress Cataloging-in-Publication Data

Sandlin, Tim.
  [Sex & sunsets]
  Sex and sunsets / Tim Sandlin.—1st Riverhead trade pbk. ed.
    p. cm.
  Originally published: Sex & sunsets. New York : H. Holt, © 1987.
  ISBN 1-57322-628-9
  I. Title.
PS3569.A517S4 1997   96-53695
813'.54—dc21   CIP

Printed in the United States of America

10 9 8 7 6 5 4 3 2 1

I wrote this for my parents,
my friend Pam,
and my partner, Emily

One is foolish to feel sorry for writers.
They're all fucking liars, and they fatten on
pain. Also, they invariably steal women.
                              —Godwin Lloyd-Jons

The need has come to explain myself to someone. First: I hear voices in running water. This communion-with-nature deal started out as mystic and romantic charm, like being on the edge of a great secret. I'd be hiking along the willow flats or aspen groves next to your typical Wyoming bubbling stream—moss-covered stones, *Lonicera* waving in the sun, air that tastes of lemon on the back of the throat—and a murmur would float over the water's surface. It sounded as if several young people were singing something, a message perhaps, or an underwater anthem. As I stood motionless, the voices grew louder and sounded like a psalm or a chant—Gregorian, if the creek was wide enough.

Enraptured as hell by the whole experience, I would sit at the water's edge for hours, knowing that if I was calm enough, and pure enough, the words would come together and some message of great importance would be revealed.

That was four years ago, when I was still married.

Then came the winter Julie boxed up her vitamins, the cookbook collection, and two drawers full of Danskins, and moved across town. Less than two weeks passed before my shower distinctly said, *"What dire offense from amorous causes springs."* I didn't know at the time, but that's the first line of a poem called "The Rape of the Lock" by a man named Alexander Pope. Rape is the recurring theme in much of my plumbing's poetry.

The morning after my shower first spoke, the flushing toilet said, *"Eat fish today."*

Of course I didn't eat fish that day. People who let auditory hallucinations boss them around wind up driving wooden stakes through the hearts of random strangers. Or tying up their mother and splitting her in half lengthwise with a chain saw. A lawn sprinkler in Cheyenne once gave me that order.

At times I shout rude comebacks at the voices—"Fuck you too, buddy"—or I stick fingers in the water while they're speaking. Nothing fazes the jerks. They laugh and trill and go merrily about the business of driving me further from reality.

I say *them* because I've counted at least eleven different water voices, and each voice has its own personality. Mostly they sound like movie stars: James Garner, Debra Winger, Kurt Gowdy, Crusader Rabbit. There's one I'm fairly certain is Thelma Ritter from around 1959.

There were other peculiar changes after Julie left. I became left-handed. I suffer days of color-blindness and lose orientation. I can't remember things like my cat's name or who was the drummer for the Beatles.

Julie only moved four blocks. She and my ex-best friend, Rick Fatt, live over by the courthouse in a yellow house with white gables. Rick must think I did Julie and him a horrible injustice, because he won't speak to me and he tells anyone who will listen that I'm crazy. He told the bartender at the Cowboy Bar that my elevator doesn't reach the top floor. What a snide thing to say.

Julie denies that she and I were ever married. I ran into her at the post office once and mentioned that we ought to think about getting a divorce. She looked me straight in the eye and said, "I was never married to you. I've never been married to anyone."

Let's establish a point right off the starting line here. I'm not crazy. Remember that. I had some doubts at one time, as did others in the community, but the insanity plea no longer washes. Everything I accomplished was done with forethought and a healthy regard for consequences.

The difficult detail in explaining yourself is where to start. This is a value judgment we all must make. I started with a voice in the shower. I could just as easily have begun with a name, which is Kelly Palamino. Does that tell any more about my life than *What dire offense from amorous causes springs?*

I was raised in Lancaster, Idaho, by fairly normal people. My father runs the only Purina feed store in Teewinot County. Mom plays viola. High school, puberty, and a busted marriage came at me in that order. Now I live in Jackson, Wyoming, gateway city to Grand Teton and Yellowstone national parks.

I wake up before noon every day, make myself a six-cup pot of coffee, water the plants, shave myself, and feed the cat. I work—I wash dishes at the Cattleman's Club and Restaurant— go to the bars, usually the Cowboy Bar, drink, dance, look for love and settle for sex—when it's offered. Usually it's not offered.

Because of a confused period soon after Julie left, I visit a therapist once a week, on Wednesdays. My therapist is a nice lady. Lizbeth gives me Thorazine and asks me what it means when the sprinkling system tells me to chain-saw my mother. It doesn't mean any more than the toilet telling me to eat fish or my Ezra Pound–quoting Water Pik, but I don't tell her that. I look very serious and stare at my shoes and say, "Hell, I don't know. I suppose it means I have some sort of repressed feelings toward my mother."

Then Lizbeth says, "What do you think those repressed feelings might be?"

So I say, "If I knew, they wouldn't be repressed."

The Wednesday before I found Colette, we had a pretty typical session.

Lizbeth sat about six feet from my chair, dressed like a young professional woman, long-sleeved blouse, and below-the-knee skirt so us crazies wouldn't get distracted trying to look up between her legs. We had our usual five minutes of her watching me while I fixated on a blinking light in the telephone at her desk.

It's real important during those silent periods not to move your hands. I try especially not to touch my face, because they take that as a sure sign of schizophrenia.

Finally she broke. "What do you think of yourself, Kelly?"

I stalled. "What do you mean?"

"What do you think of yourself as a person?"

"I never thought about it."

Another silence. "Do you think you are a good person?"

"I never do anything I think is wrong. At the time."

"Does that make you good?"

"I don't cheat at games. If a cashier gives me too much change, I give it back."

"Do you like yourself?"

"I never thought about it."

"Think about it now."

I formed my fingers into little O's like I'd read you're supposed to when you're thinking. One of her shoes had red mud on the toe. The nearest red mud in Jackson is up a canyon two miles outside of town. I wondered what Lizbeth had been doing up a canyon in high heels.

"Sure, I like myself. Somebody's got to."

That wasn't the right answer and I knew it, but I didn't feel much like cooperating. She stared some more. I fought an itch on my right cheek.

"Why did Julie leave you?" Lizbeth asked.

She was going at it from a different angle. "She said I drove her crazy."

"Why do you think she left?"

"We made love one afternoon and I didn't get her off," I said, brushing the hair out of my face.

"You couldn't have gotten her off every time for six years, could you?"

I didn't have any answer, so I shut up.

"Why do you think she left you, Kelly?"

My whole face itched. I rubbed my nose with the palm of my right hand. "She didn't love me."

"What? I couldn't hear you."

She heard me, the bitch. "She didn't love me."

"Ever?"

Lizbeth's problem was that she didn't understand that some people with inferiority complexes actually are inferior. "How should I know? She didn't love me the last year or two."

"How can you be sure?"

"She told me often enough."

Lizbeth crossed her legs at the ankles, right over left, sure body language that she thought this was the heart of the discussion. "Why did she stop loving you?"

"Because I drove her crazy."

She almost smiled. "How did you drive her crazy?"

The blinking light quit blinking. Somebody, somewhere was off hold. "I got on her nerves."

"What did you do to get on Julie's nerves?" Lizbeth was patient, I have to give her that much.

"I chewed in my sleep."

"Julie left because you chewed in your sleep?"

"I drank straight from the milk carton and I ate maraschino

cherries. I picked my teeth with matchbooks. I made major decisions based on newspaper astrology advice. Jesus, Lizbeth, what more do you want?"

"I want to know why you think Julie left you."

It seemed like bare-your-soul-to-your-shrink time. I mean, that's what they're for, isn't it? I stared at the carpet. "Every time Julie walked into the bathroom at night, she'd get her foot wet. When she left me, Julie swore she'd die an old maid before she'd live with another man who couldn't piss in the pot."

I met Colette the day of her wedding.

It was the first Saturday afternoon in April, the first nice day of spring, and I was soaking up sunlight on my porch steps. My cat, Alice, rolled on her back in the first dust since the snowmelt. Three little boys played football in front of the Episcopal church across the street. Most of the game involved waving arms and shouting names, followed by blame-fixing.

"Why didn't you catch the ball, poot-breath?"

"You threw it over my head, dildo."

I sipped on a Mello-Yello and bent down to draw a series of wavy arrows in the dirt between my feet with a toothpick. Blood rushed to my head, causing fuzz around the edges of my vision. I'd woken up that morning in a chair with my shoes on, which is a horrible way to start a day. The wheat bread I wanted to toast for breakfast had green things on each slice, and my aloneness was beginning to wear thin.

A dark car full of people wearing suits and dresses pulled up in front of the Episcopal church. Then another and another, and soon the lawn looked like Sunday morning had come ahead of schedule. The men shook hands and slapped each other's shoulders. The women hugged, offering congratulations. A few kids shuffled in and out of the crowd, embarrassed by their parents' show of emotion.

I went inside to find Alice a piece of baloney, and when I came back the people were filing into the church.

Three girls came out of the rectory and walked toward the sanctuary door. The two in front were laughing. They had on these dark blue layer-on-layer outfits and floppy felt hats that they held on their heads with their left hands.

The third girl was dressed all in white, which is how I knew this was a wedding and she was the bride. She was kind of short, shorter than me anyway, but she had exceptional posture. I noticed her posture from clear across the street. Baby's-breath flowers showed white against her thick, long hair.

One of the girls in blue opened the front door and stood in the entrance a moment, looking into the church. The other girl straightened something on the bride's collar and kissed her on the right cheek. Some organ music started, the first girl looked at the other two, then stepped into the church. The second girl hugged the bride and went in after her.

The bride, the girl all in white, opened the door and leaned to go inside, but she stopped. She turned, bent over, and picked up the football that the little boys had been throwing. As I watched, the bride slipped off her right shoe. She stood still a moment, then she punted the football over the rectory and out of sight.

The bride watched the flight path of the ball several seconds after it had disappeared. She looked up at the sky, the big cottonwood next to my apartment, then me. We stared at each other for a couple of heartbeats, then she breathed out so deeply I could see her breasts drop. She turned and walked into the church.

The girl had very nice eyes. They went well with her hair.

I stood up and walked across the street and into the church. Organ music, coming from an alcove to the left of the altar, ended as I slipped through the inner set of doors. A heavyset woman wearing way too much rouge made room for me in the back pew. She leaned into my face and whispered, "You're late."

"Sorry."

The priest stood a head higher than the wedding party. From the back, they made a pretty flashy array of dresses and tuxedoes. Moving from left to right, I spotted candle-lighters, flower girls, attending maidens of some sort, bride, father of the bride in black, groom in a slightly lighter blue than the maidens, best man, practically the best man, very young ring bearer in a tiny tuxedo, and back to more candle-lighters. I wondered where they found a blue tuxedo small enough for a four-year-old.

The priest made a vague right-handed cross sign and stepped down to crowd level, out of my sight. By leaning over the rouge woman, I could see a little of the bride's face. She didn't smile or blink or anything—just stared at a spot on the right arm of the cross. Once she raised her hand to brush hair behind her ear.

Episcopal weddings take all of three minutes if the priest drags it out. I started listening on the *If any man knows just cause* line, sat through a couple of *Wilt thous*, two *With this rings*, the Lord's Prayer, and a *Go forth and multiply*, which I think was extemporaneous because it's not in the Prayer Book. The newlyweds kissed as if they'd done it every morning for twelve years, the organist broke into an anthem I had never heard, and the whole thing was over. The couple swept up the aisle and out the door.

Of course, the rouge woman had tears in her eyes. All rouge women cry at weddings. She turned heavily on me. "Doris Hart and I were great rivals in high school." She sniffed into a scented tissue. "At one time, I could have had John."

"Who's Doris Hart?" I asked.

She looked at me over the tissue. "Danny's mother."

"Oh." I sat still a moment, then asked, "Do you know where the reception is?"

The sniffing ended in a shallow snort. "Doesn't it say on your invitation?"

"I left the invitation at home. In Denver."

"You must be a friend of Danny's then."

"Yes, ma'am, we were in the same fraternity." Anyone who gets married in a light blue tuxedo must have been in a fraternity at some time in his life.

"Funny that Danny never mentioned his mother," the woman said. "They're very close."

"We were in different classes."

"He probably never mentioned me either—Jenny Hayes?"

"I don't think so."

"Doris and I were once great rivals. I think she married John for his money."

"Do you know where the reception is?"

"I would never marry for money." Her mind wavered, drifted into the past.

"Ma'am?"

"I never married at all."

"The reception?"

Awareness snapped into the rouge lady's face. Wadding the tissue into a ball, she stuffed it into the sleeve of her dress. "It's at the Americana Inn, in the Gold Room. Do you know where the Americana is?"

"No, ma'am. I had car trouble and just got into town a half hour ago."

"I wondered why you came dressed like that. The Inn is a mile down Cache Street, turn left at the baseball diamond. You can't miss it."

"Thank you very much, Miss Hayes. I'll see you there."

I walked across the street, picked up my unfinished Mello-Yello, and sat back down on the porch, watching the friends and family load into their Buicks and Oldsmobiles, even saw a couple Mercedes. When the Mello-Yello was gone, I went inside, used my roll-on deodorant, put on a clean shirt, and wiped off my glasses. I stared at myself in the mirror for twenty seconds, then walked to the Americana.

The group from in front of the altar had gained a few mothers, an extra father, and a couple more people I don't know who they belonged to. The wedding party stood side by side against the east wall while the rest of us shuffled past and congratulated each one for whatever he or she did. I stood in line behind a group of happy girls who were kissing their way north. One of the girls whooped whenever she hugged a man. The groom's father pretended he knew me.

"Haven't seen you around the house in a while, sport. You've got to come back soon." He was partially bald, reminded me of Robert Duvall in one of the *Godfather* movies.

"My name's not Sport and I've never been to your house in my life."

"You must be with the bride then."

Shaking hands with the bride's father was like squeezing old salmon eggs between my fingers.

The groom, Danny himself, shook my hand and winked at me. "Why did you wink at me?" I asked.

"I don't know," he said, turning to the woman behind me.

When it was my turn to kiss the bride on the cheek, I didn't touch her. I tried to stare into her eyes, but she was looking down the line to see how many more people she had to be nice to.

"Where can we talk?" I asked.

She didn't hear me at first. "What?"

"We must talk. Is there a place where we won't be disturbed?"

She looked at me then. "Are you a friend of Danny's?"

"No. Listen, I'll go sit in that corner, by the piano there. See the piano?"

"Yes."

"I'll go sit by the piano. When you can get away, come over there."

I walked to the piano and sat on the bench, facing the bride and the rest of the crowd. My mouth was dry and I wanted some punch, but it didn't seem right since I wasn't invited, so I just sat and watched.

The bride shook hands with the rest of the guests, smiled at a few, hugged a few, but she kept glancing at me, then away, then back again. I looked at her good for the first time. Her cheekbones were nice, erect, out-front. I couldn't see a bit of fat under her traveling dress, but she wasn't skinny, not like me skinny. Her eyes were the nicest part. Dark brown and sparkly like a fried aggie, they bugged out a little, just enough so you noticed them. As to her dark Cinderella hair, the important question in my mind was: Natural or perm job?

Jenny Hayes was the last person through the line. She clutched the bride's hand while the bride kissed her rouge and said something, then Jenny said a long something else. Finally, Miss Hayes released the hand and shuffled off toward a six-story cake in the middle of the room. The bride chatted for a moment with her father, said something to the groom, then walked over to me.

"Do I know you?" she asked.

"I'm the guy on the porch you looked at just before you went into the church."

"I don't remember any guy on a porch."

"You are an excellent football kicker."

"Right." The bride wasn't hostile, exactly, but then she didn't recognize me as her fate either.

"Sit down, you need to hear me."

She didn't sit down, so I went ahead. "It's not too late, you can still get out of this."

She paled a little. I think. "You know it's all wrong," I said. "You don't love him. You don't want to be married to him. I can help you save yourself."

"What the fuck are you talking about?"

"I saw your face after that beautiful punt. You had the same look a lifer gets just before he goes into the penitentiary. My mother used to get that look outside the dentist's office. She always thought she was going to die in the chair."

"Twenty thousand weddings a day in this country, and the nut comes to mine."

"Look me in the eye and tell me that right before you started down the aisle, you didn't feel like you were going to your doom."

The bride's right hand closed and opened and she looked at the keyboard. "Listen," she said quietly, "I don't deserve this. Would you please leave?"

"Haven't you ever seen someone in a restaurant or a parking lot or someplace and known deep inside that here is a person who could make your life good and meaningful and you could do the same for them? Only you don't say anything because you're embarrassed, and thirty seconds later they're gone. I'm not going to let that happen to us."

"Yesterday I wrote out a list of everything that could possibly go wrong with my wedding. But I never dreamed of this one."

"The moment you kicked that ball, I knew we could save each other," I said. "Life with him will be an empty void. You know it. Come with me."

She just looked at me with those bug-out brown eyes.

"What's going on over here? You trying to seduce my wife?" Danny laughed, coming toward us. He'd changed from the blue tuxedo into a concrete-colored sports jacket with matching loafers. Danny's father was right behind him, a drink in each hand.

"I'm trying to convince . . . uh . . ." I looked at her.

"Colette. Colette Sullivan."

"Colette Hart," Danny corrected.

I started over. "I'm trying to convince Colette to get an annulment and come with me."

He looked at her. "Is this a joke?"

Her eyes stayed right on me. "He likes the way I kick a football."

"No," I said. "It's no joke. If you go through with this marriage, you'll hate each other in two years. She'll be an alcoholic and you'll be screwing your friends' wives. You should both admit it was a mistake and quit before you put yourselves through a lot of pain."

"Shut up," Danny said.

By then, a sizable crowd of guests had gathered. Danny's father stepped forward with his fists clenched. He growled at me. "Punk, I could break you in half."

"Probably."

Danny's father forgot he had a drink in each hand because one of the glasses fell on the floor and broke.

"I don't know who the hell you are," Danny sort of hissed, "but you've got ten seconds to haul your ass out of here, or I'm going to make you wish you had."

I looked at Colette's face.

"Who are you?" she asked.

"Kelly Palamino."

"You'd better go now, Kelly."

"Okay, but can I see you again?"

"No, you cannot," Danny said, that same hiss in his voice. Colette didn't move, not at all, but her beautiful eyes said yes, she wanted to see me again.

I stood up and walked home.

• • •

My own wedding was drug-induced.

During our early-seventies hippie period, Julie and I traveled around a lot. Like all good longhairs, I owned a '67 green-and-white VW van—even painted a picture from a Grateful Dead album cover on the back. I never was very original.

When we'd been together about six months—eight years ago last June 16, to get down to the details—we stopped at the house of some friends of hers outside Victoria, Texas. Julie liked them because their cats were named Today and Tamari.

The friends fed us this damp green stuff called peyote. Peyote is cut off a type of spineless cactus and it makes you sick. After you get sick, your back feels funny, then your neck. Then almost anything can happen.

Like every other night I ever wasted in south Texas, that night was hot and humid. Julie and I wandered outside to watch the full moon pulsate and the stars spin. We stood in the yard and went One with the Universe (whatever the hell that meant back then). I raised my right hand and her left.

"*Hey, God,*" I shouted. "*Hey. This woman and I are partners. We're going to stay together a while. You can write it in the book that Kelly Palamino and Julie Deere are an official unit.*"

Then Julie shouted, "*He isn't much, Lord, but I'll take him off your hands because I love him.*"

The next day, fortified with expensive Sonoma Valley wine and more peyote, we drove into the county courthouse in Victoria. It took a couple of hours of hanging around to get licensed and find out neither one of us carried any clap. We sat on the courthouse lawn, eating enchiladas and drinking warm Lone Star until I got sick again.

Julie was at the top of her life the day we got married. Sitting in the grass next to an old cottonwood, she looked so beautiful and tall in her white peasant blouse and the skirt made from cut-up blue jeans and a tapestry. Her hair and skin were alive. She laughed all day and her eyes were alert. I guess, at least for one day in there, Julie and I were happy together.

Later on, her friends drove us to an unpainted shack of a church run by a gigantic black man calling himself Father Funk. To be real honest about the whole thing, I still don't know if the marriage was legal or not. Father Funk dressed like a tourist on Maui with a collar. He put a Stevie Wonder album on the stereo and quoted a poem by an African or somebody I never heard of. Closing his eyes, he made us all hold hands—his was the biggest hand I ever held. He said golden rings were circling the room above our heads, moving in tighter and tighter.

I didn't see any rings, but Father Funk said they flip-flopped twice, I may kiss the bride, and pay him ten dollars please.

It felt real nice to be married, secure and warm. We drove to Houston that afternoon. The sky was clear and a deep blue you usually only see in water. Julie laughed and hitched the jeans skirt up to her waist and pulled down my zipper.

A hundred fifty miles of foreplay later, we stopped at a tacky motel on the north side of Houston that charged by the hour, four dollars for the first two hours, dollar an hour after that. I bought us eight hours' worth, of which we made love seven. Then we drove to New Orleans.

Julie was taller than me and we both agreed she was smarter. She was young and blond and filled to the eyes with potential, and I have no idea why she married me. All I know is she did, and I appreciated the gesture.

My last two years haven't been spent alone, exactly. The women come and go in two categories: Platonics, who behave like girl-friends, and Romantic Interests, who stay awhile, then leave suddenly, wondering what happened. My Romantic Interests are generally confused when I meet them, unhappy while we're together, then ridiculously at peace about six months later.

I have pretty much the same effect on women as shock treatments on a manic. One woman told me, "Kelly, you're the darkness before the dawn. You've got to get through it to find the light, but life sure is bleak while you're in there."

The Romantics never like the Platonics. The Plats are always very young, nineteen or twenty, and very pretty. They stay with me several months, several hours a day. The townspeople who worry about these things all think we're "together," which can be an ego thrust since they're so good looking and young, but can also frighten away possible sex objects. The categories never, ever overlap. I don't sleep with a Plat and I don't spend any relaxed time with an RI.

My current sidekick Platonic is Cora Ann. She lives upstairs, but you wouldn't know it without seeing the lease. Her toothbrush, hot curlers, and disposable tampon pack are in my bathroom. She's the best-looking Plat yet, a classic, perky blonde with that clean, glowy look of the girls in situation comedies on TV. She's strong on athletics and a great western-swing dancer, the perfect blend of sensual grace and down-home dried cowflop on her Nike tennis shoes.

Cora Ann's tragic flaw is that she eats all my food.

On the Wednesday after Colette's wedding, Cora Ann bounced into my apartment without knocking. She headed straight for the refrigerator. "There's an article in this month's *Cosmo* about men faking orgasms."

I was busy finishing a letter to the Davenport, Iowa, police department, so I answered with something along the lines of "Huh."

"Thought you might like to know how it's done. Got any cheese?"

"I never buy cheese since you started hanging out in my kitchen. Why should I need to fake a 'gasm?"

"From what I hear, it's the only way you can finish the job with honor."

I did a quick inventory to figure who ratted. "Bullshit, who told you that?"

"A little bird."

"I never screwed a bird yet that I didn't get off."

Cora Ann settled on the couch with a half-full jar of peanut butter and a full jar of grape jelly. "That's not what I heard."

"You're jealous because I last longer than an eight-second bull ride. Don't you ever get tired of those hair-trigger little boys you bring home? And what are you doing to my peanut butter?"

"Little boys are enthusiastic." Cora Ann carefully shoveled six spoonfuls of jelly into the peanut butter jar and stirred it into brown-and-purple slop.

"Sure," I said. "How many times have you heard 'I'm only like this when I'm drunk,' or 'This never happened to me before.'"

"Never. Want a bite?" Cora Ann propped both feet up on the old army trunk I use for a table and proceeded to pour the stuff into her mouth. Lord only knows why she doesn't get fat.

"I know what it's like to *wham-bam, sorry, ma'am*," I said. "I was twenty once."

"Hell of a long time ago."

I licked my envelope and sat it on the elk skull next to my TV. "How can you eat that crap, Cora Ann? Doesn't look healthy."

"When you're raised on shit, you take a hankering to it. How's the big love affair with Colleen going?"

"Colette. They're honeymooning in St. Lucia. That's in the West Indies somewhere."

"I know where it is. All the rich couples on 'Guiding Light' go there. I bet that's where she got the idea. You're strung out on a dip, Kelly."

"Am not. Look, you're dribbling slop on the floor. Want to walk over to the post office?"

Cora Ann set the peanut butter mixture on the arm of the couch. "I've got things to do, but I'll meet you in the Cowboy later. She's still a bonus-baby dip."

I picked the letter back up off the elk skull. It's a nice skull, white and smiling. "She said 'fuck' at her own wedding reception. Would a bonus-baby dip say 'fuck' at her own wedding reception? Huh?"

"She said 'fuck'?"

"Out loud."

"If some skinny wacko told her to annul the wedding and run away with him, even a dip might say 'fuck' out loud. How do you know she's in St. Lucia?"

"Her mother-in-law told me. I pulled the fraternity brother line. Even found out which hotel they're staying in before she got suspicious."

"You planning to go there?"

"Can't afford it. I sent a dozen roses."

Cora Ann gave me one of those looks she saves for tourists who don't tip. "Her husband is going to break your legs, Kelly. And rightly so. You deserve it if you try to steal another man's wife—on their honeymoon yet. You don't even know her. She might be a Jehovah's Witness or something."

I showed her the letter to the Davenport, Iowa, police department. "That's what I'm fixing to find out. According to the wedding story in the newspaper, she's from Davenport, Iowa. I've written the police, told them I'm considering hiring her for a top security job and asked what they know about her."

"That's sick, Kelly. Have you seen a psychiatrist?"

"This morning. She says I'm sick. I also ordered all the high-school yearbooks put out in the Davenport area in the last five years. Colette looks young. I don't think she graduated from high school more than five years ago."

Cora Ann laughed. A pretty laugh, kind of low-pitched. "He's gonna hang your nuts in a tree, Kelly."

"Danny'll understand."

"You bet."

Some people would wonder why a twenty-nine-year-old college graduate who hears voices in running water became a professional dishwasher.

I'm good at it. Hell, I'm fantastic at it. With one hand I can sling a stack of monkey dishes into the rack while spraying down coffee cups with the other. I handle ten-inch china plates like a Mississippi River gambler handles fifty-one cards and a joker. There has never been a burned pot I couldn't have gleaming in thirty seconds of steel wool and elbow grease.

Sometimes the whole crew—waitresses, cooks, even the cashier—will abandon their stations to watch me fly into a sinkful of filth.

And the water—the beautifully wet gallons of hot water, all of it singing for the joy of cleaning dishes. My Hobart dish machine plays entire symphonies at 160 degrees. At 180, the rinse cycle sounds like D-Day in a box, and my UL-approved Waste Disposal System can grind, chew, spit, and completely dissolve anything that has ever been alive except beef bones and avocado pits.

I've tried it all, cooking, waiting tables, I've done everything a grownup can do in a restaurant, but nothing gives me the true satisfaction, that gut-level glow, like cleaning up the mess.

My second love at work, after my Hobart, is the waitresses. Tall, short, skinny, fat, built like a poster picture in a freshman's dorm room, I don't care. Put a tray in a woman's hand and I love her. My whole life, from the day Julie said, "I won't say it was fun 'cause it wasn't," and slammed the door until I saw Colette's punt sail over the rectory, was dedicated to and obsessed by the chasing and seduction of waitresses.

Another tip: A waitress in bed is one of God's special creations. No woman is as giving, no woman will ever make a man feel as wanted, as downright good, as a food waitress. Cocktail waitresses aren't even in the same sack.

Lord knows, I wasn't always a dishwasher. I started out to become a sociologist. At least I got a degree in it. Never quite landed a job. Along about 1973, after five years of struggle and drugs, I received a B.A. from the University of Arkansas in Fayetteville. I folded up my sheepskin, which wasn't sheepskin, and shipped it off to my parents in Lancaster. That's all the good a degree ever did me. The collegiate experience was a waste of time. I was too busy saving the world and seeing how high my brains could soar to bother with class attendance. "Good Education Means Good Jobs" didn't come to dog poop set against Vietnam and mescaline.

What I'd really like to be is a writer—a novelist like Larry McMurtry or John Steinbeck. Over the years with Julie, I wrote four books, three of them westerns. My mother used to be a writer. She wrote real-life romances for *True Confessions* magazine. Country girl fakes pregnancy to test boyfriend who joins the Marines only to meet his death in a freak accident at boot camp; career woman has an affair with college boy and discovers the true meaning of family grit; that sort of thing. I was never allowed to read her stories, but my college roommate picked one up in a Laundromat and he said it was "hot stuff." Lately, Mom has switched her interests to the viola.

So—five years of college, six years of marriage, countless hours shoveling refuse into a garbage disposal and stacking plates. Two years of therapy. Where had the whole experience of being alive gotten me?

Nowhere. That move in the Americana Inn Gold Room was the first original act of my life.

``He doesn't have a father, you know,'' the woman smiled.

This boy, maybe five years old, stood at my feet, staring at me as if he'd never seen a human being before.

"His father ran away when he was only two. I guess he couldn't stand the thought of raising a retarded child." The woman sat on a park bench ten feet away, gazing at the boy.

I was lying in the grass in the town square, enjoying the warm sun on my face and waiting patiently for Colette to return from St. Lucia. I didn't really feel much like admiring a retard for his mother, but she seemed lonely, so I gave it a try.

"How old are you, kid?" I asked.

"Six," the woman answered. "Nothing's ever gone right for him. He's a triple Taurus."

The boy had that look which is considered so cute these days on TV—a grown-up head on a child's body. I liked him because his thick, horn-rimmed glasses were dirty.

"What's your name?" I asked.

"Emerson," the woman answered. "His father worshiped Ralph Waldo Emerson. He lives in Taos now, with a Mexican girl." The woman was dressed like a subscriber to *Mother Earth News* who baked cracked-wheat bread in a woodburning stove. I liked her.

"And what's your name?" I asked.

"I was born Lydia, but now I call myself Rebecca." That sounded reasonable.

"Can you talk, kid?"

Nobody answered.

"Come over here and tell me about yourself," I said, reaching out to take the boy's arm.

The woman screamed, *"Get your filthy fucking hands off my baby."*

Colette was due to return from St. Lucia on May 1. I knew because I called the airport to confirm the return reservations of Mr. and Mrs. Danny Hart.

In fact, I learned quite a bit about the Harts while they honeymooned the month away. I learned they lived on his daddy's ranch, the Broken Hart, a couple miles north of Teton Village. Danny had been working on the old two-story bunkhouse all winter, turning it into a cozy home only a hundred yards from the main house and his parents.

His father, John Hart, was president and principal owner of the Teton National Bank in Jackson. He'd come to the valley in the late thirties, bought the ranch from Depression-busted dirt farmers, and opened himself up a bank—been making money ever since.

From what I heard at the bars, John Hart was a pompous, power-crazed royal A-hole.

No one had a bad word to say about Danny though. Danny was a local boy. Quarterbacked a mediocre high-school football team in 1970. I figured their mutual interest in football was the basis of Danny and Colette's marriage. After four years of Business Education at the University of Wyoming, Danny came back to Jackson and took his rightful place as loan officer at the bank. Hobbies included golf and skeet shooting.

That much information cost me a couple of afternoons and twenty dollars' worth of free drinks for the barfly know-it-alls at the Cowboy. I ended up drunk in the process.

I learned almost nothing about Colette. Pam the bartender thought Colette used to work for one of the lodge companies in the parks, Jackson Lake Lodge or someplace. She'd heard Danny met her at the golf course club where Colette waitressed, but Pam wasn't sure. Someone had told her that Colette was "nice."

I decided not to meet the plane. There would be a lot of people around, and I didn't want a replay of the Americana. Instead, I gave them a couple of hours to unpack. Then I drove my VW bug out to the Broken Hart.

The brand for the Broken Hart is a heart with a jagged crack in it, like those necklaces guys used to give girls in junior high. The guy wore one half of the heart around his neck and the girl wore the other half and the only heart on earth that would fit right with his was hers—theoretically anyway.

To get into the ranch, you drive through an arched knobbled pine gate with the brand hanging in the middle. The driveway up to the house is real impressive, a long sweeping curve across a manicured lawn.

Colette answered the door. She looked at me and said, "Oh, shit."

From inside I heard Danny's voice. "Who is it, hon?"

"Who do you think?" she called back. Colette wore new blue jeans and a white western shirt. She was barefoot.

"Can I come in?" I asked.

"Listen," Colette said. "Thanks for the flowers, they were sweet, but you cannot do this, you understand."

"Do what?"

"This. *This*. You've got to go away and stay away."

"I was hoping we could talk."

Colette put her hand on the door frame and looked at me with what might have been compassion. "Being reasonable isn't important to you, is it?"

"What's the use?"

I think she would have said something kind, but Danny came up behind her. He didn't have a shirt on. "I don't know what your problem is, buddy, but don't lay it on us. I've been nice so far because I understand you've had some sort of mental problems, but don't bother my wife, you got it?"

"What sort of mental problems?" I asked.

"My dad had you checked out while we were gone, and he says you're a certified nut. I don't care whether you're crazy or not, just so long as you stay the hell away from Colette. I mean it."

I looked at Colette. "Do you want to talk to me?"

She stared straight back into my eyes. "No."

Danny put his hand on her back. "You heard it from her, pardner. Now, if I see you on this property again, I'll have you arrested for trespassing."

Just before the door shut, I saw him put his arm around Colette's shoulders.

I started the bug and drove back around the sweeping drive-way and past the big ranch house. John Hart walked out onto the porch and watched me. I waved, but he didn't wave back.

I moved down the drive, under the broken-heart gate, and turned right onto the country road. A half-mile later, I pulled over and sat looking at my hands on the steering wheel.

Locking the passenger door, I got out, locked my door, and hopped over the buck-and-rail fence on the right side of the road.

I had been fair, given him a chance to be there when Colette and I discussed her moving out. Now I'd have to sneak around and talk to her when Danny or his father or his mother or anyone else wasn't around.

The underbrush was quite thick between the road and the ridge that overlooked the back of the ranch. I got stuck in a chokecherry patch and had to go around. Then I fell off a little drop and scraped my hand.

A nice creek ran along the base of the hill. Because of the thick willows along the banks, I decided to walk into the creek and wade downstream toward the ranch. The water was cold. It sang "Amazing Grace," but it only knew the first verse, the part about *that saved a wretch like me*. The creek sang that line over and over.

I slipped on a rock and twisted my ankle and got wet. At first the water was so cold that my feet hurt badly. Then they turned numb and I couldn't feel anything at all, so I climbed out of the creek and pushed through the willows. My shoe caught in a hole and I walked right out of it. The shoe was stuck so tight I had to sit down and use both hands to pull it out. I untied the shoelaces, which were wet, and put the shoe on my foot and tied them again.

The twisted ankle wasn't too twisted. I could walk on it anyway, though it made me limp. My normal walk looks like a limp to some people, but this would have looked like a limp to anyone.

It was almost dark before I reached the yard behind the bunkhouse. I didn't really have a plan. I know, you should always have a plan, but I didn't have one. Originally I had intended to sneak into the house, find Colette, and talk to her alone—without Danny. However, from the bushes behind the ranch, that seemed kind of unrealistic.

I circled around to the side and crouched behind a large cottonwood tree where I could see both the front and back yards of the bunkhouse and the back door of the big house. I have never been comfortable in a crouch and doubt if I could have held this one for long, but after a while, Danny and Mr. Hart came out of Danny's house and walked up the slight rise toward the other place. They talked, but I couldn't hear the words.

This looked like what I'd been waiting for, so I stood up and started across the clearing—would have made it, too, if a German shepherd hadn't come howling around the house and attacked. He jumped and knocked me backward. On my back, I kicked him in the nose, stunning him long enough for me to roll over and run for the cottonwood tree. The German shepherd leaped on my shoulders, slid down, and bit me on the back of my leg. I shook loose and clawed bark up the cottonwood.

The German shepherd jumped high and snapped his jaws, but he couldn't quite reach me. Breaking off a branch, I jabbed him in the face. He bit the end and ripped it out of my hands.

After a few minutes of jumping and barking, the dog sat down and growled. I looked around, wondering why no one had heard the attack and come to investigate.

Colette stood framed in a second-story window with the light behind her. She was a distance away, but I could see her face. It had no expression at all, nothing. Colette didn't move from the window for a long time. The German shepherd looked at me, I looked at Colette, and Colette looked at the dog and me. Finally, way after dark, Danny came down the slope and went into the house.

Colette turned and disappeared. The light went out. A couple of hours later she came to the back door and called, "Thor, come here, boy. It's time for dinner. Come on, Thor."

The dog turned and trotted into the house.

I descended the cottonwood tree, walked past the house, and followed the driveway back to my car.

Every now and then, as a test, I pay attention to advice from the water. A drinking fountain in the library told me to buy a certain handkerchief for my grandmother for Christmas, and I did, and she seemed pleased with it. Another time, a perking coffeepot told me not to go to work that day. I didn't and I had an excellent time hiking in the woods instead.

Taggart Creek told me to bet on the Dodgers in the '78 World Series, and I did. They got clobbered. I never trusted Taggart Creek again.

The dog bite was only a surface wound, barely even ripped the flesh, and my twisted ankle was almost good as new within two days. Cora Ann painted my scratches with Mercurochrome and told me what a fool I was.

"You're an idiot, Kelly."

"I'm only sincere."

"That dog might have ripped your lungs out."

"Colette would have saved me."

"Sure."

I hung around the bank some to figure out Danny's hours before I tried the telephone approach. She answered the first time I called.

"Hi, Colette," I said when she answered the phone. "This is Kelly."

She didn't say anything.

"Kelly Palamino. You remember me."

"You're a squirrel," Colette said. "You're a wimp, a nut, an asshole. There's no chance of me ever leaving Danny for you. I can't even conceive of ever being friends with a creep like you. Stay away, shithead, or I'll have you arrested. And beat up."

"You sound hostile," I said.

"You jerk, I am hostile. You make me want to kill. I hate you. Can't you understand hatred? Do you have any idea how much I dislike you?"

"Hate is only a step from love," I said. "As long as you feel something, we're making progress."

She hung up.

· · ·

"You drink too much," Cora Ann said.

Nodding, I cut the triangular tip off the end of my cherry pie. "I know."

"And you let women walk all over you."

"You're right." A microwave oven can make a cherry remarkably hot. Tongue scalded, I choked something like *"Aighgh,"* and grabbed for the glass of ice water.

Cora Ann curled both hands around her coffee cup and raised it to her face. She looked at me through the steam. "Every time some woman is the least bit nice to you, Kelly, you start planning a wedding and a family."

"That's not true."

"It is so. You come on like a freight train. Some women don't like being run down by freight trains."

We sat in the Wort Hotel, drinking our afternoon coffee and eating my afternoon pie. It was a ritual with Cora Ann and me. She told me my shortcomings while I looked out the window at passing trucks. I didn't mind her telling me my faults. She was always right. Besides, around two the next morning, drunk, I would tell Cora Ann hers.

She blew across the coffee and sipped. "You follow women around like a lost puppy dog," she continued. "You beg for a pat on the head so you can wag your tail in gratitude."

The street was busy that day—early tourists and locals out for one last look at the center of town before the summer crush. Most of the people I could see through the window seemed to be going somewhere, not just wandering aimlessly the way they do in June. " 'Shortcomings' is an unusual word," I said. "Do you suppose it originally had a sexual meaning?"

Cora Ann set down her cup. "That's another thing. Whenever I'm serious, you start talking dirty. Get your mind off your balls for a minute and listen to me."

Cora Ann is full of sayings like "Get your mind off your

balls." I enjoy the way she tosses her declarations out, like a cheerleader at a high-school basketball game.

"Where's the waitress?" I asked.

"What do you want?"

"My coffee's cold. These waitresses disappear all the time. They go home without telling anyone."

"Take this new fantasy love of yours," Cora Ann went on, picking up in the middle of a thought I had already lost. "You don't even know her, but you're already living the tragic spurned-lover role."

"Am not."

"Are too."

I stared out the window at a parked delivery truck. She was right, of course. I'm not happy unless I'm torn apart over some woman or another, but Colette was different. She made existence meaningful. The others only made it bearable. I decided not to tell this to Cora Ann.

"Aren't you going to defend yourself?" she demanded.

Colette walked by the window. She was so close I could have smashed out the pane and touched her shoulder.

I rapped on the glass with my knuckles. "There she is," I said. Colette moved down the sidewalk, out of view.

"Who?"

I stood up and reached into my pocket. "Colette. I've got to go. There's something I need to talk to her about." Throwing a dollar on the table, I pushed back my chair and headed for the door.

Cora Ann called after me, "You're making a jackass out of yourself."

Blinking in the bright sunlight, I looked up the street in the direction Colette had been walking. The sidewalk was crowded, but she wasn't there. I ran to the corner. One direction was almost empty, only a couple of high-school kids standing on the curb, so I ran the other way.

Through the crowd, I saw the bounce of her dark hair. She was a half-block away, walking past the Cowboy Bar. I started running after her, but about twenty feet away I stopped. What was I going to say? It wouldn't do to grab her from behind and demand she talk to me. I'd get the same old squirrel, asshole, and wimp line.

Colette walked fast, as if she was going somewhere. I decided to follow and see where. I had never seen Colette from behind—except once in a wedding dress. It was interesting. She wore a dark green shirt, jeans, and wooden sandals. Her arms swung free, not touching her legs. The legs had good rhythm and just a little spring, as if she walked to music. Latin music. The bossa nova, maybe, or early reggae. Colette's butt was perfect. I couldn't have dreamed a better butt.

At the next corner she turned right, and I could see her eyes and the little indentation of her temple. I wondered what was going on in that beautiful brain. Was she thinking of me? Was she realizing the marriage was all wrong and that only I could bring meaning and happiness to her life? Maybe she was looking for me.

She seemed to be looking for someone because she crossed the street and cut into the town square, more or less doubling back on herself. She stopped at the war memorial in the middle of the square and looked at the base where the names of Teton County vets are all listed. I figured I'd saunter up behind her and say something like "Fancy meeting you here."

I came within three or four steps when Colette turned her head and spit on the sidewalk. This caused me to pause in surprise. It didn't feel proper to walk up to a woman who had just spit. She might be embarrassed. Or she might have a disgusting object in her mouth.

More than surprised, I was also kind of impressed. Colette's spit technique was forceful and solid, with a high arch and no trailing drool. It was boyish—like her punt. My God, I thought, what if Colette is really a boy? How would a sex change redefine our relationship?

While I stood there working out all the possible ramifications, Colette walked away. She crossed the street diagonally into an outdoor mall sort of thing. It had a walkway with shops on both sides and an open-air Mexican restaurant at the far end. I ran around the corner all the way to the restaurant end of the mall. Tucking in my shirttail, I checked my glasses for grease spots. Then I wandered into the mall. Keeping it casual, I walked past the Mexican restaurant, past the four or five gift shops, all the way to the other end of the walkway—no Colette.

Turning back along the line of shops, I stepped into each one and looked at the customers. The last shop was a boutique.

"Is anyone in the dressing room?" I asked the lady in charge.

She looked at me and said, "No."

"Do you mind if I just open the door and make sure?"

"What?"

"Can I look in the dressing room to make certain no one is in there?"

"No one is in there."

"Do you mind if I see for myself?"

She stood between me and the dressing room for a moment. Then she said, "Go right ahead, but no one is there."

I opened the door. The dressing room was empty. "Thank you," I said.

I walked over to the Mexican restaurant and looked at everyone eating and everyone standing in line. Cupping my hands around my mouth, I called, *"Colette."*

Some of the people eating looked up at me. I tried again. *"Colette."* She didn't answer.

Colette called me that same afternoon. I answered the phone on the second ring. "Hello."

There was a short silence. "Why are you doing this to me?" Colette asked.

"Hello," I said. "Who is this?"

Another pause. "Who do you think it is?"

I looked at the phone mouthpiece. "Colette, is that you, Colette?"

"Yes, it's me. Now answer the question."

"It's awfully nice of you to call, Colette."

"Kelly, why are you doing this to me?"

"Why am I doing this?"

"You heard me."

"Gee, Colette, I don't know. I haven't really thought about why."

"You mean you're tearing up my life and you haven't thought about why?"

"Does that mean I'm having an effect on you?"

She hung up.

I dialed her number and Colette answered halfway through the first ring.

"That means I'm having an effect on you," I said.

She didn't answer.

"You said I was tearing up your life. That's an effect, isn't it, Colette?"

"Stay the hell away from me," she said calmly.

"That's a meaningful suggestion," I said, "but could I offer another course of action? We could have lunch together tomorrow."

She hung up again. I called back and let the phone ring fifty-three times, but I guess Colette left the house because she didn't answer all afternoon.

The next couple of days, I called quite a few times—too many to count. It occurred to me that Colette was not answering the phone on purpose. I knew, though, that Danny had to have a way to get hold of her just to find out what to bring home from town every evening. That meant they had a telephone code.

Telephone codes are a snap to break. Everyone uses the same one. Wednesday, I dialed Colette's number, let it ring twice, and hung up. Then I called right back.

She picked up the phone. "Danny?"

"Gotcha," I said.

Colette hung up.

Friday night, a young deputy sheriff walked through the swinging double doors that separate the kitchen from the dining room at work. He walked through the wrong side of the door and almost knocked over a waitress. My dish station was just off the two doors.

"You're supposed to go through the right-hand door," I said.

"You Kelly Palamino?" he asked. He had sideburns down below his cheekbones.

"Did you hear me?" I said. "There's an In door and an Out door. You came in the Out door and almost upset a waitress carrying a tray."

"Yes or no, are you Kelly Palamino?"

"Let's straighten this out first. Have you ever worked in a restaurant?"

"No." The deputy walked over to the line cook. "You got a Kelly Palamino working here?"

The line cook pointed to me. The deputy walked back.

"Are you going to apologize to the waitress or not?" I asked.

The waitress walked back into the kitchen, carrying an empty tray.

I said, "Darlene, the deputy has something to say to you."

She leaned on her right leg and waited. The deputy looked from her to me and back again. "I'm sorry I came out the In door," he mumbled.

"In the Out door," I corrected.

"Okay, in the Out door. I'm sorry I came in the Out door and bumped your tray."

"Don't let it happen again," Darlene said. She walked to the line cook and called in an order.

The deputy held out a folded sheet of paper. "Here."

I took it.

"This is a warrant for your arrest," he said. "It is called a peace warrant because it does not go into effect until such time as you come within fifty feet of a woman named Colette Hart."

I unfolded the paper and read a couple of *wherefores* and *such as*'s. "Bet it covers the telephone too," I said.

"Yep. You understand, you won't be arrested unless you approach Mrs. Hart."

"What are the charges if I do approach her?"

"We'll think of something. Harassment, assault, obscene phone calls, attempted rape. We can put 'conspiracy to' in front of anything and hit you with it."

I refolded the paper carefully and stuck it into my right-hand back pocket. "That doesn't seem fair."

"With her father-in-law, it doesn't have to be fair, just close to legal. Don't go near that girl, understand?"

"I understand."

The deputy sheriff turned and walked out the door.

The next Wednesday, Lizbeth and I discussed why I act like an idiot sometimes.

"My mother pioneered the halter and leash on children," I said.

"The what?"

"The leash. The little halter goes around the kid's chest and the leash fastens in back."

Lizbeth smiled. "Why does a leash explain your current actions?"

"People made fun of me. Children used to bark behind my back."

Lizbeth sneezed. "I'm sorry," she said. "Must be something in the air. Go on, Kelly." She reached for a Kleenex and blew her nose.

"When I was twelve, Mom stopped talking to me. One night at the supper table, she said that since I didn't love her or appreciate all the things she did for me, she was never going to speak to me again. She didn't for a week."

"How did that make you feel?"

"How do you expect? I'm twelve years old. My mother says I've broken her heart. I had no idea what I'd done, I just knew it was my fault."

"What did your dad do?"

"Nothing. There was nothing he could do."

Lizbeth spoke into the Kleenex. "So, what's going to happen in your life?" *What's going to happen in your life?* was one of Lizbeth's stock therapeutic questions.

"I'll marry Colette sooner or later."

"What if she doesn't want to marry you?"

"She will." I gave Lizbeth one of those meaningful straight-in-the-eye stares. "She will."

"You can't force other people to cooperate with your dreams, Kelly."

"It's not a dream. It's fate."

"But she won't talk to you."

I crossed my legs, right ankle over left knee. "I'll wait. That marriage can't last more than two years, then I'll be around to pick her up. Besides, I have a plan."

Lizbeth lowered the Kleenex and leaned forward a little. "What plan?"

"I'm going to swoop down out of the mountains and fly away with her."

Lizbeth rapid-fired three sneezes in succession. She looked

up at me with tears in both eyes. "You're going to fly away with her?"

"Like Peter Pan."

I never expected anyone to want me enough to marry me. Even when I used to fantasize about true love and fulfillment, I didn't dare dream of a tall, blond woman. Julie was lustful. She was desired by strangers. When I suddenly found myself living in New Orleans, married to her, the feeling was unreal. I stopped thinking and got into the bad habit of saying "Jeez, Louise" many times a day.

Julie was a true child of the streets. Raised in Dallas, she came of age hustling her existence in the freak ghettos of Atlanta and New Orleans. Urban squalor was so much her element that anyone who saw us together knew immediately Julie was the person to contend with. Hippies, Moonies, and transvestites respected her to the point that I became something of a sidekick.

Which was okay by me. My own background ran to east Idaho and college-town Arkansas. Junkies intimidated me. I called pimps "sir." Julie could hardly believe my naïveté in the necessary skills of modern society.

"You don't spare-change right, you know nothing about inner-city hitchhiking. Can you tell if a bar is lesbian before you walk in the door?"

"There weren't any lesbian bars in Lancaster."

"Do you know the difference between selling blood and selling plasma?"

"No."

Julie shook her head in wonder.

"I can snowshoe up a steep hill. I can skin an elk and cook brook trout à la Hemingway. How many whores on Ursuline Avenue can do that?"

Tousling my hair, she laughed. "God must protect the helpless."

I like to think of New Orleans as our carefree period. No debts. No responsibilities. We had nothing to do with each day but live it. We met Rick in New Orleans. He was a cook at the Hilton, where I washed dishes and Julie waitressed. Most nights after work, the three of us bought a couple bottles of awful wine and roamed the back streets, watching the city put on its show.

Julie knew a blues bar where white people usually weren't welcome. We'd sit at long board tables and pass joints to old men with rose-colored eyes and catheters. A sad derelict named Babe Stovall sang raspy lyrics behind a guitar that seemed to be made from sheet metal. Sometimes Julie sat next to Babe on a beer box, moaning the harmonies. Babe let her drink from his absinthe bottle.

Before dawn, Julie would lead Rick and me through the near-empty streets to the levee along the Mississippi where we sprawled silently on the rocks, me on the right, Julie in the middle, Rick a little below us on the left. The three of us would share a last bottle of wine while the sun rose pink above the river.

Julie and I made love every day in those years. We had an apartment off Esplanade. Most afternoons we played Scrabble, then made love, then took a shower and went to work. Scrabble has turned me on ever since.

Looking back, I can see even then the romance was seeping out of the marriage. One hot, damp afternoon in August, we made love a long time—seemed like hours. Julie must have gotten off six times. Afterward we lay on our backs in the sweaty sheets and she smoked a cigarette.

We weren't touching. It was way too hot to touch. "Kelly," Julie said, staring at the ceiling, "did you ever wonder what it would be like to fuck somebody who was more than a friend?"

The day before Julie moved out, while she was at work, I tore sheets of paper into a couple hundred strips and wrote messages like *I love you and cannot live without you*, and *Hi, pal, re-member me*. I hid the strips in her stuff—between the pages of books, in pockets of clothes she hardly ever wore, between the dishes, everywhere.

I bet Julie still hasn't found them all.

Cora Ann should have been suspicious when I asked to go hang gliding with her. I mean, there are two basic philosophies about outdoor sports around here. Cora Ann's group "goes for it." They climb peaks, ski down mountains, kayak boiling rivers, strap themselves to kites and jump off cliffs—thrill-seekers.

The second group is "laid back." We hike. We cross-country ski, canoe lakes, lie under trees and watch the clouds change. Cora Ann is a jock. She could no more sit next to a stream all afternoon, listening to the water and watching trees grow, than I could plug myself into a kayak and shoot the Death Hole Rapids.

Anyhow, I spent an entire Thursday afternoon watching pretty Cora Ann jump off a bluff and float slowly to the ground. She said it was fun.

I drove to the Teton County Library and checked out *Fly: The Complete Book of Sky Sailing*, by Rick Carrier—even read most of it. He says only a suicidal fool would make his first flight from a high point without any instruction. I say only fools fall in love. Or something like that.

I waited until Monday so everyone but Colette would be at the bank. Then I stole Cora Ann's hang glider. I tied it to the top of the bug and drove toward the Broken Hart.

It was a nice day for stealing a hang glider, warm, with enough breeze that a regular paper kite could have flown easily, though I wasn't sure if a hang glider needed the same wind as a dollar K mart kite.

Aspens shimmered. Lupines bloomed. The Tetons stood there like they were posing for a postcard. About two hundred yards down from where I parked the car the night I spent in the tree, a jeep trail cut off west through the woods toward the base of the hill. I followed the track until it dipped into the creek. Then I parked the bug between a couple of cottonwoods and got out.

Untying the glider from the bug's top, I lifted it onto my right shoulder. I remembered that I hadn't locked the car, so I put the hang glider on the ground and rolled up the windows and locked the doors.

I picked the glider back up and waded through the creek and started up the hill. As I sloshed through the bubbling water, the creek did a scene from the old "Dick Van Dyke Show." It was one of those office scenes where Buddy, Sally, and Rob are working on gags. I couldn't help but wonder where the creek had heard a Dick Van Dyke rerun.

Gliders weigh in the thirty-five pound region, which is a lot to carry on your shoulder up a hill—a lot for my skinny shoulder, anyway. I climbed about halfway up the slope before realizing the library book was still in the bug, so, setting the glider on the ground, I walked back down, unlocked the car, found the book, sat in the front seat a moment, then got back out and relocked the doors and walked up to the glider.

When you forget something and must return to the house or car or wherever to get it, it is bad luck just to grab whatever it was you forgot and leave. Always, always, sit for at least ten seconds. That's one of the rules my daddy taught me that I would never think about breaking. His other rule in life was "Always put the right shoe on first."

Way up on the hill I found a nice, clear, gently sloping spot with a beautiful view of the Snake River and the valley buttes. I set the glider down and faced downwind and took a leak. My hands felt sweaty. Suddenly, jumping off a mountain seemed like a drastic thing to do, even for love.

I sat on a rock and thought about Colette a long time.

Thought about her eyes and cheekbones and her hair and the way she walked with her toes pointed straight ahead. I thought about her face after she punted the football over the rectory. The more I thought about Colette, the more I knew this was the way to win her love.

Women are impressed by desperate flashiness.

There's a trick to putting together a hang glider: Have someone help who has done it before. The construction process took most of the morning. I got the rigging wires backward. The front one was too long. The short one didn't go anywhere. The control bar attached to the control box, but I couldn't find the quick-release pin. I finally quit looking and figured I just wouldn't quick-release.

After that, things went together pretty smoothly. I swung the crossbar out at a right angle to the keel, attached the king post wire to the nose assembly, lowered the tail section, rotated my lock nut, and spread my wings. Like putting together a model airplane at home, only I had to fly in this one and I didn't get stoned on the glue.

One bolt didn't seem to fit anywhere. I decided it couldn't be important, so I stuck it in my pocket.

She looked real pretty, lying there all powder-blue in the sun, the fabric kind of glistening and sparkling. I felt good about the whole thing.

My flight plan was to take off, glide north around the edge of the hill, then cut back east toward the Hart ranch. If everything worked, I'd fly into Colette's waiting arms. If it didn't, I'd claim treacherous crosswinds blew me off course and landing at the ranch was a mistake. In my fantasy, I dreamed of scooping her up with one arm as I flew by and, regaining altitude, flying across the Tetons into Idaho. That seemed like too much to hope for.

My heavily suppressed realistic side said I'd never get the damn thing off the ground.

I crawled under the hang glider, put both hands on the control bar, and stood up. Wind filled the space under the wing and pulled me back some. It seemed easier than the guy in the book described it.

The first time I ran down the hill the front end dipped a little and the glider did a nosedive into the dirt. Almost broke my glasses.

The second time I tripped over a rock.

The third time I ran like hell, kept the nose level, elbows down, feet kicking. She took off. Floated. Glided. I couldn't believe it. The son of a bitch worked. I flew toward the base of the hill, hit a thermal or updraft or whatever it's called, and actually rose. Kelly Palamino, whose idea of sports is drinking beer and watching baseball on TV, flew like a bird—a damn buzzard.

I wanted my mom to see me and take my picture. I wanted Julie to see me and say, "Why, he's not incompetent after all."

I leaned right and the kite turned right, leaned left and went into a stall. Scared myself. I pulled down on the control bar, got something of a dive going, picked up speed, and leveled out. Stalls aren't fun. I decided not to have another one.

Slow turn north and on to the Broken Hart. How could Colette resist an eagle with blue wings dropping from the sky? I was almost bound to surprise her.

Following the creek around the corner, I angled for the ranch house. Must have been a hundred feet off the ground when I saw the buildings.

Something was wrong. I counted fourteen people and a dog standing around the lawn between the bunkhouse and the barn. There should have been one, Colette, or maybe two, Colette and Danny's mom. Instead, the whole neighborhood stood below me. I couldn't even pick out which one was her.

An arm pointed at me and all the faces turned my way. Most

of them shaded their eyes with one hand, which made it even harder to find Colette.

I had gone to way too much trouble to back down because of an audience. Besides, I was losing altitude. Besides, I loved Colette.

So I pulled the nose down a tad and aimed myself at the main house.

Colette stood off to the left toward the bunkhouse, next to Danny and Mr. Hart. She was holding something in her hands and staring up at me. The distance made it difficult to be certain, but she didn't look impressed.

At forty-five or fifty feet above the ground, I leaned into a gentle left turn, almost a hover, and went into the act.

"I love you, Colette. Come fly away with me."

John Hart ran into the house.

I had drifted past her and couldn't see Colette's face, so I turned back a full 360 degrees and came in again. *"We can live together in glory and wonder. We can change the world."*

John Hart came out of the house, carrying a rifle.

There were no thermals in sight, no way in hell to gain altitude. John pointed the rifle at me and fired.

Instinctively, stupidly, I twisted to the left to dodge the bullet. Also, I dropped my hands. Who knows why, maybe I thought I could block the shot.

Twisting left and dropping my arms put the hang glider into a steep dive toward the second story of the bunkhouse. Even then, I could have saved myself. I was diving toward an open window. I could have sailed through the window like a Hollywood stuntman, leaving the glider to crash against the wall behind me. It would have been tremendous.

Vaguely, I wondered where the quick-release pin was. Buildings, like cliffs and anything else upright, create wind disturbances, waves of air. Just before I hit the open window, the glider jerked.

I hit the wall about two feet up and a little to the right of the second-story window.

3

Cora Ann was pissed, of course. She swept into the hospital that night while I was sipping a post-Seconal apple juice.

"You destroyed my hang glider, you asshole."

"What?"

"You destroyed my hang glider."

"There's a bell in my eardrums, Cora Ann. I can't hear you."

She sat on the edge of the bed and put her hand on my arm. "I said you're an asshole, creep."

The ringing increased. "I'm sorry, it seemed important at the time."

"*Important?*" she shouted into my ear. "Important? What's important about nearly breaking your neck in the name of love? When are you going to grow up?"

"Talk as softly as you can. My headache is setting hurt records."

"How can I speak up and talk softly at the same time?" She touched one of the bruises on my face. "You're a mess, you know that? When are you going to grow up?"

I pulled a lever, which caused a whirring sound and lowered

my head back and down. "Peter Pan skipped growing up, heard fairy voices as a child, and went straight through to senility," I mumbled, fading off at the end.

Cora Ann reached over and pushed the lever back the other way. My head came up toward her. "I'm talking to you, Kelly. You ruined those people's afternoon, wrecked my hang glider, and almost killed yourself. Don't you think this has gone far enough?"

I reached for the lever, but Cora Ann grabbed my hand. "I'll buy you a new hang glider," I said.

"With what? Do you have any idea the hospital bill you've run up in the last eight hours?"

"No. Can I lie down? It's hard to breathe in this position."

Cora Ann kept her hand over mine. "Why did you do it, Kelly?"

"I'm in love."

"Do you know what would have happened to me if you'd killed yourself this afternoon?"

"You'd have to buy your own peanut butter."

Cora Ann squeezed my hand. "Asshole."

Seven o'clock the next morning, a pretty nurse in white brought me the worst breakfast I've ever eaten. The scrambled eggs tasted like half-price day-olds. The orange juice was so pulpy my hospital straw clogged at the bend. In the early daylight, I assessed myself and the room for the first time. I was wrapped around the head and ribs. I hurt all over. The room wasn't bad, though—no roommate, and it looked out on a nice view of the Tetons that probably ran me an extra fifty dollars a day. I watched the mountains awhile, then fell back asleep.

Lizbeth woke me up. "Kelly, how do you feel?" she asked, shaking my shoulder.

"I'm asleep."

"Wake up, this is costing you twenty-five bucks an hour."

"I never pay anyway. What are you doing here, Lizbeth? I thought you specialized in heads."

"Yours looks like it needs some work."

I started to laugh, which sent one of the cracked ribs through a nerve center.

"Sorry," Lizbeth said as I gagged in pain. "How are you doing, Kelly?"

"Fine. Can I have some Thorazine?"

She sat down in my bedside chair and crossed her legs. "You're already on painkillers."

"I can get stronger pills at the junior high during recess. How about some Thorazine, Lizbeth? I'm having an anxiety attack."

"You were asleep."

"It was fitful sleep."

Lizbeth studied me for a few minutes as if she was reading my psychic profile. "Is there anything I can get you?"

"Yeah, call Cora Ann and tell her to bring my spare glasses. They're in the medicine cabinet at home. No one's ever seen me without my glasses on before."

"No one?"

"No one."

She let that pass. "How are you feeling?"

"I hear bells, my head is killing me, I can't see, and if I breathe, rib splinters go through my heart. And I need Thorazine."

"How's the inside of your head?"

Sometimes Lizbeth uses trendy terms so I'll think she's one of the guys, just like me. "It's all fucked up," I said. "What were those people doing there on a Monday? Who was minding the bank?"

"Yesterday was Memorial Day, the bank was closed."

"Memorial Day?"

"All the banks and the post office close on Memorial Day. The Harts were having a barbecue, which you disrupted."

"They shouldn't have shot me down."

"Kelly." Lizbeth gave me one of those I'm-sane-and-you're-not-so-you-better-listen looks. "I'm a therapist. I don't give advice."

"But—"

"But you're screwing up, Kelly. Not just yourself, you're messing with the lives of perfectly nice people who never did a thing to harm you."

"They shot me out of the sky."

"Did you know Danny Hart brought you into town and stayed at the hospital all yesterday afternoon, until you were out of danger?"

"How do you know?"

"I was here. So was Cora Ann. People care about you, Kelly. You almost died."

"Was Colette here?"

"No."

"Danny was here, but Colette wasn't?"

"That's right."

I looked out the window at the Tetons way off in the distance.

Lizbeth continued, "You were doing so well. You have a job. You don't sleep with Julie's picture anymore. You were coming out of it until you saw this girl and decided she could save you from the loneliness. Nobody can save you, Kelly. You've got to do it yourself."

"You've said that before."

"Listen this time."

We sat in silence for a while, Lizbeth watching me watch the mountains. Finally she asked, "What are you going to do, Kelly?"

"I guess I won't bother her again."

"Good."

"The marriage is bound to fall apart. I'll just wait around and pick up the pieces."

"What if it doesn't fall apart?"

"It will. Colette loves me."

Cora Ann brought my glasses a couple of hours later, but when I put them on, everything still looked fuzzy. The Tetons seemed to shimmer, suspended in the air. It was an odd sensation— unstable mountains. The mountains have always stayed put while everything else was spinning. I closed my eyes so I wouldn't have to see them and went back to sleep.

I dreamed I was tall and wore a coarse black mustache.

"Hey, you."

"Huh?"

"Wake up, Kelly, you've got company."

"Who?"

"It's me, Colette Hart." She was standing there, right next to my hospital bed, not smiling, just looking at me.

"A wet dream right now would kill me."

"This is no wet dream. I came to tell you I don't hate you anymore."

"Do you love me?"

"No."

My vision was still fuzzy, but I could see her tan, even face. She was wearing short cut-off jeans and a T-shirt-type thing that ended above her navel. I could see a small red flower on her hip.

"You have a tattoo," I said.

"What?"

"A tattoo. Some kind of flower."

"It's a rose."

"Why would a woman with a rose tattoo settle for a loan officer?"

"Don't start, Kelly."

We looked at each other awhile. "Would you like to sit down?" I asked.

"I can't stay. How are you?"

"I cracked some ribs and dented my head. It's a thick head."

"What was the purpose?"

"I wanted to swoop down and carry you away into the mountains."

"Oh."

She didn't say anything else, so I went on, "I didn't know it was Memorial Day."

"You fucked up."

"Yeah, guess so. You have nice hands. I like long fingers."

Any other woman would have become self-conscious about her hands and moved them. Colette didn't even glance down. "I can't believe that I could cause such behavior in another person," she said. "I'm not special or unique. Why did you choose me?"

"I love you." I tried to take Colette's hand on that one, but she would have none of it.

"You don't even know me."

"That doesn't matter."

"Doesn't matter? You've made a fool of yourself—almost killed yourself. You must have some vague, insane reason for all this."

I gazed out at the Tetons. "You want the whole rap? The Palamino Philosophy on the purpose of life and why I don't commit suicide?"

"Will it take long?"

"Two minutes, tops."

"I think I'll sit down."

"Okay, sit down."

Colette sat on the chair next to my bed with her hands in her lap.

I began with some basic eye contact. "Sometimes in life we experience moments in which it doesn't matter that we're going to die someday. We escape time by living right now, past and future cease to exist. These moments of present awareness are all that matters, all that justifies existence."

"I could be outside playing."

"Usually I get this feeling of being alive now in nature or listening to music or something independent, but it is possible to find the present with another person. To share reality—that's the greatest thing that can happen to a human."

"Sounds like a line to me."

I waved at the hospital room. "Would I go to this kind of trouble to throw you a line?"

"You might."

"One more minute, okay?"

She nodded.

"Okay. You say I don't know you. That's true, but I can look at you, hear your voice, touch your hair—"

"You've never touched my hair."

"And I *know*, one-hundred-percent-for-sure, no-room-for-doubt *know*, that we can communicate, Colette. That together we can feel, be alive, make living worth dying. It may only last a day or a week, or it might go on an entire lifetime. How long doesn't matter. What matters is that we get so few chances to feel anything with another human—to touch and have it mean something. It's worth any amount of waiting, any amount of embarrassment, to get it because those moments of feeling are the only thing that means shit in life."

Colette sat very still, studying my face. "You believe that crock?"

"Yes."

She blinked twice. "I think you're desperate and lonely and you'll say anything to get me."

"Yes."

Her right hand rubbed up and down her leg. "I'm not into saving drowning men."

By then the eye contact was intense. "Marry me," I said.

"No."

"Will you see me again—after I get out of here?"

"I don't know. Maybe. I've got to admit I never met anyone quite like you before."

"There's never been anyone like me. Does that mean you'll talk to me again?"

"No. It means I might talk to you again."

"When?"

"When?"

"When do you think you might talk to me again? How about tomorrow? I get out in the morning."

"No, not tomorrow."

"Thursday?"

Colette stood up. "Call me around one, Thursday afternoon. I'll think about it."

"All right. You'll see. We're going to be together, Colette. We'll be so happy you'll be in constant bliss."

"Don't shovel it too thick, Kelly."

I tried to touch her hand, but she pulled back. "Try not to kill yourself before Thursday," Colette said.

"You have a very nice tattoo."

Colette left.

I lost my sacred virginity when I was sixteen. I was washing dishes in a small café in Lancaster for a couple named Carol and Blackie. Most of the time Carol waitressed, Blackie cooked, and I washed, but we switched around and filled in for each other on days off.

Carol was a hard little woman in her early forties. She had been in restaurants for twenty-five years and knew how to keep cooks and dishwashers in line. Blackie didn't talk much. Mostly he shuffled around the kitchen, chewing toothpicks and scratching himself.

One afternoon in October, Blackie said he was going to the chiropractor and left me to cook. Carol got suspicious. I don't know what set her to thinking, but she paced around the dining room awhile, muttering to herself. Then she threw on her jacket and ran out.

There weren't any customers, so I cut myself a piece of pie and sat at the counter, eating. I read a Marvel comic called *Red Sonja: She-Devil with a Sword*. Red Sonja had the largest breasts I'd ever seen. She wore a bikini made of chain mail, and on the comic's cover she stood knee-deep in a pile of dead natives, challenging men everywhere to slay her if they could.

I pretended Red Sonja and I were locked in mortal combat. In the struggle, her armored bikini top came off and I saw my life's dream—exposed woman's breasts. Since I had never seen real breasts, I didn't imagine nipples like on a man, but huge, swinging water balloons.

Carol stormed through the front door. "That goddamn cocksucking bastard. I'll fix that wimp. The prick is going to *pay*." She flipped the sign to CLOSED and locked the door.

"What's the matter?" I asked.

"Blackie's in the sack with that little whore, Virginia Mason." Carol pulled down both blinds, first the one to the right of the door, then the one to the left.

"Are you sure?" Virginia was a couple of years above me in high school. I kind of liked her. I couldn't picture her in bed with lumpy Blackie.

"Of course I'm sure. I saw them through the window. He's humping like a dog on a stump." With one sweeping arm movement, Carol cleared six place settings off a table. "Take your clothes off and get up there."

"What?"

"You heard me. Take your clothes off."

I put down the comic book and looked at the cleared table. "There?"

"*Now!*" Carol roared. She could be fierce when the time called for fierceness. It never occurred to me to disobey her.

I bent down to untie one shoe. "Are you trying to seduce me?"

Carol already had her blouse off and was tugging at her skirt. "I'm fucking you."

I paused before untying the other shoe. "I should probably tell you, Carol. I've never been, uh, done this before."

"There's a first time for everything, kid."

Carol stood at the table, naked, hands on her hips, and watched while I undressed. I turned around to face the dish machine while I pulled off my shorts. It was an ancient, round Jackson Sterilizer with a twenty-second rinse cycle, a lousy machine.

"What do I do now?" I asked.

"You stop shaking."

"That may be difficult, Carol. I'm not used to being naked."

She pointed. "Climb up on that table and lay on your back. I'll do the rest."

The table was cold. I arched my back and stared at the swirls in the ceiling.

Carol held my penis in her left hand. "This is the only part of you that's not stiff as a board."

"I'm sorry."

"It'll have to do." Carol crawled onto the table and straddled me with a knee on each side of my hips. "Relax, dammit."

"I can't."

She leaned down and nuzzled my right ear, then started rubbing back and forth across my body. One of her boobs hit me in the eye. I tried to picture Carol's nipples on Red Sonja.

"That's better," she said. "You're getting hard now."

"I am?"

"I knew you could do it. We'll show Blackie who gets the last laugh, won't we? There you go, nice and hard. Now, stick it in here."

"Where?"

She moved her hands between my legs. "Here, right in the old slot."

"I can't see where you want me—"

"That's it." Carol eased herself down on me. I didn't move. She could have been sitting on a tent peg in the ground for all the erotic motion Carol got out of me.

She rocked back and forth with her eyes closed, *ooh*ing and *aah*ing some. "What happens now?" I asked.

A key rattled in the lock and Blackie was there, pulling Carol off me. *"Bitch!"* he screamed.

"Bastard!" she yelled right back. "I saw you and that whore."

"So you couldn't wait to screw the first man you found."

"You bet, buddy. You fuck one and I'll fuck two."

They stood next to the table, Carol naked with her boobs hanging down, Blackie red in the face, screaming at each other. I didn't move a muscle. I figured Blackie might not notice me if I played dead.

He hit her, an open palm across the left ear. Carol grabbed his thumb and bit it, so Blackie hit her with the other hand.

"Oh my God," I moaned. I'd never come before. I had no idea what it felt like or looked like. I thought Carol had hurt something in me and I was hemorrhaging. I gasped, "I'm dying."

Blackie and Carol turned and watched me spurt all over my stomach.

• • •

I tried for three years to do it again—hours spent in my room, holding a *Playboy* foldout above me with my left hand and jerking on myself with the right. I rubbed myself raw, and my right wrist is still stronger than the left. I guess it took sixteen years to build up that first shot and three more to reload.

Finally did, though. The summer I turned nineteen, I got the trick down. Wasted half July and all August yanking on myself.

I didn't get laid again until Julie.

My brain still hadn't swollen by Wednesday, so the doctor gave me a prescription for Tylenol and codeine and turned me loose. Cora Ann came by around ten to drive me out to the bug. She talked all the way.

"The hang glider isn't as bad as I first thought," she said. "It might be possible to fix it."

"Colette came by the hospital yesterday. I think I've got her."

Cora Ann glanced at me. "You're never going to get that little bitch," she said. "Forget her."

"What have you got against Colette?"

"What have you got for her?"

She dropped me off at the bug and I drove slowly into town, trying to figure out why Cora Ann said the things she said. Cora Ann and Lizbeth were the only friends I had; they thought I was a good person, which, Lord knows, I appreciated. That good people thought I was good made a difference; but both of those women hated what I was doing with Colette. Which didn't make much sense. You'd think friends would encourage friends to pursue their heart's desire, no matter what the cost. Maybe Cora Ann and Lizbeth were jealous because I wouldn't marry them. Although that didn't seem likely.

Alice was waiting on the front porch when I got home. "Hi, kitty, kitty," I said. "I had an adventure while I was out." Alice flipped over on her back and said, *"Meow."* I reached down to rub her stomach. Alice dug into my wrist with all four sets of claws and bit the holy hell out of my middle finger.

I owned a puppy once when I was young—seven or eight years old. He was a beautiful little red setter. I named him Snoofy, an obvious attempt to steal Snoopy without being like everyone else. Snoofy followed wherever I walked and slept on the pillow next to me.

One warm evening in August, my friend and I were playing in the backyard, catching fireflies and putting them in jars for lanterns. Snoofy romped around, digging the dirt, licking his paws, being a puppy.

A great horned owl swooped down without a sound and scooped Snoofy up. I saw it. One second Snoofy was playing in the grass, the next he was being carried into the sky.

I reached my hand toward the owl. "Snoofy."

Haven't had a dog since.

Lizbeth is a Southern sorority sister name, I think, but Lizbeth doesn't look sorority-sister at all. If I had to choose an ethnic origin for her, I'd guess California Jewish. She's older than I am, but not by much. I've been talking to her for two years now and I still don't know her. I don't think you're supposed to know your therapist's personal habits.

The cat bite was the final indignity on my way into manic depression with schizoid overtones. Even the proposed meeting with Colette didn't cheer up the fact that I was wrapped in tape, hundreds of dollars in debt, and no closer to Perfect Peace or whatever the hell I wanted than I had ever been. I arrived at our session that afternoon wallowing in a wave of self-pity and despair.

"What did you hope to achieve by hang gliding onto the Broken Hart Ranch?" Lizbeth asked, staring me down.

I looked at both thumbs. "I don't know."

"You must have had some objective in mind."

"I don't know."

She paused. "How do you feel?"

Hanging my head so low the back of my neck hurt, I said, "I wish I hadn't been born."

Kindness crept into her voice. "But you were. It's time to accept that you're alive."

I looked at Lizbeth. "I almost wasn't."

"Weren't what, Kelly?"

"Born. I almost wasn't born. Mom didn't want me so I was almost aborted."

"How do you know this?"

I leaned forward, holding my hands together. "Mom was ten, twelve weeks pregnant when she decided a kid would hold her down—stifle her creative freedom. Mom's real big on creative freedom."

"How do you know she wanted an abortion?"

"She told me, lots of times. Arrangements were made and Mom drove to an abortionist in Idaho Falls. Abortion was real illegal back then."

Lizbeth crossed her legs, left over right, the sign that she didn't believe me.

"Mom sat in the abortionist's office about an hour. Just as they were ready for us, the receptionist asked her for four hundred fifty dollars. Mom started to write a check and the receptionist said, 'You can't pay with a check. Cash only.' Legally, abortionists were in the same category as hit men in 1950. They wouldn't take checks."

"What happened then?"

"Mom took it as a sign from God that she should have the baby. She did and here I am. That's why she told me the story so often, it was a *God moves in mysterious ways* lesson."

Lizbeth still looked dubious. "What do you think it means?"
I shrugged. "She should have flipped a coin."

If I'm going to blame my own peculiarities on Mom, it's only
fair to see where she came by hers. I never knew Grandma—
she fell off a cliff when I was four—but Grandpa Hawken was
a wiry, craggy little man who lived up the end of Bull's Head
Mountain Road with an old, hairless dog and thirty or forty
cats.

As with all old people who live in the woods alone, half the
town thought he was crazy and dangerous and the other half
saw him as the Wise Old Man of the Mountains—an Idaho
guru. I fit in the guru section.

Along about my seventeenth birthday, I went through my
sensitive period. I sat around the backyard, musing on the trag-
edy of life and reading syrupy poetry—Emily Dickinson and
Rod McKuen. I bought posters of sunsets and pure women and
Happy Faces. In my pimply search for Truth, I decided any old
man who lived alone in the woods for years must have found
the answer. One afternoon after school, I hopped on my Western Auto one-speed bike and pedaled up the mountain to find
Grandfather.

Grandfather Hawken was short, not much over five feet tall,
but he had the forearms of a college wrestler. Whenever I think
of the old man, I see those thick, hairy forearms and the tiny
black eyes that skittered across his face.

He was sitting on a buck-and-rail fence in front of his shack,
staring west, into the sun. I picked my way through the cats and
sat down beside him.

"Who're you?" he demanded.

"I'm your grandson Kelly. Mavine's boy."

He nodded a couple of times. "Yeah, I remember. Mavine
only had one. I see you're still a shrimp."

I caught him up on all the news about Mom and Aunt Vera. He didn't seem too interested. Then I got down to business.

"Grandfather Hawken," I said, "you've been around a long time. What have you learned in this life?"

He kept staring at the Big Hole Mountains in the west. His mouth moved, like he was chewing the words before he spit them out. "I can mend a fence and fix windmills. Know how to shoe a horse, tan a cow, and stick a pig. Can roll a real tight Bugle cigarette. Used to be able to drive a car, but can't anymore."

I thought about this. It wasn't the answer I had in mind. "But what's important, Grandpa? What are the priorities of your value system?"

"Value system?"

"What matters?"

The little bent man squirmed around on the fence, waving his head from side to side. He lifted himself up on his hands, then lowered himself again. He seemed angry. He shook one finger at the sun. "Do you see that?" he said urgently. "Do you see what's going on over there?"

"The sun's going down."

His wiry fingers clamped hard on my wrist. *"The sun is going down,"* he shouted. "That's a fucking miracle, boy. A miracle. It'll be an even bigger miracle if it comes back up tomorrow. You ain't never going to see anything more amazing than a sunset." He released my wrist.

Grandpa shook so hard, he almost fell off the fence.

"Now look at this," he demanded. "Look at it." Grandpa held his penis in both hands. It was a giant of penises, a leathery rattlesnake crawling from between his legs; even the head was snakelike. "This is for sex! Use it every chance you get. Never, ever, pass up a chance to stick this in a woman. This"—he shook the snake—"and sunsets are all there is. There ain't nothing else."

"By that do you mean appreciation of nature and romantic love?"

His eyes shook and popped. *"You idiot,"* Grandpa thundered. "I mean sex and sunsets. You take in some of each every day, and you'll never go crazy."

"Are you crazy, Grandfather?" I asked.

"Of course not," he said, stroking the great coil.

Grandpa Hawken was the only member of my family Julie ever liked—including me. It used to make me jealous, the way each knew what the other was thinking. I never could understand either one of them, but he told me once that Julie was just like Grandma Hawken only taller and with bigger tits.

I make it sound like Mom's family was the sole contributor to my particular form of oddness. That isn't exactly true. The Palamino clan also coughed up its share of loose screws.

Back in the late sixties, a Boise doctor installed a pacemaker in my Uncle Homer's chest. He farmed and drank and drove his truck without missing a tick for years before some cowboy told him that a microwave oven could short-circuit his pacemaker and drop him dead on the spot.

After that, Homer quit eating in restaurants, then going to people's houses. Then he stopped going out at all. He stayed in his cabin way off in a field, defending himself against microwaves.

A well-meaning friend drove out to the cabin and told Uncle Homer that a microwave wasn't any more likely to short his pacemaker than a CB radio. This didn't comfort Homer. Almost every truck in Teewinot County sports a CB antenna.

Homer took to sitting in an old straight-backed rocker all day, holding hands with himself and waiting to die. After a few weeks, the fear of sudden death got so much worse than the dying itself that Uncle Homer loaded his antique derringer and blew his pacemaker into the kitchen drapes.

I found the body and the gun.

Colette checked out clear with the Davenport police department—no arrests, no outstanding warrants, they'd never even heard of her. Most of the yearbooks I'd ordered never arrived. They don't normally print extra copies, I guess. Colette wasn't in any of the seven I did receive, so I still didn't know if she'd been a homecoming queen or student-council representative. It didn't much matter. I loved her either way.

I called Thursday around noon, but no one answered. Suspecting another code, I tried various combinations of two rings, hang up and call back, three rings, wait, one ring, wait, then seven rings and hang up. At one o'clock she answered.

"Where have you been?" I asked.

"Having lunch with Doris. Is this Kelly?"

"Of course it's Kelly. Who's Doris?"

"Danny's mother."

I waited. Colette was breathing kind of heavy like she had run to answer the phone. "Did you run to answer the phone?"

"I heard it ringing when I came through the door, and I was afraid whoever was calling might hang up before I reached the phone."

"Then you did run to answer my call?"

"Yes."

"Oh."

I waited a while longer. "When can you meet me?" I asked.

"What?"

"When can you meet me? You said you'd meet me."

"I said I might meet you."

My glasses slid down my nose. I pushed them back up. "Are you or not?"

"Am I or not what?"

"Going to meet me."

"I don't know."

The alarm clock in my bedroom started ringing. "Excuse me," I said. I walked into the bedroom and turned off the alarm, then carried it back to the phone.

"What was that?" Colette asked.

"My alarm clock."

"Was it ringing?"

"Yes."

"At one in the afternoon?" The answer seemed obvious, so I didn't say it. "Why did you set your alarm for one o'clock?"

"I don't know."

"Sometimes I set mine for nine in the morning and it goes off at nine at night, but I've never set an alarm clock for one, day or night."

Propping the phone between my shoulder and ear, I wound the clock. "What are you doing this afternoon?" I asked.

"I'm supposed to exercise Dixie."

"Why does Dixie need help to exercise?"

"She's a horse. Danny's father gave me a horse for a wedding present. She's beautiful."

"I'd like to meet her."

"Who?"

"Your horse. I'd like to meet her. Bring her with you this afternoon."

"Where?"

I thought. Taggart Creek ran a couple of miles north of the Broken Hart. "Do you know where Taggart Creek is?" I asked.

"It's in the park," she said. "First creek up from here."

"That's the one."

"There'll be tourists all over the place."

"There's a bridge on the main trail. Right before the bridge, an old jeep trail goes up the hill. About a half-mile up is a real small dam and reservoir. Meet me there."

Long pause. "I don't know."

"Don't know what?"

"I haven't said I'll meet you at all yet."

The conversation seemed to be circling itself. "Will you or won't you?"

"I don't know."

"You aren't too quick on decisions, are you?"

"I guess not."

I set the alarm clock on the smiling elk skull. "Listen, I'll be at the dam at three. You come tell me what you decided."

"What if I decide not to see you?"

Time for a threat. "I'll come there."

"Jesus, don't do that."

"Okay, see you at three."

"Maybe."

After Colette hung up, I listened to the phone, waiting to see if she would pick it up again. Then I took a shower.

Colette was right about the tourists. Jackson was built to hold five thousand rural people. That's all the room there is. An average summer we'll move over four million tourists through town in twelve weeks. Makes for a manic city and a neurotic populace. Once a year we suffer the culture shock of moving from small town to frantic city. Then every fall it happens again in reverse. No wonder so many of the natives drink.

June came while I was hospitalized, and with it came the Winnebagos and Airstreams, funny hats and rubber spears, fathers thrown together with families they haven't seen in fifty weeks, American children without television. People out of their natural element cause chaos.

I waited five minutes to turn left onto the highway that leads to Grand Teton and Yellowstone—five minutes at an intersection where I usually don't even slow down. Finally I claimed local-license-plate privilege and cut in front of a Continental.

Once in traffic, though, the pace didn't pick up much. The out-of-towners average three miles an hour, craning their necks to see the sights, taking pictures through rolled-up windows, stopping suddenly to let the kids out while Daddy drives around the block in search of a parking place. Fat chance of finding one.

I showed tremendous, uncharacteristic patience by not killing myself and as many of them as I could take with me. On the north end of town across from the A&W, a tall girl in jeans and a sweater stood by the road with one thumb hooked in a belt loop and the other thumb pointing toward traffic. I eased in the bug's clutch and brake and stopped. The guy in the Continental honked rudely.

"Hi there," the girl said, sliding into the front seat.

I moved the gear shift into first, eased back out on the clutch, and pressed on the accelerator. Then I shot something we used to call the bird at the car behind us. "How far you going?" I asked.

"Colter Bay," she said, shrugging her body into a comfortable position.

"You work up there?" I shifted into second.

"Yep, just started a couple of days ago." She was a skinny, tall girl, maybe nineteen years old, with short brown hair, probably from Utah.

"You from Utah?" I asked, skipping third and moving straight into high gear.

"Yeah, how'd you know?"

"I don't know." I didn't know. After all these years of working tourists, I can feel where they're from. It's a game most of us locals play. I hardly ever miss. "How do you like working at Colter Bay?" I asked.

She moved around on the seat to look at me. "It's fun so far. The boys are awfully immature, though, if you know what I mean."

"No, I don't know what you mean." I hadn't considered

what to say to Colette, and this seemed like an important meeting coming up, so I was thinking more about what was fixing to happen than what was happening. I didn't hear the hitchhiking girl's next words.

"What?" I asked.

"The boys that work for the lodge company. They're all so young and looking for girlfriends, you know, steady relationships." She said *girlfriends* like it was a dirty word. She swept the short brown bangs out of her face. "I mean, I like to have fun as much as anyone, more even, but I can't up there because all the boys are so serious and want to get so involved. Besides, they talk and they'll spoil my reputation. I need a good reputation this summer."

"Oh." I rolled down my window and rested my arm on the open edge.

"I'd give anything to meet a guy who doesn't want to get involved. I mean, I'd like a little fun."

I reached down and turned on the radio. "Do you know what time it is?" I asked.

"No."

"I have an appointment at three o'clock. I would hate to be late for my appointment. I wonder what time it is." The radio station was playing a song about a Rocky Mountain High. I hummed along.

"Could I ask you a personal question?" the girl asked.

"How personal?"

"It has to do with what you want or don't want."

"Okay, what's the question?"

"Do you want a blow job?"

The song ended and the disc jockey said it was 2:25 and sixty-six degrees. "From you?"

"Yeah. I'm so frustrated, and I don't know who I can trust at Colter Bay. I mean, all those boys are so serious."

I turned off the radio. "Okay," I said. It had been a while, and I thought a blow job might make a nice drive through the park even nicer.

That Utah girl knew her business, all right. Lots of girls just clamp on the end and go at it like a milking machine. Their mouths get all tired and they get cranky if you don't get off right away, but this girl had read books or something. She treated me like a Popsicle. Started way down at the bottom and tongued her way up, putting on more pressure as she went.

I felt fine, driving along with one arm out the window, watching the beautiful Teton Mountains and having myself sucked by a connoisseur. I took it as a sign. Everything would be great between Colette and me. We'd be married by the Fourth of July. We could have a picnic and invite my parents. Her parents came out for the first wedding, so I didn't know if they could fly back for ours or not. I made a note to ask Colette about it.

There was some confusion at the entrance gate to the park. I was real close to coming and I didn't want the girl to stop. She had moved up into the gentle end-licking stage, but the gate was right there with a perfect view of my front seat. Twisting around, I grabbed a blanket out of the backseat and threw it over her. Then I eased in the clutch and stopped for the gate. It was my first time in the park since they started collecting entrance fees that summer, so I had to dig around in my pocket, which was about knee level, to find some change. I bought a one-day pass instead of the season pass I'd meant to buy. For a local to buy a one-day pass is a waste of money.

The girl in the gate station handed me a map of the park and a Johnny Horizon barf bag and said, "Have a nice day." I don't think the blanket fooled her.

A mile or so up the road, I came—came real strong because it had been a while and I must have built up a good load. The girl didn't swallow it.

"How was that?" she asked, raising her head. She sounded out of breath.

"Very good. You do nice work."

"Thanks." She rolled down her window.

"Do you feel better now?" I asked.

"Sure do. I think I can make it through the summer if I hitch to town once a week."

"I hope so. I know I'll be glad to give you a lift any time I see you on the road." We were almost to the Taggart Creek turnoff. "This is my turn," I said, pushing down the clutch and brake and steering for the right side of the highway.

"Hey, wait a minute. You're leaving me out here in the middle of nowhere."

"I have a three o'clock appointment."

"How about a few more miles for services rendered?"

"You said you didn't want to get involved."

The girl called me an asshole and slammed the door. I turned left past a sign that read SERVICE ROAD ONLY. NO ADMITTANCE.

I always park in maintenance men's parking lots instead of the tourists' lots. It makes me feel a step above the mass.

Before going off to meet my true love, I pulled up my pants. They were kind of sticky. Then I locked the passenger door, opened my door, and got out. I pushed the lock button on my door and slammed it shut. I tried opening it again to make sure the lock worked.

The walk up Taggart Creek to the dam is short, maybe a half-mile, and pretty—lots of aspen and early larkspur. I saw a couple of black-capped chickadees and what I thought was a killdeer. They look so much like plovers it's hard to tell. As I crossed the bridge, the creek sang an old Up With People theme song, then toward the top of the moraine it recited the liner notes from an album called *The Patsy Cline Story*.

"She was the hard-luck kid, hillbilly equivalent of Edith Piaf,

Billie Holiday, and maybe a little Judy Garland. Like all of them, Patsy lived hard, had more than her share of bad luck. . . ."

A thin shriek whistled down the hill. The creek shut up and we listened as it came again—a ground squirrel in the talons of a hawk perhaps, or mating ravens. Or Colette in trouble.

I ran up the last of the rise, around a bend in the jeep trail, and straight into a light brown horse tethered to a bearberry bush. The horse whinnied and sidestepped toward the creek. I bounced into the bush.

"Do you practice these entrances?"

Colette sat on a rock next to the reservoir with her knees hugged up to her chest. Above the knees, her hands were clutched in the first position of "Here is the church, here is the steeple."

"I heard a sound and thought you might be in trouble." Some of the bearberries had squished onto my clean shirt.

"A sound?"

"A squeal."

Colette blew into the gap between her thumbs, making the shriek sound.

"It was you," I said.

She laughed, friendly-like, and opened her hands to show me a wide blade of grass stretched into a reed. "My brother taught me this when we were kids. I can still work it."

"I always wanted to whistle through grass."

"No one ever taught you?"

I shrugged as if to say no, but that was misleading because my dad spent hours showing me different whistles. My failure was my own fault. By shrugging, I avoided a lie. Lying to her wouldn't have been right.

Colette sat watching me as if she expected me to do or say something. I didn't know what to say. I just stood by the bearberry bush, looking at her. She had on a satiny-looking black shirt and pointy-toed boots the same color as her hair.

My hands felt awkward. I held the left one with the right one, then I put the right in my pocket and let the left one dangle.

"I like your horse," I said.

Colette smiled. "She's beautiful, isn't she? I love her so much, I don't know what I'd do without her."

As Colette gazed at the horse, I stepped across the clearing, then stopped. The soft expression on her face might mean it was time to take her into my arms, or it might not. Our futures could be ruined if I made my move too soon.

Colette glanced back at me. "You want to sit down?" She moved over some so there was room for me on the rock. I put my left hand in my other pocket.

"What's her name?" I asked.

"Who?"

"The horse."

"Dixie." Colette pulled a strand of hair behind her left ear so I could see the whole ear. It was pierced. There was a hole, but no earring in it.

"Yeah, Dixie. You told me that over the phone. How's Doris?"

"Will you sit down, you look nervous."

"I'm not nervous."

"Well, I am, this is very peculiar for me."

"Why is it peculiar?"

"Jesus, Kelly, sit down."

I sat on the rock next to Colette. The upper parts of our arms were touching. Neither one of us said anything for a while. I think we were both wrapped up in sexual tension.

Taggart Creek spoke up: *"Did you bet on the Dodgers?"*

"Doris thinks she's got psoriasis," Colette said.

"Psoriasis?" I put my hand on her leg, just above the knee.

"Yeah, she's scared to tell John." Colette picked up my hand and set it on my own leg, then let go of it.

"Why?"

"John will be mad at her." Colette shifted to look at the water spilling over the concrete dam. The dam was real small, probably twenty feet across. Branches had piled together across the outlet.

"Do you love Danny?" I asked.

Her arm moved. "Could we talk about something else?"

"What would you like to talk about?"

"I don't know, small talk. We hardly know each other."

Taggart Creek read aloud, *"On this day in history, 1924: At forty, Franz Kafka dies in Kierling, Austria."*

"Did your brother teach you how to kick a football?" I asked.

Colette nodded. "I was the first girl in Iowa to win a Punt, Pass, and Kick competition. Would have been the Chicago Bears' thirteen-year-old champion if I hadn't shanked my last punt."

"Nineteen twenty-six: Poet Allen Ginsberg is born in Newark, New Jersey."

"Did you know this is Allen Ginsberg's birthday?"

"Who's Allen Ginsberg?"

I started a long explanation of *Howl* and beatniks and the relevance of gay poets in the fifties, but the subject kind of petered out on neo-nihilism. Colette wasn't listening closely anyway. I made another grab for her hand. She pulled away.

"Was your brother at the wedding reception?" I asked.

"No."

"Where was he? You guys must have been close as kids for him to teach you whistling and kicking and things."

"We were close. Dirk was my only pal." Her eyes turned vulnerable and faraway.

"So why wasn't Dirk at the wedding?"

Colette did the hair-behind-the-ear hand movement again. "Dirk died two years ago, bone cancer in his leg."

I watched the water awhile. "Is that why you married Danny?"

"What?"

"Maybe you went looking for a replacement."

"What are you, a shrink? Listen, Kelly, I know the difference between a brother and a husband."

"If you had something really important you wanted to talk about with somebody, who would you want to go to first, Danny or Dirk?"

"This isn't small talk, Kelly."

"Are you going to leave Danny?"

"No, I'm not going to leave Danny." Colette stood up and stepped to the creek bank. "It was nice and peaceful here," she said. "I was comfortable. Why did you have to start in on me like that?"

I stood up also. "I'm sorry about your brother."

Colette hooked both thumbs in her belt loops and stared up the hill. "So am I."

I stood next to her, watching Dixie graze on some kind of weed. A squirrel chattered on the other side of the creek. Above us, a jet left a white vapor trail across a lake-blue sky. Colette's dead brother changed the situation in some way. All along, I'd been thinking about what she could do for me, how much I needed her. I hadn't considered that Colette had a past also.

With her breathing quietly beside me, the entire scenario spread itself out like a made-for-TV movie—the idolized brother dies, leaving a giant hole in pretty Colette's life, she drifts west to start anew, but the emptiness grows until it's almost unbearable. Along comes pleasant, polite Danny with his money and family and football letter jacket, volunteering to take care of her, be the things her beloved brother was. Blinded by pain, Colette mistakes gratitude for love and makes a terrible choice to marry Danny. Now she's stuck, miserable and unhappy, in a promise she can't keep.

What a selfish ass I'd been. All I worried about was me, my true love, my life. The relationship with Julie turned to pus long before she left, but Colette and her brother were separated at the height of their closeness. How much worse that must be than my self-imposed melodrama. Colette needed me more than I needed her. The way was now clear. My calling in life was to save this beautiful woman from her calamitous marriage. I would hound her into loving me for her own good—not mine.

Colette walked over and patted Dixie above the nose. "Sorry I went heavy on you there," she said. "Whenever I think of Dirk I feel sad. I guess I don't really understand death."

I loved Colette more than ever. "You shouldn't apologize for feeling heavy. I eat up heavy. Anything less seems . . ." I couldn't think of a word. ". . . less."

Colette hugged Dixie's neck. It should have been me. "You want to go for a walk?" she asked. "Dixie will be okay, and I don't feel like sitting."

"I just realized that we should get married."

"No."

Colette tested Dixie's reins, slapped her lightly on the shoulder, and walked off up the hill. I followed.

"It's for your own good," I said. "With me, you'll be happy when you're an old woman. If you stay with Danny, you won't be."

The hill behind the reservoir is kind of steep. I had some trouble with loose rocks and only caught up with Colette as she was climbing over a downed log. She said something I couldn't understand.

"What?" I asked. "What was that?"

"How do you know all the answers? I never know anything for sure."

"I know you don't love Danny."

Colette stopped, but she didn't look back at me. "I didn't say that."

"Say what?"

"I didn't say I don't love Danny."

I reached for her arm. "Do you?"

Colette turned around. "Keep it trivial, Kelly, nice and light, okay. I'm not the type for scenes."

Gently, I eased Colette toward me. She almost came into a hug, but then she jerked away.

"This is crazy. I can't talk to you like this. I just got married last month. I haven't even written all the thank-you notes yet."

"Thank-you notes for what?"

"Presents, wedding presents. Come on, let's walk." She started back up the hill.

"What kind of wedding presents?"

"You know. The usual shit."

"No. I don't know. I never got a wedding present."

Colette broke a twig off a blue spruce as we walked past it. "Silverware, towels, bonds, Dixie."

"What kind of bonds?"

"I don't know. John wants us to buy land and have babies."

"You mean bonds to pay for those kinds of things?"

"Yes."

We were nearing the top of the hill. I could see blue sky behind the trees ahead. Taggart Creek said, *"Gil Hodges batted .289 in 1958,"* which I took to be a lie.

"Which do you want first?"

Colette stopped again. "Between babies and land with Danny?"

"Yes, which do you want first?"

She leaned her head back and exhaled. "I can't imagine having a baby by Danny."

"How about me?"

"How about you."

"Can you imagine having a baby by me?"

"No."

At the top of the rise, we turned and looked at the view below. It was nice—bubbling brook, valley floor, dark green mountains in the distance. I touched Colette's hand again. She didn't pull back.

"Let's sit down," I said.

She looked around. "Where?"

"Over here." I pointed with my free hand. "There's a grassy spot where we can sit and watch the sky."

"The sky?"

"Yes."

I sat cross-legged on a clump of grass with a little bank behind it so I could lean back should the occasion for leaning back come along. Colette sat next to me. I had to let go of her hand in order to sit down, but as soon as she got settled, I picked it up again.

"Don't do this, Kelly," she said, but she didn't move her hand.

I shifted around so I was facing Colette and picked up the other hand. I turned her palms so I could look down at them both. "Do you love him?" I asked, looking at her hands.

"I don't know. Maybe."

"Do you love me?" I raised my eyes to look at hers. Her eyes seemed hurt.

"How could I?"

"That's not what I asked."

"God, Kelly, I don't know." We sat there awhile, staring at each other's eyes. "Everything is so complicated," Colette said.

"What's complicated? You don't love Danny and you do love me."

Colette broke the eye contact. "Jesus." There were tears in

her eyes. On the outside corners, then underneath the pupils, tears formed.

"I love you," I said.

"Jesus." She blinked twice and turned to the side. I released her left hand and put my arm around her shoulders. She leaned against me. "I'm so fucked up," Colette said. "What am I going to do?"

A tear came out of her eye. It left a little trail down to her cheekbone where it stopped. I let go of her other hand and reached over to touch the tear.

"You're okay," I said.

Colette looked at the sky. "Jesus." She kind of slid down until she was lying mostly on the grass with her head in my lap, facing away from me, toward the valley floor. I touched her ear and brushed the hair out of her face.

"It's pretty here, isn't it?" Colette sniffed.

"You're safe with me."

"Dirk would have liked you. He liked weird people." She stared out at the clouds coming up behind the mountains on the other side of the valley. "I can't leave Danny. He loves me. We've only been married a month."

"I know."

She didn't move for a long time. "But you are right. I don't love him—not the way I'd want to love a husband. He's such a nice guy and he takes care of me, but I just don't feel what you're supposed to feel."

I said, "You love me."

Colette turned her head to look up at me. "I don't see how that's possible. But maybe I—" A funny look came across Colette's face. "What?" She raised her head and put her hand on my jeans zipper. "Did you whack off on the way out from town?"

I put my hand next to hers. The jeans were damp and a little sticky. "Oh, that. Some hitchhiker gave me a blow job."

Colette sat up. "Male or female?"

"Male or female what?"

"Did a male or female hitchhiker give you a blow job?"

"Female. She just got into the valley, works at Colter Bay and doesn't know anybody. She seemed kind of lonesome."

"So you let her suck your cock?"

I didn't answer. Colette jumped up and started running down the hill. I caught up with her partway down in a real steep spot. The creek said, *"A wise patient never mixes an anticoagulant with an anticonvulsant."*

I grabbed Colette's arm. "What's the matter?"

Colette was crying. She threw my hand off her arm. "Fuck off, Kelly."

"I just want to know why you're acting like this."

She spun to face me. "You tried to convince me to leave my husband. I was almost listening, and five minutes ago you pulled your dick out of some slut's mouth."

"She didn't look like a slut. She was from Utah."

Colette pushed me away. She turned and ran down the hill too fast. Partway down, she tripped, falling forward and rolling a long ways. By the time I got there, she was up and crashing through the trees.

I stopped at the spot where she fell. Cupping my hands on the sides of my mouth, I called, "You didn't sleep alone last night."

Down by the dam, Colette stopped for a moment. Her voice floated up the hill. *"Go to hell, Kelly."*

I stood with my arms at my sides while Colette pulled Dixie's reins off the branch, jumped on the mare's back, and rode away. The creek tumbled and sang, *"You screwed that one up good."*

4

Julie always gave horrible blow jobs. I think she was bad on purpose so she wouldn't have to give them often. They came on Christmas and my birthday—holiday orals. The best job I ever had was from a real young girl in Blackfoot, Idaho. She couldn't have been over thirteen. Had an unbelievably long tongue that she wrapped around me as if I was a corndog.

I heard our scoutmaster in Lancaster gave good head, but I never found out if this was true or just vicious rumor. I've always felt I missed something by not having a homosexual encounter in the scouting movement.

Early in the summer of 1975 I sold an ounce of marijuana to an undercover policeman and Julie and I had to leave New Orleans quickly. There was no time to pick up the last paychecks from work, tell Rick we were leaving, or even gas up the bus. We pulled out five minutes ahead of the parish narcotics squad.

I watched the rearview mirror all the way to Shreveport, where we sold the bus and crossed the state line into Texas. We hitchhiked to Oklahoma City, bought the VW bug, and drove on to Dumas, Texas, where we checked into a motel that advertised CLEAN RESTROOMS and TORNADO CELLARS, and slept for the first time in forty-eight hours. The next day we drove to Jackson Hole.

I say we drove, though I did all the driving. Julie never learned how to operate a car. She said it was too much responsibility. The trip across Wyoming on Interstate 80 was not very pleasant. The wind blew the bug all over the highway. Every time a semi passed, we were almost sucked under the rear wheels.

On top of that, Julie was in a foul mood. She didn't want to leave New Orleans and blamed me for our forced departure. I think she was angry about leaving without saying anything to Rick. She sat against the far door and bitched all the way from Laramie to Rock Springs—two hundred miles of continuous nag.

"It's all your fault."

"I know."

"Look at this. There's nothing. No trees, no buildings, I could die out here."

"You could die in a city."

"At least people would know I was dead. If I die here, no one will find the body for decades."

Julie's whole life had been led between Austin, Texas, and Atlanta, Georgia. She had never seen Wyoming—never had any desire to see Wyoming. My theory is the emptiness, all that vast nothing of the Red Desert, threw her off center. Like a Siamese cat, Julie liked cozy boxes, definite edges to her territory. She wanted to feel that she fit into a special niche in the universe, and Wyoming, with its hundreds of miles of rolling desert, intimidated her. So, swamped by insecurity, she took it out on me.

Finally, tired of her complaints, I pulled into the Outlaw Inn in Rock Springs for a drink. At that time Julie and I, like thousands, maybe even millions, of old-line dope fiends, were making the inevitable transition from drugs to alcohol, and like practically everyone else in our generation, we wasted some time on the missing link between the two—tequila. First we drank it straight and pure, the way a true drug abuser always takes his medicine. Later we moved on to tastier forms, sunrises and margaritas, before finally graduating to the real middle-class-alcoholism drinks, scotch or bourbon and water.

That afternoon in the Outlaw Inn, we had just left the hippie period 1200 miles back down the road, so we took our tequila straight with salt and lemon. Julie and I sat on padded barstools, throwing down shots and admiring the photographs of dead desperadoes until after dark. As the glow rose, Julie's sense of companionship rose with it, and she became a friendly insecure woman instead of a bitchy insecure woman. She leaned against my arm and kissed me once in public, something she would never have done in New Orleans. She told the bartender she was going to stick with me in spite of me being a dunce. He said that was nice.

Smashed, I bought a pint for the road and jammed the bug in gear, heading north. Julie propped the bottle between her legs and talked.

When I first met Julie, she had been waiting all her life for someone to talk to, someone who would listen to her. She came from a large family where no one talked much and no one listened at all. Maybe that's what she saw in me. I can't think of any other attractive traits I had back then. At night, after making love, she would settle into the hollow below my collarbone and tell me about herself. Jumping from subject to subject, skipping fifteen years in a breath, she let out everything she'd been saving since childhood. For hours, sometimes all night, I lay beside Julie, feeling her against me and listening.

A lot of nights I didn't hear the words so much as the music, the rhythm and melody of her voice as it rose and fell, turned and rose again. I loved her for it.

That was the way she talked the night we drove drunk the length of Wyoming in our new VW bug. She told me about her first teacher, her father, her lost virginity, her lost kitten, high school in Atlanta and Dallas, a year at SMU, brothers, boyfriends, whores, oyster bars in Mobile. Some of it I had heard before—gay roommates, her crazy aunt. Some of it was new—a sex dream in junior high, a dinner on Padre Island. The bug hummed. The stars leaped. Mountains loomed far to the north, above the desert, and all the while Julie talked.

I think the Wyoming emptiness made Julie feel lost again, the way she'd felt as a little girl, scared and lonesome. That early summer night, rolling drunk across the sagebrush desert, was the last time Julie ever talked to me about anything that really mattered.

I spent two weeks with Julie's family one Christmas. Her parents were divorced, so I never met her father, but her mother, Eve, was an energetic, critical little woman with a tongue like a needle-point spur. I came from a one-child family. Nothing in my background prepared me for the shock of six kids competing for everything from toothpaste to recognition. They fought a lot. They screamed and slammed doors. Those kids knew each other's weaknesses and ripped into exposed nerves without mercy.

At first I thought they hated each other, but later I found them fiercely loyal to the family when outsiders got involved. Christmas Day, I heard Julie call her overweight little brother a fat slob because he wouldn't get out of bed for breakfast. Later I asked her why one brother was fat and the others skinny like me.

She lit into me, ending with, "If you ever insult one of my family again, I'll burn those lousy books you write."

Before that, I didn't know she thought my books were lousy.

Above all else, Eve hated ugliness and mediocrity. To her, there was no excuse for either. More than once I heard her say any mother who gives birth to an ugly baby should drown it. In her mind, I flunked both tests, so Eve had no use for me at all. She took for granted that I gave Julie drugs because there was no other possible reason why a daughter of hers would live with a scraggly-haired bum with poor posture, and since Julie had a high opinion of her mother's disdain, it turned into a long two weeks. Mostly, I played solitaire at the kitchen table.

It was that hatred for weakness and mediocrity that made the family appear so cold. To become good at something, you must be bad at it first. Right? Eve didn't see it that way. Fear of failure and ridicule made most of the kids never try anything. The others hid their talents. Julie's oldest brother played baseball. He was good, but he never told his mom he played until the day he signed with the New York Mets. Even then, she made fun of the Mets. Another brother is an artist. He makes a good living, but he has yet to show Eve a single painting for fear she'll laugh at it. She would, too.

No wonder Julie opened up like a washed-out dam when I listened to her. She could tell me her secret fears and aspirations without having them flung in her face the next morning in a fight over who drank all the orange juice.

To this day, she hasn't told her mother we were married. Julie and I slept together in the room next to Eve's. She must have heard the springs, but we pretended it was all illegitimate. Better to live with a bum than marry a bore—though sometimes I wonder if maybe I'm not a bum or a bore.

Lizbeth asked me about it once. "Why do you think Julie wouldn't tell her mother she was married?" Lizbeth asked.

I gave my usual "I don't know."

"Was she ashamed of you?"

"No. No, I'd say she was embarrassed. I was a skinny, dirty-haired dishwasher, and Eve would have been terribly hurt to think her daughter settled for scum."

"Who said you were scum?"

"Julie's mom. I suppose Julie agreed at the time. Eve's contempt was pretty forceful. I never saw any of the kids disagree to her face."

"Why was Julie embarrassed by you?"

"Why?"

"Yes."

"She sold herself short on me. It wasn't just her mom. She never told any of her high-school or old street friends we were married. Julie and I were Mr. and Ms. Palamino in New Orleans, Wyoming, and Idaho, but in Dallas we were 'traveling together.' "

"How does that make you feel?"

"Hell, she denies it to everyone now. Cora Ann met her in the secondhand store once and asked, 'Aren't you the girl who used to be married to Kelly Palamino?' and Julie looked her right in the eye and said, 'I've never been married in my life.' Cora Ann believed her."

"How does that make you feel?"

I stared at the pattern of the rug. "Sometimes I wonder if I didn't dream the whole thing. Maybe we weren't married. We never divorced. Maybe I got some bad peyote and hallucinated Father Funk and Victoria, Texas, and the ride to Houston. Maybe Julie and I didn't weather bust scares and sit up all night with sick cats. I mean, Julie says it never happened, and who am I to disagree? She doesn't go to a psychiatrist. She's not crazy. Maybe it didn't happen."

Lizbeth leaned forward. "If it didn't happen, where were you those six years?"

"God, I don't know."

•   •   •

My own mom had an attitude a lot like Eve's during the long-hair years. She wrote a letter while we were living in New Orleans, before she and Julie ever met.

She said, "This girl couldn't be a very nice person or she wouldn't be seen with anyone who looks like you."

You would think Colette shouting, "Go to hell, Kelly," and riding into the south would have pretty much bottomed out my day. I could have adopted an at-least-nothing-worse-can-happen-now attitude and relaxed. Humiliation doesn't work like you would think.

That night I was walking across the town square, heading for the Cowboy Bar and a drink with Cora Ann, when three kids blocked my path. One had longish red hair, the other two looked like early-sixties rednecks. All three wore wool caps.

The redhead demanded, "How old are you?"

"Twenty-nine," I said. "How old are you?"

"We're in the sixth grade and we're going to stomp you," he said. The other two moved forward.

"Why?"

"Because you're twenty-nine."

It wasn't a bad beating, as beatings go. The little redneck on my right swung a hook into my crotch and the others dived high and low—a well-choreographed fight. I wasn't their first victim.

I rolled into the fetal position and protected my glasses while they kicked my back with those pointy-toed cowboy boots of theirs. When I didn't scream or fight back or whatever they wanted, the kids got bored and wandered off to knock down somebody else.

Over the years, I've taken beatings for hair too long, hair too short, talking, not talking, being twenty-nine or just being, and they all end the same—fetal position. That means something about something.

•   •   •

I thought if I lay there long enough someone would come by
and save me. A few people walked through the square, but they
must have mistaken me for a wino or a dead person or something because no one stopped to turn me over.

The pain was considerable. One of the little punks had
landed a solid boot toe to my taped-together rib cage. Breathing
was a problem and the high ringing in my head was back. I
wondered if there might be a reason why some lives are consis-
tently more bizarre than others. I mean, what are the odds
against being sucked by a hitchhiker and beat up by sixth-
graders on the same day?

I drew my knees up under my chest and pushed myself into
the crawl position. By holding on to a tree trunk, I managed to
raise myself more or less upright. When I bent over to brush the
mud off my jeans, blood dribbled from my face. It spattered on
the sidewalk in almost the exact spot where Colette had once
spit.

I unbuttoned my shirt, shrugged it off, and draped it over a
tree branch. My undershirt took more care on account of the
pain when I raised my hands over my head. I hurried as much
as possible, considering the situation. June nights are cool in
Wyoming. Also, I hate for people to see me without a shirt on.
I'm so chest-shy I often wore a pajama top when Julie and I
made love. That was another one of her complaints.

Leaning forward, I pressed the undershirt against my nose
until whatever is supposed to coagulate coagulated. Even in the
dark, anyone would have been able to see the undershirt was
ruined, so I decided to abandon it in the tree. My regular shirt
wasn't nearly as bad as the undershirt, only a few dark spots
on the collar. I put it back on, buttoned all the buttons except
the top one, and tucked the tail into my jeans. I wiped the blood
off my glasses and crossed the street to the Cowboy Bar.

Cora Ann had already ordered a drink for me. "Why don't

you clean up?" she asked, pushing my VO and water down the bar.

"Did you catch my horoscope in the paper this morning?"

"There's grass coming out of your ear."

"I'm having a very strange day."

Cora Ann said, "I don't want to hear about it," nipping an interesting story in the bud.

I slumped over my drink and stared into the mirror behind the bar. The Cowboy is kind of peculiar. The stools have been replaced by saddles. Hundreds of silver dollars are embedded in the bar. The woodwork is all polished, cancer-warped pine. Drinks are expensive, and if you don't tip, the second is mostly water.

The owners run the place as a basic Old West tacky tourist trap for the out-of-towners. By mid-July, vacationers would be sweating all over each other for the fun of polluting themselves in a bar packed full of strangers—no reputations to uphold, no histories to slow down the moves. I've wasted several hours of most days the last few years drinking, dancing, and doing my part for the fantasyland atmosphere.

Lizbeth once told me that if I did normal things in normal surroundings, I might become a bit more normal. Being tragic and crazy is sometimes boring, but I'm not sure I want to try normal yet.

The drink did wonders for my ribs. VO helps any problem. Looking at Cora Ann in the mirror, I asked, "So, what's happening?"

She set down her glass. "For a writer, you talk trite, you know that, Kelly?"

I figured she'd lecture me about something soon enough, so I kept my mouth shut.

"Do you have any idea how many times a day you say 'What's happening'?"

I thought a moment. "About as often as you say 'You're looking at it' or 'Nothing much.' "

"At least I have two answers."

"Well, what is happening?"

"Reword it."

"Hell. Is there anything in which I might be interested occurring in the bar tonight?"

"That's better." Cora Ann flipped her blond head toward the lower lounge. "Your bonus baby is here."

"My what?"

"Colleen and her pals."

"Colette's here? Where?"

"There's a whole table full of social climbers down that way."

I stood up. "I need to talk to her."

Cora Ann held out her right hand. "You know what the peace bond says, Kelly. Two steps closer and you've invaded her territorial waters. Imagine the shame of a criminal record."

I sat back down and picked up my VO. "We had a misunderstanding this afternoon. I need to talk to her."

"She's surrounded, Kelly. Have a drink."

I drained the first one. "You buying?"

"Cheap bastard." Cora Ann ordered another round.

The bar wasn't very crowded, slow for June, even though it was early on a Thursday night. Most of the customers stood grouped around the pool tables. The rest, a few tourists and Colette's table, sat in the lounge. The band was an Arizona group called Two Week Notice. They're the best around for dancing western swing.

"Want to dance?" I asked.

Cora Ann handed me another drink. "I'm not going to help you impress your honey. You'll be watching her instead of dancing."

That's one of Cora Ann's peeves. Sometimes I tend to watch

the crowd and forget what I'm doing. "No, I won't," I said. "I promise."

She looked down at my mud-caked shirt. "Can you dance all taped up?"

"I can always dance."

As we walked to the floor, I checked out Colette and her friends. Cora Ann was right about their belonging to the privileged class. The guys wore forty-dollar chamois shirts and Tony Lama cowboy boots. The other two girls at the table had more invested in their hair than I did in my summer wardrobe. One of them was done up in cornrow braids like a black person from Jamaica. By contrast, Colette was fresh air in a perfume factory—a spring columbine in a field of VFW paper poppies. Given the opportunity, I would have married her on the spot.

I can dance western swing—it's my one talent outside of washing dishes—and Cora Ann can out-twirl, out-dip, and out-spin any woman in Jackson Hole. We make a colorful pair skimming across the floor: Cora Ann, young, beautiful, and happy; me, round-shouldered, assless, shirttail always half in and half out.

The band played a Bob Wills song called "San Antonio Rose." I didn't look at Colette's table because I knew they would all be admiring us. Cora Ann and I put on an act too—pretzels, triple twirls, death drops, front dips, moves so complex they don't even have names. I think Cora Ann tried harder than usual. We could have danced on "The Lawrence Welk Show."

The dance ended with a flashy inside-tuck-type thing where I catch Cora Ann and bend her over backward until her hair brushes the floor. I positioned the move so I could dip Cora Ann and look up into Colette's loving eyes. Only she wasn't there. Danny and the two couples were right where they should have been, but the third chair from the left was empty.

I panicked. "Cora Ann, she's gone."

"Let me up, my spine doesn't bend like this."

"Where's Colette?"

Cora Ann leaned farther back so she was looking at the lounge upside down. "She probably went home."

"Without Danny?"

"Let me up, dammit."

I straightened, pulling Cora Ann up with me. "She's in the bathroom," I said.

"Women like that don't go to the can alone." Cora Ann walked toward the bar and our drinks.

I followed. "You don't know Colette. She's in the bathroom. I can tell."

"So what?"

"Will you go tell her I want to talk to her?"

"Hell, no." Cora Ann stuck two fingers into her drink and popped an ice cube into her mouth.

"No?"

"No. I won't give her any messages. I'll have no part of your soap opera."

"Traitor."

The bathrooms at the Cowboy Bar are off a hallway downstairs. One says COWGIRLS on the door, and the other says COWBOYS. I pushed open the door marked COWGIRLS and walked in.

The walls were painted a different color from the men's room, and the sinks were on the wrong side. Bending over, I looked under the doors of all the stalls.

I said, "Colette?"

Her voice came from the end stall. "Ardith?"

I pushed against the stall door. It wasn't locked, so I walked in and closed the door behind me.

Colette said, "Oh shit."

"Who's Ardith?"

"Kelly, you can't do this. My pants are down."

"You wouldn't piss with them up."

"Leave. I don't want to talk to you."

I leaned against the metal partition between the stalls. "If you didn't want to talk to me, you would have locked the door."

"You think not locking the door was some kind of Freudian slip?"

"Yep."

Colette looked at me a moment. "Jesus, Kelly, you're probably right."

"Sure, I'm right. Who's Ardith?"

"The cowgirl Rastafarian out there. She wouldn't understand this. You've got to leave now. What if somebody walks in?"

As if on cue, the bathroom door opened. I sat in Colette's lap and propped my feet on the toilet-paper dispenser.

We heard footsteps, then water running in the sink. Colette's hand made fists on my legs. There were more footsteps, then the door opened and closed again.

"I'm back to hating you again," Colette said.

"We need to talk. We had a misunderstanding this afternoon, and I don't think either of us will sleep peacefully until we clear it up."

"Misunderstanding, hell, you had a woman give you a—you know."

"Why can you say 'fuck' and 'shit' without blinking, but you have trouble with 'blow job'?"

Colette smiled. "Maybe I'm not a very oral person."

"Is that a joke?"

"What?"

"I'm not an oral person. Was that a joke?"

"Of course it's a joke. You're not an idiot on top of everything else, are you?"

"Because if that was a joke, you couldn't hate me. I read that no one ever tells jokes to people they hate."

"Don't believe everything you read. Now get up and get out. I'm not listening to you anymore."

"You'll never leave this bathroom if you don't listen."

"Is that a threat?"

The door opened again and a girl's voice said, "She's a little whore."

Another, higher voice said, "Did you know she went down on three different guys in the last band that played here? Where did you get those shoes?"

"Idaho Falls. I hate the straps. They look queer."

Someone opened the door to the next stall and a pair of feet walked in and turned around. A pair of jeans settled around the ankles. The girl was right. The shoes did look queer.

Colette leaned back against the toilet tank. She seemed relaxed, considering. She watched my face a moment, then started laughing—hysterical laughter.

"What's so funny over there?" the girl in the next stall asked.

Colette gasped and tried catching her breath, but that only made her laugh more. Finally she got out, "The graffiti."

The voice at the sinks asked, "What's it say?"

I leaned back so Colette could read the door. "I'd rather have a bottle in front of me than a frontal lobotomy."

"That's an old one," the girl in the stall said.

The girl at the sinks said, "Not worth going to pieces over."

Colette giggled. "I never heard it before."

The jeans went up and the toilet flushed. Then the feet moved away. I heard running water and one of them said, "Let's go see if the little twit will buy us a drink." The bathroom door opened and closed again.

Colette started laughing uncontrollably.

"I do not see what is so funny," I said.

"Will you get up?" she laughed. "My legs are asleep."

"What's so funny?" I asked, standing up.

"This doesn't strike you as strange?"

"What?"

"Sitting on me while women go to the bathroom. You don't think that's funny?"

"No. We had a misunderstanding and I'd like to clear it up. Nothing strange about that. I couldn't come to your table, you know."

Colette picked something out of her crotch. "You're all muddy."

"We must talk, Colette. This could seriously damage our relationship."

"We can't talk here. They'll send someone down to look for me soon."

"Where then?"

Colette raised her hand and showed me a chunk of dried mud between her thumb and index finger. "How am I going to explain muddy pubes to Danny?"

"Where can we meet?"

She spread her legs and dropped the mud into the toilet. "If I don't agree, you'll sit on me all night, won't you?"

"Yes."

"Jesus, you're weird, Kelly." She thought awhile. "How about Jackson Lake Lodge? I used to work there and we never saw any locals."

"When?"

"Tomorrow?"

"I have to work tomorrow."

"It'll have to be Monday, then. Danny has the weekend off."

"Okay, Monday afternoon, one o'clock."

Colette stared up at me with those all-alive eyes. "You are remarkable, Kelly," she said. "I think you've got a chance to win me over."

I opened the stall door. "Of course I'll win you over. It's fate."

I walked to the sinks and leaned forward to look at my face

in the mirror. A dark-haired girl walked in the door. She backed up a step, reopened the door, and read the sign that said COW-GIRLS. She looked at me and said, "Excuse me."

I said, "Quite all right," and left.

"Danny's suspicious," Cora Ann said when I walked back to the bar.

"Of what?" The ice in my drink had melted so the VO tasted watery.

"He practically cricked his neck looking for you or Colleen."

"Colette."

"Did you get to her?"

I leaned over the bar and waved a finger at Pam, the bartender. "Could I have another one? With less water this time."

"Did you get to her?"

"Yep. I'm forgiven. She's mine for the picking up."

"Forgiven for what?"

Pam brought my drink and I handed her three one-dollar bills. "We had a misunderstanding. It's cleared up now."

"I bet."

"Bet what?"

"I bet it's cleared up," Cora Ann said with some sarcasm.

"Okay. Ten bucks says she's living with me by Labor Day."

"That's in September?"

"Yep. Ten bucks or get off my back."

"You're mixing metaphors again."

"You're evading."

Cora Ann leaned against the bar, looking past me. She smiled. "It's a bet." Nudging my elbow, she nodded toward the lounge. Colette and Danny were slow dancing, waltzing across the floor. They were kissing each other. On the Cowboy Bar dance floor, right out where the whole world could see, Colette and Danny were kissing.

I was disgusted. "She's only doing that so he won't be suspicious."

Cora Ann said, "Sure," but I could tell she didn't mean it.

I finished the evening by drinking a lot of alcohol and going on a rampage of social blunders. I poured someone else's beer on my head and shouted, "Drinks are on me." I barked at a guy who was trying to pick up Cora Ann. I made a pass at somebody's grandmother. "Didn't we ball on the Champs Elysées the night the Allies liberated Paris?" I asked. The old lady thought it was cute, but her grandson was offended.

At one point, a man threw me out of an all-night café for offering to sell my shoes to a family of tourists. At another point, I came to on the ground in a cemetery with my jeans around my ankles. The Earth mother Rebecca who used to be Lydia was crouched by a marker, holding her dress over her face and crying. She blamed her unhappy life on a domineering father.

Much later, I heaved a rock through Cora Ann's bedroom window. Worst of all, I slept in my shoes and muddy clothes.

5

One reason I wash dishes instead of cook is because I don't have the attention span to grill a medium-well steak—or hold any job that requires alertness. I transcend details. My mind wanders the cosmos, moving effortlessly from past to future and back again, rarely ever stopping in the present.

The only way I know if I've brushed my teeth is to feel the toothbrush. If it's dry, I brush. If it's not, I don't. When walking across intersections, I miss curbs. I'll fall off the first one and think that going down one curb means I'll have to go up another one in a moment, but then I'll start worrying about Hemingway's theme or Willie Nelson's contribution to the world, and bang into the up curb—or walk into a stop sign.

I wake up from these reveries and don't know where I am. I'll be considering the proper way to live when I become rich, and realize I'm staring into a skillet full of black hamburger, or I buy a movie ticket from the girl out front and lose it before I come to the guy who tears them in half.

At various times in life, I blamed this habit on booze, drugs, my mother, my Higher Purpose, fluoridation of the water, but I think I may have always had it. Maybe I was born lost.

The first mind-skip I can remember came in the bathroom right after my thirteenth birthday. I was sitting naked on the toilet lid, wondering whether dead people float or not, when I realized I didn't know why I was sitting naked on the closed toilet. My clothes lay in a pile in the corner, under the towel rack. After some thought, I decided I must be preparing to take a bath.

I plugged in the stopper, turned on the hot water, waited a few moments, then turned on the cold. When the tub was about a quarter full, I stepped in and sat down.

Mom walked into the bathroom. "What are you doing?" she demanded.

"I'm naked, Mom," I said, covering my privates with a wet washrag.

"I've seen you naked your whole life, now what's the idea?" She stood above me, arms crossed over her chest, something like a fundamentalist God on Judgment Day.

"I'm taking a bath. Is there something wrong with taking a bath?"

"There is when you took one ten minutes ago. I heard the water run the first time. What are you trying to pull?"

"Nothing. I'm taking a bath."

"You were doing something dirty and you thought you could cover it by taking another bath."

"What could I do dirty in the bathroom?" I was once naïve enough to say that with a straight face.

"What are you doing under that washrag?"

"Nothing, I'm modest." Thank God Mom never caught me with an erection. I think she would have cut it off with the pinking shears. So far as I can tell, she still doesn't know I've ever had one.

She stared down at me in the tub for a full minute. Then she said, "It's not my fault you're growing up evil. You'll pay for this someday." She stomped out, slamming the door.

Lizbeth says I don't pay attention. Cora Ann, who can't communicate with anyone over twenty-two, says I'm "spaced out." Sometimes I think I act this way because being nebulous is easier than taking care of myself.

The day I woke up with my shoes on, I went into the blackout period at work. I was washing dishes like a demon, slinging plates, stacking cups, listening to the Hobart sing the blues. My mind rested somewhere else: up on the hill studying Colette's hands, outlining her fingernails, which go almost all the way to the first joint where they widen just a little. I was remembering the lines across the palms, trying to decide what it means when the two main lines don't touch, and wondering about that small lump of flesh between Colette's thumb and the rest of her hand.

Somewhere in all this meditation, a giggle seeped in. I looked around to see the whole crew standing by the pickup counter, staring at me the way people stare in dreams when I've gone outside without any pants on.

"What's the matter?" I asked.

Joe, the manager, asked, "What are you doing, Kelly?" This made a couple of waitresses burst into laughter.

"Washing dishes."

"Is there something wrong with the dish machine?" Joe is a well-enough-meaning guy for a manager. He puts up with my eccentricities, so I try to humor him when I can.

"Not that I know of."

"You're washing the same dishes over and over."

"Huh?"

"Look at that plate in your hand. Why are you loading it into the wash rack?" I looked at the plate. It sparkled. As the saying goes, it was clean enough to eat off of.

"I've already washed this plate."

Joe nodded. "Right, why are you washing it again?"

I looked back at the plate. "I forgot I already washed it."

"You want to take a break or something?" Joe asked.

"No, I'm fine. I'll only clean them once from now on." The waitresses stared at me as if I was some kind of a freak. I guess I made them nervous.

That first weekend in June was gray, rainy, cold, rotten. The tourists hid in their motel rooms, watching cable TV and chewing candy bars. Locals stood around the bars and shot pool and drank to fight off the terminal boredom. I rehearsed speeches to give Colette, knowing if the words were dazzling enough and the love undying enough, I could hook her like a rainbow trout on a dry fly. I even practiced a few lines on Alice. She turned her back and washed her face.

Monday, however, the world changed. The sun came out. The Tetons sparkled in air so pure, so clean, the city folks' lungs must have ached just to breathe it. Driving through Grand Teton Park, I rolled down the windows, turned the radio up full blast, and absorbed life. I was so busy absorbing that I almost ran down a camera-toting tourist who stood on the highway, focused on a buffalo. I swerved between him and the buffalo, frightening all three of us and ruining the picture.

Jackson Lake Lodge sits on a hill overlooking a flat willow swamp with Jackson Lake behind the swamp and Mount Moran behind Jackson Lake. The doors open onto a long room where guests register for cabins and float trips and horseback rides; then there is a wide stairway up to a huge, high-ceilinged place full of overstuffed chairs and old, wealthy people in off-colored slacks.

The bar is behind the stairway. A sign over the door says THE STOCKADE ROOM, NO MINORS ALLOWED. The lounge is made up to look like a wilderness fort from Daniel Boone's days, all vertical log walls and animal furs, a couple of carved mountain men in full regalia. The ceiling is painted black and the lights are little inset twinklers. It's supposed to be the night sky over Wyoming. Opposite the entrance is another set of doors opening onto an outdoor deck with chairs and tables.

I sat in the far left corner against the wall.

"You're my fourth customer of the summer," the cocktail waitress said. She wore a short skirt, cut jagged at the bottom like a Hollywood version of the happy Indian maiden, and long boots.

"What?" I said.

"We only opened today. You're the fourth customer."

"Oh."

"I guessed where the other three were from. Didn't miss a one. Want me to guess where you're from?"

"I'm from Jackson."

She leaned on one leg and studied me. "I bet you're from Wisconsin," she said. "You have that Wisconsin look."

"I'm from Jackson."

"Come on, nobody's from Jackson. You were raised in Wisconsin, right?"

"No."

She didn't believe me. I ruined her perfect record. "What do you want?"

"VO and water."

She wrote it down and walked away. A cardboard pyramid stood in the middle of the table with a specialty drink described on each of the four sides. Turning it slowly, I read about each one. They all sounded sweet.

"Two dollars," the cocktail waitress said.

I handed her two-fifty. "Do you know what time it is?" I asked.

"Around one. Will that be all?"

"Yes, thank you."

She walked back to the bar and began talking to the bartender. I sipped the drink. It was mostly water. The waitress with her guess-where-you're-from game rankled me somewhat. For one thing, it was my game. For another, she was a seasonal employee—a summertime native. Resort areas worldwide maintain strict social caste systems based on how long each member has lived there, the idea being that "anyone who came after me is an outsider." The system rates the seasonal employee somewhere above the tourists and below horses. No skinny-legged college girl working through summer vacation had the right to ask me where I was from. The bitch.

As I fumed about the cocktail waitress, a man came in wearing a checked sports coat. He picked up an accordion and began to sing. Since I was the only customer in the bar, he glanced at me from time to time to see if I appreciated the songs. I smiled and nodded.

"Any requests, kid?" the man said.

I thought. "Do you know 'Oklahoma Hills Where I Was Born'?"

"No." He broke into "Climb Every Mountain," leaning into each stroke on the accordion.

"You want another one?" the cocktail waitress asked.

I looked up. She was pretty, for a college girl, but the scowl marred her face. "Do you know what time it is?"

"One-thirty, do you want another drink or not?"

I fingered my glass. Most of the ice had melted. "Actually," I said, "I was born in Milwaukee, lived there till I was twelve."

"I knew it," she gloated. "I can spot Wisconsin every time. Listen, since it's opening day, the next round's on me." She twirled and scampered back to the bar, anxious to tell the bartender that her perfect record was still perfect.

I started drink number three before Colette walked through the door. She stood in the entrance, waiting for her eyes to adjust to the bar darkness. She was wearing the same white

western shirt she'd worn the first day I drove to the Broken
Hart. Her hair was in a ponytail.

I waved my arm to get her attention. "You look nice today,"
I said as she slipped into the chair next to mine.

"I don't feel nice. I'm only here because you trapped me in
the toilet, and I knew if I didn't come, you'd think of something
even worse to subject me to next time."

I raised my glass to my lips and sipped. "You don't sound
in as good a mood as you were Thursday night."

She picked up the cardboard pyramid and turned it around.
"I had all weekend to think. When I think, I get sane and realize
what you're doing to me."

"The waitress is a smartass. When she guesses your home
state, tell her she's right."

"Why?"

"Why are you so late?"

Colette set the pyramid back down. "None of your goddamn
business. You look drunk." She seemed to have worked herself
into a fury. The eyebrows, usually so relaxed and wide, were
drawn together low over her eyes. Her shoulders were raised,
tight. This wasn't the Colette I knew and loved.

"I was on time. There's nothing to do in this bar but drink."

"How many have you had?"

"I'm on my second."

The cocktail waitress walked over with her tray braced between one hand and her hip. "Hi. What can I get you?" she
asked.

Colette brushed her hair behind her right ear. "I'll take a
double Grand Marnier, on the rocks."

The cocktail waitress didn't move. "Say 'I have to go to the
market.' "

"Why?" Colette asked.

"Say it," I said.

"I have to go to the market."

The cocktail waitress put the tip of her pencil on her upper lip. "Southern, right. East side of Tennessee."

I jumped in before Colette could answer. "Damn, you're good. How'd you do that?"

"I deal with a lot of tourists. I am right, aren't I?" she asked Colette.

"Yeah, I guess so," Colette muttered. When the waitress was gone, she turned on me. "You sure lie easily."

I drained my glass. "I do what it takes to get a decent drink."

"Do you do what it takes to get a decent woman?"

"What the hell's eating you?"

Colette looked away, toward the bar. "I'm pissed."

"So I noticed. I'm Grumpy. Do you always drink Grand Marnier?"

"Is there anything wrong with that?"

We observed a moment of silence until the cocktail waitress brought the drinks. "Together, that's seven dollars," she said. Colette looked at me. I dug into my pocket for a five and two ones. I handed them to the waitress, but she didn't leave. "You're honeymooners, aren't you? I can always spot the honeymooners."

Colette scowled. "No, we are not honeymooners."

I put my arm around her. "Aw, hell, honey, let's admit it. We can't fool this little girl."

"I knew it," said the waitress, then she went off to tell the bartender.

Colette shrugged my arm off her shoulder. "You've got a lot of nerve, Kelly."

"She's seasonal." I drank, then put down my new glass. "What's gotten into you anyway? You're a whole different person."

Colette was in a horrible state, all worked up and emotional. She looked like she might cry. "How dare you tell her we're honeymooners."

"Jesus—" I started.

"Don't Jesus me."

"So, you want to be honeymooners?"

"I'm warning you, Kelly, don't start that shit."

"We'll have to get married first."

Colette breathed deeply a couple of times. She tossed down her drink, five dollars' worth of sticky liqueur in one chug. "It's all over, Kelly," she said. "The game has lasted long enough."

"What do you mean?"

"Danny loves me. I can't and won't leave him."

I tried making eye contact, but she would have no part of it. "We're meant for each other," I said.

"No, we aren't. You do bizarre things, and I'm impressed because somebody's willing to make a fool of himself over me, but that's not love or fate. That's just you acting like a fool."

"What bizarre things have I done?"

She looked at me. "You don't know? You sat in a tree outside my house half the night, you literally crashed my father-in-law's barbecue, you trapped me in the toilet. That's not bizarre? Not to mention that stunt at the wedding reception."

I looked around the bar, not knowing what to say. Another couple had come in, the accordion player was taking a break, the waitress and the bartender huddled in the corner. Nobody seemed to care that my life was draining onto the floor. "I'd rather not live without you."

Colette stared at her empty drink. "You'll have to get used to it."

The cocktail waitress approached us, carrying her tray up on her shoulder. The accordion player bounced along behind her, grinning. "Free drinks for the newlyweds," the waitress laughed, setting another VO and another Grand Marnier on the table. She stood next to me, smiling.

The accordion player planted both feet, pulled his hands apart, closed his eyes, and broke into "Some Enchanted Evening." His voice was a good octave higher than Ezio Pinza's or whoever sang it first. And he pronounced "enchanted evening" like Lawrence Welk—"Enchandid Efening." "I love you, Colette," I said over the music. "I'll die without you."

The accordion's volume rose and fell and rose again. Colette smashed her empty glass on the floor. "How dare you say that to me. How dare you dump the responsibility for your life in my lap."

"I can't help it."

"You make me so mad I could slug you." Colette gulped down her second drink. The cocktail waitress stood very still. The accordion player went into verse two, winding up for the big finish.

Colette was crying, "I can't stand it anymore."

I yelled, "*I love you.*"

"*I'm married!*" She swung a right hook that struck me on the left cheekbone, knocking me to the floor.

The accordion player held the last word of the song, which was "go," about seven seconds. "Go-o-o-o." Then he sighed and opened his eyes, expecting applause or a tip or something other than me on the floor.

Colette covered her mouth with one hand. "Oh, I'm sorry, Kelly. I got excited." She turned to the cocktail waitress. "I got excited. I'm sorry. He's frustrating sometimes, and—"

"You aren't really honeymooners, are you," the waitress said.

Colette looked back down at me. "Uh, no, not really. I mean, I am, almost. I was a couple of weeks ago—but not with him."

The cocktail waitress walked away. The accordion player didn't move. Colette said, "Get up, Kelly. I said I was sorry."

I felt the side of my head with my hand. "Loving you has been tough on my body."

Colette laughed. "I'm better now, I needed that. Let's walk out on the deck and have a drink—on me."

"Are you going to hit me again?"

She stood up. "Nope, I promise. It's all out of my system. You go outside and I'll clean up the broken glass and buy us another round."

"I still have a full drink."

"I'll get you another."

Close to drunk, I stumbled past the accordion player and out the door onto the deck. What kind of woman had I chosen for my life mate anyway? I mean, I was crazy, but at least I was consistent about it. Colette always did the unexpected. Laughing when we were trapped in the toilet, slugging me for no reason, running away just because my zipper was sticky. Thursday afternoon she yelled, "Fuck off, Kelly." Thursday night she said I might win her over, Monday afternoon she flattened me, then bought me a drink. Colette wasn't any more stable than I was. We'd be perfect together.

"The waitress was nice, considering," Colette said, walking onto the deck. "She didn't seem mad at all about the glass." Colette had a drink in each hand. Hers was a double.

"She's probably confused," I said. I set the new drink by my other one. "Your brother teach you how to punch?"

"No, I'm afraid that was spontaneous violence."

"You've got fighter's instincts."

"Thank you."

Colette sat next to me, watching the tourists move in and out of the parking lot. We could see sunbathers at the pool behind the lot and farther off lay the valley and the Gros Ventre Mountains. The sun felt real good on my skin. I closed my eyes.

"What's that mountain over there?" Colette asked.

I opened one eye. "Mount Leidy."

"It looks lonesome all by itself."

"Everybody's lonesome all by themselves."

Colette giggled and sipped her Marnier. "You sound drunk."

"I am drunk," I said. "I have a confession. I had three drinks before you came, not two."

"You do lie easily, don't you?"

I closed both eyes again. "Maybe."

We sat in silence some more. I took Colette's hand and she squeezed once.

"Damn, it's nice here," she said.

I settled deeper into the chair. "You'd have to be crazy to live anywhere but Jackson Hole."

I could hear Colette sucking ice from her drink. "John says you are crazy. He says you were locked up awhile."

"I was hospitalized, not locked up."

"Why?"

"They said I tried to kill myself."

"What did you do?"

"Do you really want to go into this?"

"Sure, what did you do?"

I opened my eyes to look at Colette. She was so beautiful. "I hit three shots of tequila in the Cowboy Bar bathroom one night."

"Hit?"

"Shot up."

"You injected tequila into your bloodstream? With a needle?"

She didn't seem shocked or anything, just curious. "Yep. I wasn't trying to kill myself, I only wanted to cop a buzz."

"What's 'cop a buzz'?"

"Get drunk."

Colette cleared the hair out of her eyes. "What happens when you inject that much tequila?"

I picked up one of my drinks and drained half of it. "Your eyes and ears bleed and you fall down and stop breathing."

"Is that what happened to you?"

"I don't know. That's what they said happened to me. I woke up with tubes down my nose and my wrists tied to the bed."

"What happened then?" Colette asked.

I drank the rest of the VO. "A judge told me to see a psychiatrist once a week until I got well."

"Are you well now?"

"I never was sick."

Colette looked off at the pool. "Do you still see a psychiatrist?"

"Yep. Why did you spit in the square the other day?"

"When did I spit in the square?"

"The day you telephoned me. You were standing in front of the war memorial and you spit."

Colette leaned her head back and closed her eyes. I think being with me made her feel at ease. "I was sealing a wish."

"People don't seal wishes with spit."

"I do, it's another one of Dirk's habits."

"What did you wish for?"

Colette's eyes flickered open, then shut. "Nothing. Stupid stuff."

"Come on and tell me. I'm interested in this sort of thing."

Colette exhaled—almost a sigh. "The names on the memorial are sad. I wished for world peace."

I was amazed. "Jesus, that's major."

"It was more wishful thinking than a real wish."

"I generally wish for money or sex or something for me, but world peace? Isn't that a bit much?"

"I didn't expect it to come true."

I thought about the kind of person who makes wishes for world peace. What if Colette did stuff like that regularly? The implications were complex and disturbing. A mosquito landed on Colette's thumb and I let go of her hand long enough to brush it away. Colette reached over and took my hand back. I almost cheered.

"Are you going to leave Danny?" I asked.

She looked down at our hands. "No."

We sat in silence. I closed one eye and tried to focus on a woman on the diving board, but she was too far away. Colette pulled her hand from mine and held her Marnier in both palms, staring into it like a tea-leaf reader.

"Why not?" I asked.

She shrugged. "I married him. He loves me and I make him happy. I never made anyone happy before."

I closed both eyes. Yellow sunspots sprang up all over the insides of my eyelids. "What about you?"

"What about me?"

"Have you ever made yourself happy?"

Colette didn't answer. I heard her lean forward. "Oh, shit," she said.

I opened my eyes, but the sunspots didn't go away. They spun slowly, counterclockwise.

"Oh, shit," Colette said again.

"What's the matter?"

She pointed at the sidewalk below us. "It's John."

"John?"

"My father-in-law John. What's he doing here?"

I leaned forward and looked over the rail. It made me dizzy. "Why does he walk like his ass is sunburned?"

"John Hart always leads with his crotch." Colette grabbed my right arm below the elbow. "I think we should do something about this."

"Huh?"

"We can't let him catch us here."

"Oh."

She stood up, pulling on my arm. "Come on, Kelly. We've got to get out quick."

"I'd rather not move. I'm comfortable."

"I'm not, let's go." She walked into a chair and banged her thigh. "Shit." Colette held her leg and turned back to me. "Kelly, you've got to come with me."

We helped each other through the doors leading into the Stockade Room. As we passed the bar, I said, "I've never been in Wisconsin in my life." I don't know if the cocktail waitress heard me or not.

John was almost to the top of the stairs. He seemed to be with a couple of other men because all three wore double-breasted suits.

"What do we do?" Colette asked.

I looked around. "We could hide in the bathrooms."

"Not on your life."

I nodded. "Try that door."

Colette dragged me through the door. I leaned against the wall while she peeked out. "They're coming this way."

"Figures."

We ran and stumbled down a long hall to a dead end at two doors marked MEETING ROOM A and MEETING ROOM B.

"You know damn well whichever door we pick will be the one he's going to," Colette said.

"Want to split up?"

She shoved open door B. "No way. We live or die together on this one."

"You knocked me down twenty minutes ago and said it was all over."

"It is all over as soon as we get out of this."

"We should have stayed in the bar."

Meeting Room B contained one long table surrounded by eight chairs. At one end of the table was a wooden lectern.

"Where's the fire escape?" Colette asked.

"Where's the window?"

She put her ear to the door. "They're coming."

I sat in one of the chairs. "We're fucked."

"You're never fucked till they stick it in." Colette grabbed my arm, pulling me out of the chair.

"What does that mean?"

She dragged me toward the end of the table. "The lectern is hollow. We'll hide in it."

"The lectern is four feet tall."

"We'll bend over."

"My ribs don't bend."

"*Kelly.*"

Colette curled into a ball at my feet. I picked up the lectern and lowered it over my shoulders, stooping down until my knees rested on her back. I whispered, "I can't do this for more than thirty seconds."

"Shuddup," Colette hissed.

The door opened. A high, scrawny voice said, "They aren't here yet."

John Hart's voice boomed. "They will be. He needs us more than we need him." He talked as if every word was being written down somewhere.

Chairs scraped back and forth, somebody cleared his throat, a pencil tapped a four-beat rhythm on the table. Inside the lectern, I wasn't anywhere close to comfortable. My ribs were killing me. Colette seemed to be breathing all the oxygen because I sure wasn't getting any, plus I had this ugly sensation I would soon throw up on her.

The door opened again—more footsteps and a lot more chair-scrapings. John Hart said, "Mr. O'Henry, Mr. Spinelli, meet my associates, George Patterson and Donald Shultz."

"Pleased to meet you," the scrawny voice said.

Chairs were pulled out and in again. I caught clicking sounds like briefcases being opened. I tightened my grip on Colette's shoulders, knowing I would pass out soon and wanting to warn her.

"Did you have a good flight from New Jersey?" John asked.

A voice with a sickening Northeastern accent answered. "Do you mind if we get down to business? I'm booked to L.A. tonight and I'd like to get this over with quickly."

But they didn't get it over with quickly. At first I tried following the conversation. It seemed that John and the bank wanted to pass off some land and the Easterners wanted to build condominiums—lots of condominiums. From the talk, it sounded as if they wanted to build an entire city. I heard terms like *shopping complex, zoning ordinances*, and *sewage-treatment plant*. The Easterners had a deep fear of "environmental assholes" slowing down the project, and John kept assuring them that environmentalists were "no more bother than the mosquitoes."

Twice I heard him say he had the county commissioners "by the balls," and they would "zone the cemetery for a roller disco if I told them to."

As the discussion turned to interest rates, stock options, commissions, and kickbacks, my ears started ringing, inhalation became pretty much impossible, and both calves turned to charley horses. My lower back hurt quite a bit. I felt horribly sober. Sweat dripped onto Colette. I put my palm on her back to see if she was still breathing, but I couldn't tell. I tried to imagine how the janitor would feel three days later when he smelled something funny and lifted the lectern to find two dead bodies.

We should never have left the deck. Colette and I could still be out there in the sunshine, getting soused and discussing my insanity. It's always a mistake to move quickly. I knew that. It was one of my mottoes. When faced with a problem, if possible, do nothing.

I might have been unconscious, I don't know, but someone rapped on the lectern next to my ear, scaring the hell out of me.

"Knock on wood," John Hart said. The others all laughed. Briefcases clicked, chairs scraped, a voice said, "I'll buy you a drink," and another voice said, "I could use one." Shoes scuffed across the floor. I heard the door open.

The footsteps drifted into the hall, then I heard John Hart's voice. "I'll catch up in a moment, George. I forgot some papers." The door closed and a single set of footsteps walked toward us.

The lectern slid off my shoulders. Colette and I fell sideways, to the right. We lay on the hardwood floor, gasping for breath, bathed in sweat. She was cadaver-green and stuck in the frightened-armadillo position. I lay on my back with my knees and feet in the air, choking.

John Hart demanded, "Get up, Colette."

Colette shuddered and made a moaning sound.

"Get up."

She rolled over with her knees tucked under her chin and most of her weight balanced on her forehead. The moan deteriorated into a whimper. John reached down, grabbed the back of Colette's shirt, and yanked her to her feet. She almost fell.

"Wait in the hall," John said, shoving Colette toward the door. She looked back at me with pitiful fawn eyes. She seemed about to say something. Her mouth opened, but nothing came out.

I lay on the floor spread-eagled like a crucified Jesus and stared up at a fluorescent light fixture in the ceiling. I expected John to stomp my face and ribs—hell, everybody else had that week—and I desperately needed to clear my head before he smashed it.

John Hart's pinched-up, dirt-brown face hovered above me. "You're scum," he said. "You're worse than scum."

I didn't protest or defend myself. He was probably right.

"If you aren't out of this valley—out of this state—in twenty-four hours, scum, you're going to wish you had never been born. I'm a powerful man, scum. I can make your life miserable."

He stared down at me for a while. "Twenty-four hours, got it?"

I nodded and braced myself for the kick I knew would follow. Instead, John spit on my face, my forehead to be specific. A long, wet glob of spit landed right over my left eyebrow. I was so glad not to be getting stomped again, I almost thanked him.

Later I stretched my aching body onto my couch and listened to various drips and drains argue the situation. The water heater was worried about Colette, but the kitchen hot-water faucet raved on, totally pissed at John.

"Put sugar in his gas tank. Throw a brick through his window. Spread the rumor he has pinworms," and on and on.

In television commercials, everything talks—roaches, stomachs, carrots, dogs, germs, even baking-soda boxes—so I suppose it is only natural that we grow up expecting dead objects to speak with cute, high voices, but sometimes auditory psychosis is nothing but a bother.

Maybe mass murderers only want a little peace and quiet.

The next day, while I sorted silverware, Joe came out of his office and stood at the head of my dish machine. "I need to talk to you, Kelly," he said.

I was listening to a Leadbelly song playing in the rinse cycle and didn't hear.

"Kelly," Joe said. "Come into the office."

"Can't it wait? I'm doing forks. The girls are short on forks to set up tonight."

"No, it can't wait."

As I turned off the Hobart, the overflow drain sighed and sang the last chorus of "Goodnight Irene." *"I'll see you in my dreams."* The gurgle was kind of mournful, as if the machine knew it was saying good-bye for the last time. I felt closer to that Hobart than any other dish machine I've ever worked with.

Joe sat in his chair with the tips of his fingers touching. I leaned against the edge of his desk. Joe's face flushed red; kind of a deep rhubarb color. I had known him long enough to know what it meant.

"Why?" I asked.

Joe wouldn't look at me. "I'm sorry," he said.

"I'm the best dishwasher in Teton County."

"You're the best in Wyoming, maybe even the whole Rocky Mountains."

"Then why fire me?"

Joe rubbed his fingers in small circles. "John Hart."

"Oh."

"It's not just all the money I owe him, though I owe a lot. The health inspector owes John money also. And everyone on the county planning commission, my milk and meat suppliers, people at the phone and electric companies."

"I understand."

"He could shut me down in an hour, Kelly. In fact, he will if you're not gone by four."

"I understand."

"I'm really sorry, Kelly."

I moved farther onto the desk so I was sitting more than leaning. Joe's eyes slid across me and focused on the wall to my left. His fingers moved back and forth, interlocking, then pulling apart.

"When can I get paid?" I asked.

He pointed to an envelope on the desk. "There's your check."

I picked up the envelope and looked at the front. It had *Kelly Palamino* written on it in blue ink.

"Guess that's it," I said.

Joe looked at me, then away, then back. He still seemed uncomfortable, red. "There's one other thing I wanted to tell you. It's not really any of my business, but I suppose it's yours, so I ought to tell you."

"What's none of your business?"

He hesitated. "I'm pretty good friends of Julie and Rick, you know."

"How are they? I never see them anymore."

"They're fine, but when I first hired you, before you even

came to work, Julie dropped by and tried to talk me into firing you."

"What?"

"She said she wouldn't come around the restaurant if you were here."

"I know we aren't friends now, but this is surprising. I always thought Julie wished me well."

"She and Rick are spreading around that you're insane and dangerous."

I looked at Joe. "Do you think I am?"

He wouldn't look back at me. "I don't think you're dangerous."

"Thanks."

"Most people believe her. They can't see any reason why Julie would lie."

I turned over the envelope and looked at the back. It was sealed. "Why would she lie?"

Joe moved his hands to his sides, pushing on the edge of the chair. "I like Julie and Rick a lot, but they are kind of strange. They're buying some land. Rick's talking about opening a sporting-goods store. They're going middle-class respectable, and it embarrasses the hell out of them when you get drunk and tell people about panhandling in New Orleans or that hocus wedding in Texas."

"It wasn't hocus."

"Yeah? Julie says it was all a put-up job for your mother. Anyway, you're Julie's dark, secret, ugly past and she can't stand having you around reminding her and everyone else she was ever like that."

"The wedding wasn't hocus. Why does Julie say we're not married?"

"She doesn't want to think about you. She wants you out of town."

I stood up to leave. "There's not much she can do about it. I'm in town."

Joe finally made a little eye contact. "Julie's been talking to your mother."

I sat back down on the edge of the desk. "My mother?"

"Julie says between them they can get you institutionalized."

"What's that?"

"Committed. Out of the way."

"Why would my mother want me in an institution?"

Joe shrugged. "How should I know? She's your mother. Julie probably has her believing you're a potential child raper."

"I'm not."

"I know that. Convince your mother."

"How?"

"If Julie teams up with John Hart, you could be in a mess of trouble. I'd hate to have those two for enemies."

I thought a moment, but nothing made sense. My mother and Julie had never agreed on anything. Why work together now? And why lock me up? "What should I do?" I asked.

"You could leave town for a while."

I stood up again. "I can't do that. I'd shrivel and die if I left Jackson Hole."

"Think about it, Kelly. You're a fantastic dishwasher. I'd hate to see you locked away in a nuthouse the rest of your life."

"Thanks."

Joe shook my hand. The waitresses lined up and kissed and hugged me. The cook wished me well. I walked away from my beautiful Hobart without looking back.

Even though it was only Tuesday and my appointment was for Wednesday, I drove straight from work to see Lizbeth. I was upset about things, and I figured I might be able to milk the firing for some legal drugs.

Luckily, someone had committed suicide or something because Lizbeth had an open half hour. I told her about Julie's plan.

"I'm Julie's dark, secret, ugly past, and she can't stand having me in town reminding her and everyone else she was ever like that," I said.

"Like what?" Lizbeth wore brown that day, I remember. Brown blouse, brown skirt, brown shoes, dark hose. The shoes were open at the toe.

"You know the stuff. When I drink, I tell anyone who will listen the same things I tell you."

"Like what?" she repeated.

"The cross-country hitchhiking, selling plasma at the blood bank between the Salvation Army and the liquor store, drug deals, summers spent living on the street and pissing in alleyways."

"She's ashamed of these things?"

I thought. "It doesn't fit her new image. Also, now that she's been away awhile, Julie sees me for the true spook I really am, and it infuriates her to know people point at me and say, 'That skinny little nerd used to fuck Julie Deere.' "

Lizbeth watched me a moment. "Does Julie think you're a spook and a nerd?"

I scratched my upper left arm. "Rick hates me for it. He can't stand everyone knowing I used to lay on top of Julie and stick my dick in her."

"Can you blame him?"

"I don't know." I stared at Lizbeth's toes in the stockings. They looked unnaturally short and stubby—funny toes. "It kind of hurts that Mom is going along with this mental institution idea."

"Why?"

"It doesn't seem the motherly thing to do."

Lizbeth tucked both her feet under the chair. I think she was self-conscious about her short toes. "What do you think your mother is thinking?"

"God, I don't know. I've never been able to understand her thought process. I suppose Julie told her about the hang glider accident. Mom always believes other people's versions of what happened over mine."

"Did you tell her your version of the hang glider accident?"

"She wouldn't understand."

"Do you ever tell her your version of anything?"

"When I was little and had fights with neighbor kids, I tried to tell her my side, but she took for granted I was lying."

"You haven't told your mother your side since you were a little boy?"

I thought about Lizbeth's question and decided to change the subject. "Can they do it?"

"Do what?"

"Lock me away."

"It's very doubtful unless I testify that you're dangerous to yourself or society, and you know I won't do that because you aren't."

"Thanks." I thought of something. "Has Mom or Julie contacted you yet?"

"I can't tell you that, Kelly. It's unethical," Lizbeth said, nodding yes.

"John Hart's out to get me. He could threaten to cut off the clinic's state funds if you don't declare me insane."

Lizbeth's face was serious. "I promise you that won't happen, Kelly."

I trust Lizbeth. When she promises, I believe.

Lizbeth continued, "He asked to see your files."

"Asked?"

"Demanded."

"What happened?"

"We refused."

"Thanks again."

Lizbeth pulled her feet out from under the chair. "He won't get to you through the clinic."

I stared at those stubby little toes under the dark hose. "John Hart and Julie would like each other."

Mom and Julie didn't like each other. They didn't get along right from the beginning. Not that they openly and actively hated one another. They were much too subtle for that. They acted more like two top gunfighters drinking in the same bar. They respected each other's skills too much to open fire, but each always knew just where the other stood, and they over-reacted to any suspicious moves.

After the first summer in Jackson, Julie and I rented a trailer outside of Lancaster, Idaho, ten miles from my parents' house. Lancaster is county seat of Teewinot County, a small, isolated valley between Jackson Hole and Idaho Falls. The women still wear beehive hairdos. The men chew in church.

Mama was born a Hawken, which meant she had over two hundred relatives living within rifle range. I guess all those backward in-laws made Julie nervous. Whatever the reason, bits and pieces and, later, whole chunks of the marriage collapsed during the year and a half we hibernated in east Idaho.

It didn't collapse from any lack of togetherness. For an unexaggerated fact, the first six months we lived in the trailer, Julie was never out of my sight for over forty-five seconds. There wasn't even a door to the bathroom or a curtain for the shower. Neither one of us worked. Neither one of us did anything outside the trailer that I can recall.

Julie was in command. Our lives were as organized and compartmentalized as the staff at a brand-new McDonald's. She made the coffee, watered the plants, dug the garden. I dealt with the outside: landlords, mechanics, Mother. Every morning Julie cooked breakfast, I ate it while reading a book, then I sat at my desk and wrote until lunch.

She fed me again at lunch and together we watched an Andy Griffith rerun. In the afternoon I shoveled snow or Mom came over or something happened to pass the time. Later we'd drink a bottle of sherry, watch the weather on TV, fuck, and go to sleep. Whole days passed without more than twenty words being spoken out loud.

I wrote three of my four novels in Idaho. They were sagas of the Old West: broken gunfighters, drunk sheriffs, women hard as quartz with hearts of ice cream.

The books obsessed me. While working on a novel, I lived, talked, and ate with the characters. I had wet dreams about the women I created. I lived in a world Julie couldn't enter and I guess she resented being locked out.

One time she threw an entire first draft out in the snow and screamed, *"Talk to me, you shit. I can't stand playing second fiddle to a lousy novel anymore."* I managed to save most of the book by drying the pages on the oil heater.

Once every month or so we drove forty miles to Jackson and saw a movie and drank in the Cowboy. I remember lots of cold, drunken drives home over Teton Pass through blowing blizzards. The second winter, I worked a few nights a week at Blackie and Carol's, drawing beers and cleaning ashtrays while an old lumpy cowboy named Dusty Pockets sang heartbreaking country songs for spare-change donations. A few couples danced in a cleared spot by the cash register. Other people played table shuffleboard or penny poker. It was fun. Julie always came along and sat at the bar. She never talked to anyone and no one talked to her. I encouraged her to sit next to Dusty and sing along like she used to with Babe Stovall, but I guess to Julie Idaho was different from New Orleans.

Julie never forgave me for making her live so close to Mom, and of course Mom told me over and over that it wouldn't work, that Julie would leave me soon. She said Julie couldn't keep a house clean and would bear me autistic children.

Mom bought me a hypoallergenic pillow for Christmas. Julie threw it out the back door. Mom made me a meat loaf. Julie fed it to Alice. They both tucked my shirttail in for me in public. I was an off-color pawn in a battle between the black and white queens. They treated me like a retarded boy at the center of a child-custody suit—each wanting control of me in spite of the fact that they considered me a helpless idiot.

I did hear them agree on something once. It was in the Bicentennial summer of 1976. I was helping Dad build a bookshelf in the bathroom. Mom loves bookshelves in bathrooms. She fills them with *Reader's Digest*s in case constipation ever hits and there's nothing around to read. I popped my thumb with a hammer and went off to find Julie to have her fix it. They sat in the kitchen, drinking coffee and deciding what kind of shoes I should wear that summer. I stood at the door, listening.

Mom said, "Lord only knows what Kelly would do without us to look out for him."

And Julie answered, "He'd fall apart and die within two weeks. Kelly couldn't eat if I didn't feed him." I decided to bandage my own thumb.

Julie was right, of course. She was always right. I didn't die of starvation two weeks after she left, but I came reasonably close. Two and a half years later, I still got by on the things Julie did for me. I wore the same clothes Julie had picked out. The same pictures hung in the same spots where she had put them. Except for a gradual deterioration and wearing thin, the apartment was exactly like it had been the day she walked away—down to a half-full box of tampons on the side of the bathtub. I wanted Julie to feel at home should she ever come back.

• • •

I'm almost certain Julie was never unfaithful while we lived together. She was never out of my sight long enough to screw anyone else. Also, right before Julie left, at a time when she had no reason or desire to spare my feelings any pain, she said, "To think I spent six years being faithful to you, never even talking to another man. What a waste of time."

I did cheat on her once.

It was at the county fair rodeo in Montpelier. I drove over with Rex Lyle and Bobby John Jefferson one Saturday night in mid-August. I'm not sure why Julie didn't go. She hated rodeos, but that didn't stop her from going most places. Julie hated a lot of things she did for entertainment.

Bobby John liked beer, so we bought a couple of cases and I drank my share. I don't normally drink beer. It makes me pee too often. During the bareback riding, I got the urge for about the third time in an hour, excused myself, and went down under the stands where I met a barrel racer from Tetonia named Shirley.

I stood against a low fence, cupping it between my hands and listening to the stream, when she walked up—five foot three, dark pigtails, white hat, gum.

"Hi," she said. "My name is Shirley. I'm a barrel racer from Tetonia."

I shook twice and tucked myself back in. "I'm Kelly, a novelist from Lancaster."

She nodded. "That's a nice dick you've got there."

"Thank you." I had heard about Tetonia girls and barrel racers; both are supposed to be good fun, and I suppose my loyalty to Julie had always been based more on lack of opportunity than any sense of duty. Anyway, as soon as the girl started talking dirty, I perked right up.

"I'm riding in a few minutes," she said. "If I win I'm going to get my brother's teeth fixed."

"Oh."

"A horse stepped on his face."

I had too much beer in me to be clever. "His face, huh?"

"The horse didn't do it on purpose. Leopold shouldn't have been lying there."

"Leopold is your brother?"

Shirley leaned forward and scratched behind my ears and down along my neck. "Yeah, I've just got to win for Leopold."

I didn't move. "I hope you win, Shirley."

She scratched and patted and stuck her finger in my ear. "I ride a lot better when I'm relaxed."

What an opening. "How can I relax you?"

Shirley smiled. "Want to go for a ride in my horse trailer? It's got a mattress."

I almost came in my pants. It was so easy. Julie had me convinced that no woman would ever want me besides her. I mean, she was the first unless you count that tabletop revenge fuck with Carol. In fact, Julie was the only woman I'd ever come in. I'd always wondered what it would be like with someone else—someone shaped a little different. Was I any good? Did other women scream and moan like the women in the movies? What would other asses feel like in my hands?

I didn't even think about the fact that Shirley must do this fairly often if she took a mattress to the rodeo. I didn't worry that she probably had crabs or clap or she might call me in four to six weeks to say she'd skipped her period.

All I thought was, Damn, I'm going to get laid by someone other than Julie. Anyone, it didn't matter who. It was time I got my piece of the forbidden kingdom.

Shirley led me across the parking lot to a blue-and-gold single-stall horse trailer. On the back of the trailer was a sign that read MADE IN CHICKASHA, OKLAHOMA, and a bumper sticker that read COWGIRLS HAVE MORE FUN. She let down the ramp and led me into the stall. Evidently, it was an old mattress and the horse rode standing on it, but anything felt smoother than a haystack or a manure-filled pasture, which were the places I'd always heard loose cowgirls prefer.

I still can't figure out how she got her jeans off without removing her boots. All I know is I turned away to take off my pants—I never pull down anything facing a woman. I hopped first on one foot, then on the other, yanking off my sneakers. Then I shrugged off my shirt, and when my jeans were finally kicked into the corner, I turned around to find Shirley lying on her back, one knee raised seductively, wearing nothing but pointy-toed boots and a white cowboy hat.

That was my first indication she might be kinky. The second came when I climbed on board and tried to kiss her. She would have none of it. Shirley raised her legs, stuck me in, and took off.

I mean, I like passion, but I was accustomed to slow starts, gradual builds through the use of tongues and fingers and other implements of foreplay. With Julie, I pushed the right buttons and kissed the right spots and after thirty or forty minutes her breathing got real intense, she moaned, and came in a stifled shriek.

Shirley came out of the chute shrieking. She grabbed my ears and humped like we'd been going at it for hours. I held on. After a few seconds she pulled my right ear down, hard. Then she kicked with the heels of her boots. Thank God she wasn't wearing spurs. Another few seconds and she pulled the other way, on my left ear. Then more writhing and kicking.

I didn't know what to do. She wasn't anything like Julie. Nothing in porno literature had prepared me for a barrel racer.

Shirley jerked hard on the left ear again, then she humped like crazy, double the intensity of anything before. She made a noise, a high whine with gasps and things like *"Go, baby. Move."*

I don't know where she got the stick. Her right hand moved off my back for an instant and the next thing I knew she was whipping me across the lower ass with a stick—a riding-crop-type thing. I stopped moving and she hit me real hard and yelled, *"Go!"*

I went. Shirley hit me a couple more times. She raised both legs and arms straight up above my head and screamed.

I stopped again. She pushed me out and off her. I lay against the trailer wall, watching her little breasts heave up and down. Sweat trickled across her neck and into her armpit.

"Are you going to hit me anymore?" I asked.

Shirley exhaled everything at once. "Eighteen seconds flat."

"Is it over? I didn't come yet."

She sat up. "Eighteen seconds, I can feel a winner tonight." Shirley leaned over and kissed me friendly-like on the cheek. "You just fucked a champ," she said.

She gathered up her clothes, slid her jeans on over the boots, buttoned up her shirt, and left. I lay on the mattress in the horse trailer for a long time, thinking.

Julie found out, of course. I lay on my stomach in the middle of our bed while she rubbed Johnson's Baby Lotion on the welts across my ass. Her hands were very gentle. Not once did Julie say "Serves you right," or "That'll teach you for screwing around," or "Why, Kelly?" or anything.

When we made love later that night, Julie was very careful not to touch any of the sore spots.

In Idaho, Julie and I gave up the last remnants of our hippie lives. The painted microbus was gone. I cut my hair. Julie threw out the books on *I Ching* and *Sensual Massage*. The waterbed had been abandoned in New Orleans along with the pink rolling papers and a three-hose water pipe. Everything tie-dye, Day-Glo, or red, white, and blue went to the dump. Julie shaved her legs. I watched Cubs baseball on the cable TV.

We even stopped smoking pot. By then, marijuana wasn't a

freak habit anyway. Everyone smoked—cowboys, rednecks, old retired couples, politicians—the only groups who didn't smoke pot were ex-hippies and Mormon missionaries. It wasn't a conscious today-we-stop-getting-high decision. Somehow, without consulting each other, Julie and I realized it wasn't fun anymore. In fact, being drugged didn't feel good at all. It felt rotten.

We discovered the joy of being alert. I had never been alert before—at least as far back as I could remember. Also, after eight years or whatever of committing several felonies a day, it felt nice not to be scared. We no longer panicked at a knock on the door.

Nowadays, I'm a pot hater. As far as I know, so is Julie. I won't allow the stuff in my house. If I see kids smoking in the park, I go over and testify to what a horrible habit marijuana is, offering myself as an example of how it can ruin a man.

I quit all other drugs—pills and powders—even before Idaho.

It was on account of a pop festival in a frying pan-hot baseball stadium outside of Dallas. The temperature in the stands must have been 110 degrees. Even Julie sweat. In the bathroom I met an emaciated, scraggly-haired kid. He couldn't have been over fourteen. He wasn't wearing a shirt and he looked skinnier than me.

He held out a huge clear capsule filled with red beads and said, "Ten dollars."

I picked it up. "What is it?"

"All the belladonna from four packs of Contac time capsules. Took me six hours to separate the decongestant from the antihistamines."

"What's it do?"

"Makes you hallucinate. You'll think you can fly and talk to the dead."

I turned the pill over and held it between my thumb and

forefinger. "Makes you think you can fly, huh? I'll give you two dollars for it."

"Two dollars don't even cover the costs of the Contac." The kid's skin color was pale, kind of translucent, the color of a television screen when it's turned off, or the cadaver of a hepatitis victim. People that color need money.

"Two dollars," I said.

"Shit," he mumbled. "Okay." He wadded up the two dollars and crammed it into his right front pocket. Then he blew his nose on a paper towel.

Whatever was in that pill was strong. I remember holding my head under the cold tap to wash it down. As I was leaving the bathroom, a woman dragged in a screaming kid. She held his arm and pulled. He dug in both heels and yelled, "But I don't have to go! I don't have to go!"

She shouted, "You'll damn well go when I tell you!"

Then a very fat midget walked up and said, "God sent me to tell you everything is all right. He planned this."

My mouth got dry. Everything fun for the body causes drymouth, but that pill took dry further than my imagination thought possible. My whole body dried up.

I blacked out.

I came to naked, lying under a sheet on a cot in the first-aid tent. A man with long, shiny blond hair and one hoop earring was leaning over me holding out a metal cup. Joni Mitchell music was playing.

"Drink this, brother," the man said. "It's chamomile and dandelions." He wore a light blue sari and a turquoise ring. He seemed calm and gentle.

I sat up on the cot. Lifting the sheet, I ripped it down the middle and shouted, *"There's no fucking meat in this taco."*

Julie found me a couple of hours later, which turned out to be fourteen hours after I swallowed the pill. All she said was, "You blew it again, Kelly."

She wrapped half the sheet around my body and led me to the car.

I couldn't lick my lips for two days or focus my eyes for four. I thought the pill had blinded me. Praying, I made a deal with God that if he let me see again, I would never eat unauthorized chemicals, no matter how cheaply they were offered. Gradually, my eyes accepted light and learned to focus once more.

I found out later from a woman who actually enjoys belladonna that my sight would have returned even if I hadn't made a deal with God, but I kept my word. I never abused pills or powders again. Neither did Julie.

The night after John Hart forced Joe to fire me, I pulled a chunk of concrete out of my rotting porch, walked to the Teton National Bank, and heaved it through the glass front door.

I've lived in Jackson enough years that I know without sticking around what this action caused. Three blocks south, an alarm sounded in the Jackson police department. The dispatcher radioed the all-night Western Cafe where the graveyard shifts of various Wyoming law-enforcement agencies had gathered to swill coffee and relive gory car wrecks. Within two minutes, four city police units, two county deputy sheriffs, and an off-duty highway patrolman converged on the scene of the broken glass.

Two men crept through the front door—pistols drawn.

By then—long before then—I elbowed my way through the crowd at the Cowboy Bar and ordered a VO with water. As the officers searched the dark bank, I sat on a saddle, sipping my drink and trying to see down a pool-shooting cowgirl's tank top. I found the cowgirl erotic. In her boots, she stood about six-three and she blew on her cue tip before each shot.

Ninety days of continuous rodeo action had begun that evening, and two senior-citizen "See America by Bus" tours clogged up both sides of the doorway, so the Cowboy was a real mob scene. I heard a woman in a pink pantsuit and a hat made from sections of Budweiser cans ask, "Do you think these cowboys are all hired actors, Marlene?"

"Of course they are, Hedy," said the woman I took to be her sister because they both had the same silver-blue hair. Marlene kept looking from the stuffed animals and knotty pine to a book in her hands. "I can't find this place on the checklist. We're not supposed to be here if it's not on the list."

"This must be a sight. Look under *nightlife* or *local color*."

"It's not on the list. I think we're wasting time, Hedy."

Cora Ann swept past the line of out-of-towners like a bouncy blond Queen of Egypt scattering badly dressed slaves. I half expected her to snap her fingers at the doorman. "Clear a table, Butch, a big one by the dance floor."

Instead, spotting me, she glided over, the crowd parting before her. Cora Ann's first words were exactly what I knew they would be.

"Fucking turkeys."

I laughed. "What's the matter?"

"There should be a separate entrance for locals—a separate bar with free drinks."

In every tourist town on earth—Jackson, Wyoming; Key West, Florida; Paris, France—natives laugh at, persecute, and generally hate outsiders.

"What would we do without tourists?" I asked.

"Go on welfare." Cora Ann ordered a drink. She paid and took a long swig. "So how's your day been?"

"I got fired."

"Yeah? Want to play Space Invaders?"

"I threw a rock through the window at the bank."

"Why?"

"My kitchen sink told me to."

Cora Ann nudged me and pointed to the Hawaiian-print

slacks on a passing retiree. "Would he wear that crap back in Pennsylvania? I thought you ignore orders from talking water."

"I decided to listen this time."

"Oh. You want to play Space Invaders or not? It's too crowded to dance."

"I'd rather drink."

"Okay, let's drink."

We drank a good deal. Cora Ann met a kayaker from Alaska and took him home. I danced with Hedy and Marlene. They both said it was the high point of their vacation.

Later I stumbled back to my apartment and dressed up two pillows in an old cotton nightgown of Julie's. I stuck Alice on them so it would look like they were breathing, and pretended I was sleeping with Colette.

I dreamed all my teeth fell out. They crumbled into small bits and mixed with saliva so that I was afraid to swallow. I spit pieces all night.

7

The next day, Wednesday, Lizbeth Day, I awoke with one arm over the pillow-stuffed nightgown. Alice had moved and I was sober, so the whole thing looked stupid.

I coughed a couple of times and wandered into the bathroom and threw up. In something like a stupor, I flushed the toilet with one hand and brushed my teeth with the other. I shook food into Alice's bowl and went back to bed. Drifting off to sleep, I pushed the dummy onto the floor.

I didn't wake up again until after nine. This time I put on my glasses and telephoned Colette.

"Good morning, darling," I said cheerily into the phone.

"What?"

"It's a beautiful day out."

"Who is this?"

I switched the phone to the other ear. "Who else calls you 'darling'?"

"I'm asleep. Who is this?"

"Kelly." Colette didn't say anything, so I said, "Kelly Palamino."

"I know which Kelly you are. Why did you wake me up?"

131

"Because you're beautiful."

I heard a long yawn followed by, "Horsepoop. I can't talk to you anymore, Kelly."

"We nearly died together in that box. You've got to talk to me."

Another yawn leaked through the phone lines. "I told you in the bar it's all over. You passing out on the back of my neck doesn't change a thing. It's time for me to quit this game and grow up."

"But you love me."

"I never said that."

I stared at the dial on the phone for a moment. "You never denied it either."

"I don't know how I feel about you, Kelly. You confuse me. I hate being confused."

I switched the phone back to the original ear. "We need to talk about the other day," I said.

"Why?"

"For one thing, John threatened my life."

"What's that got to do with me?"

"I risked everything for you."

"Did I ask you to risk anything? Did I encourage you in any way? Leave me out of this. I've got enough trouble with John on my own."

"What kind of trouble?"

"None of your business." I didn't have a comeback, so after a moment, Colette continued in a singsong voice, "I like you, Kelly. I'll never forget you, but . . . but. You know the words of that speech. I'm sure you've heard them before." I had. "The last line is that I can't see you anymore."

"I've got a great idea," I said. "Let's eat breakfast together."

"Kelly, you aren't listening. John will kill you if we're seen together again. And he'll do worse to me."

"What?"

"What what?"

"What will he do to you?"

"I don't want to talk about it. You've caused enough trouble already, Kelly. It's time for me to settle down and become a Happy Homemaker until Danny retires or dies or both."

"How can you say that when you're in love with me?"

"I rehearsed."

"Meet me for breakfast."

"No. It's too risky."

"You could come here, to my apartment. No one will see you here."

"No."

I dropped the phone on the floor. When I pulled it up by the cord, Colette asked, "What was that?"

"I dropped the phone."

"You should be more careful. You'll break it."

"Colette. Listen. This is the last time. I promise. Lord, I love you. I live for you, Colette. At least give me one last good-bye."

She didn't answer for a while. "You'll get all mushy."

"No, I won't. I swear. No mush, no fuss."

Another pause. "You'll never bother me again?"

"Never. Promise. See me one last time and you'll never see me again."

This pause was longer than the other two combined. About the time I thought Colette had gone back to sleep, she said, "Shit. I'm a fool to trust you, but okay. I'll be there in an hour. How do I find your apartment?"

Gotcha, I thought.

"No, you don't," Colette said.

Another nice thing about Colette is her posture. I'm big on posture, probably because mine is so horrible. Colette walks with her shoulders straight, her chin up. When she's in a hurry her arms hang back a little with the knuckles facing forward—kind of streamlined. I like that. I tried to walk Colette-style, but it looked like I was falling instead of walking.

After she hung up, I went into the kitchen and washed a mountain of dishes. Inspired by the Mad Hatter, I own lots of dishes, hundreds of dishes, enough to eat daily for weeks without washing any. They pile up and stink. Live things, moss or mold or something else disgusting grows in the bottoms of the glasses. I'm not very proud of my personal hygiene habits.

Something special had to be cooked for Colette's breakfast. Something that would make her come back for more. I was torn between down-home—biscuits, grits, and eggs—or flashy—a flaming crepe dish. While I stood in the kitchen deciding, Colette knocked on the door.

She was ravishing, beautiful, all brown eyes, dark hair, and posture. God's own woman.

"Do you like grits?" I asked.

"Grits?"

I nodded. Colette wore a T-shirt, a red one with nothing stupid written on it.

She looked over at the church. "Can I come in, Kelly? I'd just as soon not be seen out here."

"Oh, yeah, I forgot." I stood aside and let Colette walk past me and into my apartment.

"Nice place," she said. "What do you pay for it?"

I stood behind her and put a hand on her shoulder. "One-eighty plus bills. Come here." I turned her. Colette made a sighing noise and we hugged.

I mean, we both hugged. She hugged back. Then we kissed. I tried slipping some tongue past those cared-for teeth, but she wouldn't go quite that far, so we returned to a mutual hug.

I kissed her lightly on the ear. "Do you like grits or not?" I asked.

"Hate 'em. Kelly, do you mind if I ask a question?"

I pulled away with both hands still on her shoulders. "Anything."

Colette looked me in the eyes. "Why aren't you wearing pants?"

"Pants?"

"Pants."

I looked down at my pinstriped boxer shorts. "I just woke up."

"You called me over an hour ago." I didn't answer. Colette continued, "You're taking this spaced-out eccentric act a little far."

"I guess so." I let go of her shoulders. "Don't leave. I'll get dressed."

I shut the door behind me as I went into the bedroom. My jeans lay in a pile under the desk. "So what do you want for breakfast?" I called.

"Coffee."

"Coffee. I would have thought you're a big breakfast eater. Pancakes, waffles, cantaloupes filled with cream."

"Shows how much you know about me," Colette answered.

Checking my zipper twice, I opened the bedroom door. "I know your soul," I said. "That's the part that counts."

"Do you honestly expect me to swallow crap like that? Who's this?" She held up the elk skull. One of the teeth fell on the floor.

"That's Sherlock. She's my pet skull."

"She? How can you tell it's a she?"

"I don't relate to males. Even dead ones. Coffee's all you want?"

I walked into the kitchen and dug under the counter for the coffeepot. It was an old camp pot, all black on the bottom.

Colette leaned against the door. "You don't have any men friends, do you?" she said. "That seems odd."

"I don't trust men. They lie. Their crotches don't know right from wrong. They give women drugs and presents and expect kinky sex in return." I turned back to Colette. "I can't find the guts to the coffeepot. They were here yesterday."

She pointed. "Over on the drainboard."

"Thanks." I picked the long piece out of the drainboard and fit it into the pot.

"I've been here three minutes and you're already asking me where things are," Colette said. "You must be awful to live with."

I turned on the cold water and let it run a moment before filling the pot. "Did John tell Danny about catching us together?"

"He wouldn't dare."

"Why not?"

"Didn't you hear the meeting Monday?"

The plastic lid wouldn't come off the coffee can. I had to sit down and clamp the can with my knees and pull the top off with both hands. That had never happened to me before. "I was fighting for survival in that box. It didn't seem polite to eavesdrop."

"John's planning to subdivide the Broken Hart. He's literally selling his mother's grave. Danny will disinherit the old fart when he finds out they're building a condo city on the family homestead."

"I don't think a son can disinherit his father."

"He can't?"

Carefully I spooned eight tablespoons of coffee grounds into the metal bowl. "No. A father disinherits a son, but not vice versa. The son can get mad or run away, but that's about it."

"Whatever. Danny's not going to like it, and if John tells on me, I'll tell on him."

"Danny's bound to find out when the bulldozer knocks down the fence."

"That won't happen for months, long after there's anything he can do to stop it."

The first match sputtered and died, but the second burned. I lit the burner and set the coffeepot on the heat. "Then we've got something on John. He can't stop us from seeing each other."

Colette brushed the hair out of her face. "Yeah, but he's got a lot more on me than I've got on him."

"What?"

"He told me yesterday, something happened after the wedding."

I would have followed up with another "What?" but someone knocked at the door. They didn't knock. They rapped hard, the way the police rap when they suspect you're flushing evidence down the toilet.

Colette jumped about a foot. "This is it," she said.

I had a sudden urge to be somewhere else. "Maybe not. Maybe not. Maybe it's census takers or religious fanatics. Go in the bedroom and shut the door."

"But if it's John, I'll look even worse when he finds me in the bedroom."

"If it's John we're both dead anyway. Shut the door, crawl under the bed if you have to."

Whoever it was knocked again, even louder.

"Hold on," I shouted.

A fist banged on the door. Colette went into the bedroom and closed the door. I checked to make sure it was shut tight.

I guess I expected John or the police. Instead, a man I'd never seen barged in.

"I've come for your phone," he said, looking around.

"Huh?"

"Where's the phone?" He spotted it on the trunk and walked

over and picked it up. He was a big man wearing a chain belt with all kinds of tools hanging off his hips.

"Why do you want my phone?"

"Orders are orders. Guess you didn't pay the bill. Is this the only one?" He began wrapping the cord around the base of the phone.

"Are you with the telephone company?"

The man stopped wrapping and looked at me. "Of course I'm with the telephone company. Why else would I want your telephone?"

"I don't know."

He worked quickly. The phone was the kind that plugs into a jack in the wall, so it disconnected in no time at all.

"If I pay the bill, will you put it back in?"

"Sure, if you put up a new deposit."

"How much is that?"

"Once you've been cut off, it usually takes a couple hundred bucks to get back on." The man grinned. "But I have a feeling that it might cost you a good deal more."

He tucked my phone under his arm and left.

Colette walked out of the bedroom, carrying the two pillows dressed in the nightgown. She carried them in her arms like a baby.

"I liked that phone," I said.

"What's this?" She held up the pillows and the white night-gown. It was a very nice nightgown. I don't know why Julie left it.

"You," I said. "I was pretending to sleep with you. Did John send that guy?"

"What do you think? Why am I on the floor?"

I kept looking at the spot where my phone had been. It didn't seem right that it was gone.

"Kelly?"

"I sobered up and you'd stopped breathing, so I kicked you out of bed."

"Oh." She looked back at the pillows. "Doesn't look like me."

"That's why I threw you on the floor."

Colette gently laid the dummy of herself on the couch. "You'd better hurry with that coffee," she said. "I imagine the gas and electricity will go soon."

I went into the kitchen, but the coffee hadn't started to perk yet, so I walked back to the couch and Colette.

"He wouldn't do that," I said.

"Why not?" Colette was picking at the elk skull. She carried it to the couch and set it against the dummy. It looked kind of obscene. "There. You should have given me a head."

I wondered why I hadn't thought of that. "What's John got on you?" I asked.

Colette sat down. "Oh, it's a bunch of crap. I didn't know anything about it."

"About what?"

"After the wedding—after you threw that scene in the Americana—Mr. Hart offered to loan Daddy a bunch of money to open his own tap-dancing studio in Davenport."

"Tap dancing?"

"My dad teaches tap dancing. He's very good. John loaned him ten thousand dollars at a ridiculously low interest rate to open his own school."

"I never laid a girl whose daddy was a tap dancer."

Colette scowled. "You never will with that attitude. Anyhow, way down in the fine print of the loan agreement there's a clause that says if Danny and I split up, or I'm unfaithful, or I do anything at all that John Hart considers behavior unbecoming to his daughter-in-law, the note comes due immediately."

"What an asshole."

Colette didn't look happy. Her eyes drooped like an unwatered African violet. "I called home. Dad's already spent the whole ten thousand."

"On tap-dancing equipment?"

"He's competing against a Jazzercise franchise. Dance lessons are a tough business." She looked at me. "This new studio is the first thing Dad's been excited about since Dirk died. I can't take it away from him."

I sat next to Colette and took her hands in mine. She pulled her right hand loose and tucked hair behind her ear. "I think Daddy would like you. You're kind of like Dirk. Dirk didn't care what anybody thought of him so long as he was happy."

"That's a good attitude."

Colette smiled. "Once when President Nixon came to Davenport, Dirk dressed up like a rat and tried to shake his hand."

"I'm not too political myself."

"The Secret Service threw Dirk on the ground and handcuffed him. Daddy had to go downtown with bail money. He acted real mad, but I think he was secretly proud of Dirk. The newspaper article is framed on the wall in Mom and Dad's bedroom." Colette looked me full in the face. She put her free hand back in mine.

"Do you want to be with me?" I asked.

She didn't blink or sniffle or anything. "Maybe," she said. "I don't know how—it's so impossible. I can't ruin Daddy, and you can't live here with John after you."

A truck from the gas company pulled up outside. I could see the logo through a crack in the curtains. It was an orange flame with words printed underneath—TETON GAS.

"John Hart is the only thing standing between us and happiness," I said.

"That might be an exaggeration."

"Okay, he's the only thing standing between us and any chance at happiness. You agree to that."

Colette looked down at my hands around hers. "I don't know. It's all impossible."

"Do you love me?"

"I don't know, don't ask me these questions. I'm confused. I don't know anything anymore." Colette raised her face. I could see straight into her brown eyes—eyes soft and alive enough to make a poet sober. "I love you, Kelly," she said.

I almost passed out. "My God, I did it."

"Yeah, you did it. You got to me, you son of a bitch."

Doubling my fist, I hit the trunk. *"Fuck, I did it."* I danced. I sang. I knelt on the rug and sanctified the couch. But Colette did not look happy.

She stood up. "This is it, Kelly," she said. "No matter how I feel or how you feel, we can't see each other ever again."

"Bullshit, you love me."

"That doesn't matter."

"Like hell it doesn't. Where are you going?"

"I won't destroy my father or Danny, or you either. I'm leaving."

The little bitch left.

I sat staring at the skull-headed dummy on the couch, wondering if tennis shoes on the bottom would take the whole thing a step too far.

I couldn't believe I had her. I talked all self-assured—"It's fate, someday you will love me, you and I are inevitable"—but I don't know if I meant it or not. It was too good a line to know if it was true.

And now Colette had said right out loud, "I love you, Kelly." Knowing Colette, she would deny it tomorrow, but that wasn't important. She had admitted to herself and me that she loved me. That was enough.

The only remaining problem was that yeast infection in the womb of Mother Nature, John Hart. His bulky ass stood between Colette and happiness, me and happiness, even Danny and happiness. Danny would never find contentment while living with Colette. The most perfect woman in Wyoming isn't worth day-old piddle as a wife if she doesn't love you. I know.

The one, the only, impediment between me and perfect peace was the fat banker. Time for the Avenging Angel to fly down and take possession of my body. I could say the shower made me do it. John, Julie, and Mom thought I was sanitarium fodder. Why disappoint them? Temporary Insanity would please everyone except John, and after six months of Thorazine fog, I'd be back in Colette's arms before she missed me.

As I sat staring into Sherlock's eye sockets and musing on the convenience of Being Crazy, the gas man finished tying off my pipes and a big yellow truck from the electric company pulled up. By noon he'd have me powerless, waterless, and up the creek paddleless.

Time to pop somebody's cork.

I possess—have possessed ever since the death of my Uncle Homer—an exact replica of the 1880 Box Lock Percussion .41-caliber derringer, also known as the "muff gun." Gentlewomen used to carry this pistol in their hand muffs to blow the prostate glands off would-be rapists.

It's a cute gun, a muzzle-loader. It came with a leather bag that contained lead balls, patches of cloth, a tiny rammer rod, percussion caps, an even smaller bag of powder, and a coke-spoon-looking thing made out of horn—the all-around assassination kit for munchkins.

The derringer had an effective kill range of twelve feet. Past that you could cause more pain with a thrown rock. To my knowledge, Uncle Homer tried to shoot the gun five times and it misfired twice. That gave John pretty good odds in case God wanted to keep him alive.

I pulled the gun from its secret hiding place in the closet, set all the parts on my living room trunk, and went to work: measure of powder (to be on the safe side I put in two hornfuls), patch of cloth (wool), then the lead ball. Out came my rod and I rammed the ball down the hole in authentic sexually frustrated frontiersman style. I sorted through the percussion caps for the one most likely to work and, saying a little prayer over the one I chose, stuck it on the nipple—another symbolic part of the black-powder gun.

I shrugged into my red windbreaker, stuck the loaded, primed, and ready-to-kill gun in the right-hand pocket, and walked to the bank.

Everyone would be real surprised. No one, not even Julie or Lizbeth, knew about my muff gun. It was my one secret never spilled onto a barroom table.

His secretary didn't try to stop me. Hands in jacket pockets, I walked straight into John Hart's office—red shag carpet, desk the size of a '63 Chevy Impala, antelope heads mounted on the wall paneling.

John sat behind the desk. For maybe a tenth of a second he looked surprised. Then he said, "Yes?"

The man had purple jowls. *Jowls* is a disgusting word. Does it rhyme with *pals* or *towels*? But to actually have them hanging off your cheeks. . . . Nobody likes a man with purple jowls.

"My name is Kelly Palamino," I said, tightening my hold on the muff gun.

John played it straight. He shuffled a couple of papers and pushed them aside. "What can we do for you?" We? Who the hell was "we"?

"I need a loan."

John looked relieved. I had approached him in his element. He opened the middle desk drawer and removed a pad of paper. "How much would you like to borrow?"

"Six or seven hundred dollars. My utilities got cut off and I need deposit money to turn them back on."

He smiled. I've seen truer smiles on Miss Teenage America contestants. Door-to-door magazine salesmen. TV preachers. Inside my jacket, I pointed the muff's barrel at John's Adam's apple. As if it knew, the apple bobbed up, then down.

"What is your weekly income?" John asked.

"Nothing."

"Nothing." He wrote this down. "Do you have anything to use as collateral?"

"A '71 Volkswagen."

"Oh? You still have a car?" The apple bobbed again. It knew. I might not kill him, but he'd talk with a little box pressed against his throat for the rest of his life. Let's see him threaten me with a voice like a worn-out Barbie doll.

"What is your address, Kelly?" he asked, bending over the paper.

"Box 1974, Jackson, Wyoming, 83001."

This is it, I thought. It's prove-you're-a-real-man time. Nothing happened. I tried again. Okay, *now*. My finger refused to squeeze. John sat at his desk, alive and pompous as ever, scribbling my name and address on his pad. I decided to try a countdown. Three, two, one, *fire*.

"Do you have any credit references?" he asked.

"Not that I know of."

He asked my parents' names and what they did for a living. I told him about the Purina feed franchise in Lancaster. When he asked for marital status I said, "Separated." John looked at me as if he didn't believe, then he wrote something on the pad.

God knows, I tried to shoot him. My palm was sweaty, my elbow tingled from the strain, but no trigger slammed the pin into the nipple, igniting the percussion cap and blowing John's neck into the antelope heads. Something was terribly wrong. I knew in my soul that killing John was right, but my body refused to act.

Finally, John finished the notes. "I'll have to take this up with the other loan officers. We'll see what they say. Can you call in the morning, say around nine?"

The turd. I had as much chance of getting that loan as leaving the earth and circling the sun before lunch. "Sure, why not?"

He smiled again, his jowls fracturing like snow crust. "Unless you're planning to leave town?"

"I'm not planning to leave town." My arm went limp. All that I valued about myself as a creature of honor and nobility drained onto John's shag carpet. I couldn't kill him. The one true test of my beliefs and I'd failed.

John leaned his bulk back and made a tent of his ten fingers. He eyed me over the peak of the tent. "Why did you come here?"

"To borrow money."

"I'm ruthless," he said. "Did anyone ever tell you that I'm ruthless?"

" 'Ruthless' wasn't the word they used."

His forehead flushed a bit. "I'm ruthless," he repeated. "That means I'll stop at nothing to force you out of Teton County."

I blinked. My trigger finger was dead. My spirit would soon follow.

"Do you know what I mean by nothing?" he continued.

"Yes."

"Then you will leave."

"I'll think about it." I stood up.

John leaned forward and placed his weight on both hands on the desk. "Think real hard about it, sport. I can make your worst nightmares seem like fun."

I walked away. Passing through the bank lobby, I dropped the muff gun into a garbage can.

I crossed the street and the square, managing to avoid the transient hordes, the bike packers, backpackers, Teen Tours from Long Island. A million acres of virgin wilderness stretching in every direction, and the tourists jam up like blowflies on a dead horse.

Nausea rolled up from my stomach. Killing John had been the ethical thing to do, but I hadn't pulled the trigger because I couldn't. It felt wrong. I could no longer trust myself. I didn't know right from wrong or beautiful from ugly. What if I had become a bad person?

Halfway across the square, I threw up on the grass. A girl holding a Frisbee stared at me. She was wearing white shorts. I wiped my mouth with the back of my hand and walked on.

I needed help. Crossing another street, I cut into the Wort Hotel, first phone booth on the right.

Colette answered on the fourth ring.

I said, "Hi."

"You promised not to call ever again."

"That was before you said you loved me. Things have changed."

She sighed, a long, sad kind of sigh. "I knew that was a mistake."

"Loving me is a mistake?"

"Telling you was a mistake."

I didn't know what to say. Tourists walked in and out through the lobby doors. A bellman glanced at me and went upstairs. Listening to Colette breathe, I flipped the switch that turned on the fan in the phone-booth ceiling. Checking the coin return, I found sixty cents.

"I just found sixty cents in the coin return," I said.

"What?"

"Sixty cents. Somebody left sixty cents in the slot."

"Calling me wasn't a total waste after all."

I stuck the change in my right front pocket. "I need to see you, Colette."

"No. You've got to pack up and leave Jackson today. You aren't ever going to see me again."

I turned to face the wall side of the booth. "I just tried to kill John Hart."

"I don't believe you."

I leaned against the side of the booth and looked down at the butts and old gum on the floor. The glass felt cool against my forehead.

After a moment Colette said, "Oh, crap, Kelly. I do too believe you."

"I couldn't kill him."

"That's good. What made you think you could in the first place?"

"I want to make you happy."

"Kelly," she said, "don't ever murder anyone for me. Understand?"

"Yes, Colette." I paused. "Colette?"

"Yes, Kelly."

"What should I do now?"

She sighed again, this time even louder. "Put your stuff in suitcases, throw your cat in the car, and leave."

"Do you want me to?"

I counted seven wads of gum on the floor, two green, one orange, and four indistinguishable black. Colette answered, "Yes."

"Where could I go?"

"Go to your parents. That's what moms and dads are for."

"My mom wants to lock me up." Colette didn't comment. "I don't feel very good, Colette."

"What's the matter?"

"I don't know, I feel crazy."

"I'm sorry."

I noticed I was crying.

After Colette hung up I closed my eyes and felt the glass on my forehead, the phone still in my hand. She was probably right. I could stay at my parents' house. They only lived fifty miles away, but I hadn't seen Mom and Dad in a year, or talked to them in a couple of months.

I called collect. Mom answered.

"Hi, Mom," I said.

"Kelly? Is that you?" I guess I was still in emotional turmoil from the conversation with Colette, because as soon as I heard Mom's voice, I felt like crying again.

"Yeah, it's me."

"Why are you calling? Is everything okay?"

"Sure, Mom, everything's fine. I just hadn't heard from you in a while and figured I'd call." The phone is in the kitchen on a counter by the breakfast nook. Mom would be sitting down, facing east, probably holding a cup of coffee.

"Are you still washing dishes?" she asked.

"Yes, Mom."

"How long is your hair?"

"I got it cut a couple weeks ago. How's the viola practice coming along?"

"That stopped months ago. I've decided to concentrate all my energy on dancing."

A picture of Mom wearing tights jumped into my mind. "What kind of dancing?"

"Ballet was my first choice, but my teacher says a woman in her fifties is too old, so instead I'm getting into modern. She thinks if I'm committed and stretch out every day I might make it on television."

"Gee, that's great, Mom. Dancing sounds like more fun than the viola."

"Your father moved all the furniture out of the den so I can rehearse. He says I have natural talent."

"Dad's usually right about these things. How's he doing at the store?"

"There's some kind of regional sales meeting in Rexburg

today. I don't think he wanted to go, but the home office made him."

"That's too bad." I'd run out of chitchat and couldn't think what to say next, so I waited silently, hoping Mom would talk. The subject of an invitation home seemed difficult to approach.

"How's the weather over there?" I asked.

"It couldn't be much different from the weather in Jackson. Kelly, are you in trouble?"

"Of course not, Mom. What makes you think that?"

"We've been hearing things. They say you've been acting the way you did before the accident." Mom always calls the suicide attempt an accident. She thinks I was on drugs. No child of hers would ever kill himself from unhappiness. In fact, predictable as mud running downhill, the next question was, "You aren't on dope, are you?"

"Of course not, Mama."

"We heard you had a prescription for dope."

"Who told you that? Did Julie tell you I'm on drugs?"

"You were a fool to lose her, Kelly. No other woman is ever going to take care of you the way she did."

I guess I exploded. "I didn't lose Julie. She left. And she lies, Mom. I'm not on drugs. I'm not crazy. Everything she tells you about me is lies."

"Why would Julie lie? Her only concern is your welfare."

"She hates me."

"Don't shout at your mother."

"I'm sorry." I haven't had a conversation with Mom in over twenty years in which I didn't apologize at least once. "She hates me," I repeated.

"Don't be silly," Mom answered. "You shouldn't take the split-up so personally. Julie told me all the details. She was just creatively stifled, that's all. I've been creatively stifled and I know how she feels. It had nothing to do with you."

"My wife's leaving had nothing to do with me?"

"Yes, and if you'd quit moping around and feeling sorry for yourself and cut your hair and dress decently, you could land yourself a real job, using your degree."

"Yes, Mama."

"I only tell you these things because I love you, Kelly."

"Yes, Mama."

"It breaks my heart to have a son who's a failure. You're almost thirty years old. It's time to grow up."

"Yes, Mama."

Our conversations always end with me automatically saying "Yes, Mama," until she winds down and tells me not to call collect in the daytime, wait until after five, then hangs up.

Afterward, I stood in the booth a long time trying to think of someplace I could go other than Idaho.

The appointment with Lizbeth was set for one-thirty, and it wasn't quite noon, so I figured I'd wander home and take a shower with the last of the hot water. Later I could find Cora Ann and work out a bathroom-and-kitchen-privileges deal while my utilities were off. There would be a heat problem next winter, but that was months away. I had to get through Wednesday first.

I found Alice sitting on the front porch, watching the landlord change my lock. Mr. Hiatt, the landlord, is shaped like an upright freezer. He always chews on unlit cigars and says "fucking" before nouns.

"What's going on?" I asked.

Alice said *Miaou*.

Mr. Hiatt said, "Fucking lock won't come out." He was kneeling on the porch, blocking the door, fiddling with a Phillips head screwdriver.

"I haven't used it in three years," I said. "Why do you want it out?"

"Got to change the fucking lock. You're moving." The

screwdriver slipped and skidded across the door. A hailstorm of curses spewed from Mr. Hiatt's mouth.

"I can't move," I said. "All my stuff is here."

"Anything left in this apartment tomorrow goes to the dump." Mr. Hiatt turned the screwdriver over and began beating on the keyhole with the blunt end.

I sat down, facing the church across the street. For four years I had been sitting on the porch with Alice, watching the sky and the trees change. It seemed hard to believe I couldn't do it anymore.

"Why?" I asked.

"Orders. You have a key for this place?"

"A dog swallowed it." I rubbed Alice's forehead. For once, she acted like she enjoyed my attention. I was so used to my apartment, my plants and pictures, the holes in the walls, faucets that wouldn't turn off, windows that leaked. My bed.

"Why did he have the utilities turned off if he meant to have me thrown out anyway?"

"Damned if I know." Mr. Hiatt drew back his fist and punched the lock clear through the door and onto the floor inside. "Got the sucker," he snorted. "I put the rest of June's rent and your deposit on the trunk in the goddamn living room. Don't spread it around that I gave back your fucking deposit money. John wouldn't like that."

"Why did you then?"

Mr. Hiatt took the cigar out of his mouth and looked at me for the first time. "You're a damn nice kid, Kelly. I hate to see you in trouble. Maybe you can use the fucking money to set yourself up in a new town."

"I'm not leaving the old town."

8

I drove to the Mental Health Center and sat in the lobby for over an hour, reading pamphlets with titles like *What is Depression?*, *Alcoholism*, *The Shame of the Battered Woman*, and *How to Tell If Your Child Is on Drugs*. Those brochures are like the *Reader's Digest* articles on swollen livers and colon cancer. I can't read the symptoms without noticing a few in me.

Sitting on the couch, I tried to remember what life was like before the day of Colette's wedding. I know I drank, danced, washed dishes, chased waitresses. I talked to Cora Ann and Lizbeth. I listened to music, looked forward to Doonesbury, ate hamburgers plain with ketchup, but I couldn't remember how I felt—what it was like to wake up in the morning. What I thought about whenever I was alone for a moment.

Colette had become everything. The first thought in the morning to the dreams at night. I couldn't conceive of what I'd been before her. Or what I might be after her.

I mentioned this midway through the session with Lizbeth. "I'm unbelievably happy when I'm with her and miserable when I'm not with her."

Lizbeth sat less than four feet away, looking at my face. She wore green. She had cut her hair a new way, which threw me off a little. Psychiatrists and mountains aren't supposed to change. Too many people depend on them.

"What's that mean?" she asked.

"Means I should be with her all the time."

"You shouldn't base your happiness on something outside yourself."

"Why not?" After a couple of years of therapy, I'd learned what not to say to Lizbeth. I don't know if those exasperated "grow up" looks were real or imagined, but I imagined she was giving me one then. I kept my eyes on the floor.

Lizbeth went into the speech we'd both heard so often: "If your happiness is based on something external, you can lose it, or you can become so afraid you might lose it that you aren't happy anymore."

I wanted to lie down real bad. Emotion wears me out. "What if your outside base is stable?" I asked.

"Is Colette stable?"

I thought about her eyes and hair and the way she walked. "She's not consistent, but if she loved me and lived with me, I think she'd stay—a while."

I could see Lizbeth's hands. The right index finger moved up, then down, then out. Maybe she did isometrics to stay in shape while sitting all day listening to crazies whine over the same things hour after hour.

Lizbeth tried a different angle. "Have you slept with Colette yet?"

"Of course not. She's married."

"So?"

"It's unethical to sleep with a married woman."

"Is it ethical to steal a married woman from her husband?"

"If it's for her own good."

"You're doing this for Colette's good then?"

"She needs me."

"It's right to convince Colette to leave Danny, but not right to sleep with her."

"Not while she's living with him. Listen, could I lie on the carpet? I'm tired. My mind feels too fuzzy to hold me up."

Lizbeth looked at me a moment. "Go ahead."

I slid off the chair and onto the floor. Lying on my back, looking at the spackle bumps in the ceiling, I tried to remember if I'd slept last night. I must have, but I couldn't remember. I felt real sleepy.

"What's going to happen in your life?" Lizbeth asked.

"I'll marry Colette and write novels that change people for the better and raise babies into good grownups."

"What if she doesn't want to?"

"She wants to."

"What if she doesn't?"

"I'll either go crazy or I won't." The floor felt comfortable, warm, like an electric blanket. It had been too long a day. I talked on, more to myself than Lizbeth.

"My life is this bouncing ball, see. Every bounce it flies higher and comes down harder. It's only a matter of time before I come down too hard and shatter—or bounce so high I lose touch with earth forever."

"Cute metaphor."

I couldn't tell if Lizbeth was being sarcastic, but nobody likes a snotty shrink, so I went on. "The drama of me is this. Can I hold my brain and body together long enough to write a good book, find a good woman, accomplish something that makes this manic bullshit worth the trouble?"

I leaned back and looked at Lizbeth's ankles, expecting a reaction to my wise words. They didn't move.

Her voice came from above. "Would writing a book or finding a woman get you off the bouncing ball?"

I thought awhile. "No. I'd still go way up and come way down at pretty much predictable intervals, but maybe the bottom wouldn't be such a shock, and a steady woman might keep me in touch with reality or whatever."

I lay flat, thinking and drifting, exhausted. After a minute, Lizbeth spoke: "You talk about women as though they're tools of the trade equal to typewriters and paper. Do you want Colette or do you want to use her to write books?"

"What?"

"The end, the goal. Do you want her or what she brings?"

"Given a choice, I'd prefer to be happy."

I knew Lizbeth didn't take that as a satisfactory answer, but she didn't press it. I pretended someone had set a great weight on my forehead, at least forty pounds. A giant thumb was squishing out my third eye. It felt good.

"What are you going to do?" Lizbeth asked.

"Right now?"

"The next two hours, the next two days. Colette won't see you anymore. John has made it pretty much impossible for you to stay in Jackson. Are you going to leave?"

I didn't want to go anywhere. I wanted to crawl under Lizbeth's desk and go to sleep. "I wouldn't stand a chance right now, away from the familiar."

"How will you live?"

"It won't be hard. John doesn't know he's dealing with an old-line hippie. I'm highly trained in surviving without an income or a place to live. So long as I've got the bug I'm in fine shape."

Lizbeth didn't comment.

Flashing lights pulled me over less than a block from the Mental Health Center. It was the young deputy with the sideburns who had pushed in the Out door and served the peace warrant three weeks earlier. I slid from the bug and walked toward the deputy sheriff's car where he waited, tall and smiling. Every policeman's smile I've ever seen meant I was in big trouble.

The deputy peeled off his sunglasses. "Most people drive on the right side of the road."

I looked back at the VW, which was parked against the left curb. "Which side was I on?"

"The wrong side." He stood watching me. He seemed to expect some kind of an explanation.

"I have a lot on my mind today," I said. "Guess I forgot about right and wrong sides of the road. Are you going to give me a ticket?"

"Nope. We'll forget about it this time." The deputy leaned against his car door and crossed both arms. He was enjoying himself. "I've got a proposition for you," he said.

"A proposition."

"Yep. An either/or type deal you can't turn down."

I put my left hand on the hood and looked through the windshield at the rifle on the gun rack next to the driver's seat. "So what is it?"

The deputy was in no hurry. "We've got a file of parking tickets on this vehicle from three, four years ago," he said, nodding at the bug. "What with interest and all, we figure you owe the city at least a couple of thousand dollars."

"Two thousand dollars for parking tickets?"

"That's right. Now, legally, I should impound that automobile right now, but you're a good kid with a clean nose. We thought we'd give you a break."

It grates my nerves to be called a kid by someone younger than me. "I could use a break," I said.

"The city is willing to forget all those fines and interest if you will hop in your car and follow me to the county line, where I'll stop and you won't."

I looked at the bug. It was off-white with a dent in the passenger door. The trunk lid and hood were held on by bungee cords. Because of a small fire, it didn't have a backseat. "What will I use for gas money?"

The deputy reached into his breast pocket and pulled out a roll of bills. "Since this is the county that cares, I have been authorized to give you one hundred dollars for traveling expenses. That ought to get you clear of Wyoming and then some."

Mr. Hiatt's rent and deposit money was stuffed in my back pocket. Combined with the hundred and my last paycheck, I could go pretty far—or double back and set myself up again.

"Is there any legal basis for this deal?" I asked.

"If you can afford a lawyer, and if you can find one that will take the case, I'm sure we could come up with something," he said. "Do you have a job or residence?"

"No."

"That's vagrancy right there." The deputy stared off at the aspens on the hill over town. "Look, Kelly. I know something about your problem with John Hart. You're holding the raw end of the stick, but there's nothing I can do. If I didn't like you, you'd be handcuffed and fingerprinted by now, so don't push your luck. Take the offer and get out. No woman is worth prison, and I promise you that's the next step."

"What about my cat?"

"What cat?"

"I can't leave Alice."

He held out the hundred dollars. "Take the money, Kelly. Get in your car and follow me. If you don't, I'll have to do my duty and impound the automobile."

I've noticed that people tend to personify Volkswagen bugs more than any other car. I wonder why that is. The bug and I had been friends for a long time. I'd miss her.

"I wouldn't want to stop you from doing your duty," I said. "The keys are in it."

The deputy put his sunglasses back on. "Are you this much in love, or just a stubborn jackass?"

"Both."

· · ·

As I walked home, for some reason I got to thinking about my mother. It seemed like a long time since we'd talked, so I stopped in a phone booth across from the post office and called Idaho.

I called collect. Mom answered.

"Hi, Mom," I said.

"Kelly? Is that you?" Her voice sounded kind of worried.

"Yeah, it's me."

"Why are you calling? Is everything okay?"

"Sure, Mom, everything's fine. I just hadn't heard from you in a while and figured I'd call."

She didn't say anything for a minute. When she did speak, she sounded disgusted. "Kelly, you're doing it again."

"Doing what?"

"Behaving like a fool."

"What'd I do?"

"You called less than two hours ago."

"I did?"

"Julie's right. You are on drugs, aren't you?"

"No, I'm not on drugs."

"How could you forget calling if you aren't on drugs?"

Fair question. "I called you two hours ago?"

"Right."

I stood in the phone booth, watching the American flag in front of the post office. There didn't seem to be anything to say. "What did we talk about?"

"Kelly," Mom said, "don't be such a fuckup."

That was the second time I had heard Mom say *fuck*. The first was at Grandpa Hawken's deathbed. On July 4 of the Bicentennial summer of 1976, a dirtbiker from Salt Lake City ran over Grandpa Hawken on a trail up on Bull's Head Mountain.

The bike mangled Grandpa's insides. It split his spleen, ruptured a kidney, poked a rib through a lung. The Teewinot County sheriff's department carried the old man off the mountain and rushed him to the hospital in Rexburg, where we all gathered to see Grandpa once more before the doctors performed a last-gasp operation that no one expected him to survive.

We stood in a horseshoe around the bed, Julie, me, Mom, Dad, and Aunt Vera and her husband, Tom. Mom and Vera tried to convince Grandpa that he wasn't dying, but he knew better. He lay there breathing through his mouth, an ancient head on top of a midget wrestler's body. His arms were over the sheets, not moving. He stared at Julie, thinking of Grandma I suppose.

Grandpa's mouth moved up and back down like he was chewing. "Get some paper," he said.

Aunt Vera said, "What for? What's he want paper for?"

Julie went to the nurses' station and borrowed a pad and a pen. She came back and stood by Grandpa's right ear. Mom stood on the other side. I was next to Julie where I could see his darting eyes.

Grandpa looked at Julie. "I've got some last words."

Mom mumbled, "Oh, Daddy. You're not going to die."

"Shuddup, Mavine," Grandpa Hawken said without moving his eyes from Julie's face. They were green eyes—bright green.

"It's a poem," he said. "The first poem my mama taught me. My mama was beautiful."

Julie nodded. She stood straight, not bending toward Grandpa at all, with the pad in front of her. She looked ready to take a business letter.

Grandpa Hawken's eyes fluttered a moment, as if searching his memory for the proper words. He licked his lower lip and began in a sea-chant rhythm:

> *Tiddlywinks young man*
> *Catch a woman if you can*

If you can't get a woman
Get a clean old man.
Well, the women in Gibraltar
Ain't got nothing left to offer
So you better get a slice before the boat goes down.

Then the old man winked at Julie.

From the other side of the bed, Mom leaned over Grandpa's face and said, "Daddy, don't be such a fuckup."

The thing I'd always looked forward to the most was checking the mail. That's because, before Colette anyway, my real day-to-day existence had been pretty much limited to cleaning dishes, looking at the mountains, and trying to trick some waitress into bed. I always thought any excitement or opportunity that might enter my life would have to come through the mailbox. I'm not unique in that attitude. For many people, the postal system matters more than the life they see and live every day.

So far, no one had mailed any excitement or opportunity my way, but where there's a post office there's hope, and hope is always better than despair.

Since Colette's fateful punt, however, I'd stopped checking the mail two or three times a day. In fact, I couldn't remember the last time I'd been in the post office—although my not remembering didn't mean much. My own mom had just called me a fuckup on account of my memory. I did remember that.

I unlocked the post-office box and pulled out a handful of junk mail—a flyer from CondoShares, a Coast-to-Coast paint-sale ad, some credit agency that was irate because I hadn't paid on my student loan in several years. Cleveland Amory wanted me to send him money to help save rabbits in Idaho. Some guy offered a free test of my short story talent. Wendy's promised a twelve-ounce Coke with my purchase of a fish sandwich. No

excitement or opportunity there. Julie had a Burpee's seed catalogue addressed to Mrs. Julie Palamino. I had a postcard from
the library saying *Desert Solitaire* was six months overdue and
I should pay for a new copy.

I wandered over to browse through the army enlistment of-
fers and the wanted posters. No one I went to high school with
was wanted, so I dumped all the mail except the seed catalogue
into a green garbage can and left.

It took a half hour or so to find Julie and Rick's place. I'd
seen the house once before when I followed Julie home from
work soon after we split up, but that was two years ago in
winter, and everything looked different now.

Julie came out the door as I crossed the lawn. She was wearing white slacks and a jersey top and carrying a brown leather
daypack.

She said, "I didn't invite you here."

"It's nice to see you again," I said.

"You better leave. If Rick thinks you're bothering me, he'll
hit you."

I stood on the grass, looking up at Julie. She'd always been
a couple of inches taller than me, but the steps made her much
taller. Even though we lived four blocks apart, I hadn't seen her
in several months. I hadn't talked to her in over a year. She
seemed older than I remembered. The little double muscle that
runs between her nose and upper lip had sagged. Her hair was
a lighter blond and she wore eyeliner.

"Here." I held out the seed catalogue. "You got some mail."

Julie reached down and took it from my hand. She glanced
at the label and handed it back. "That's not for me."

I pretended to study the address. "Has your name on it."

Julie's eyes flashed scorn. "Does not." *Scorn* is the perfect
word for Julie. Her entire long-legged, big-chested body oozed
with scorn.

"You aren't Mrs. Julie Palamino?"

"You know damn well I'm not, and I demand you stop telling people I am."

I held up the catalogue. "This proves we were married."

Julie snatched the catalogue, opened the door, and threw it inside. Closing the door, she turned back to me. "It proves you're using that name to order stuff through the mail."

"What happened in Victoria, Texas?"

A kind of mask slid over her face. "I've never been in Victoria, Texas, in my life."

"How about Father Funk?"

"Father who?"

I was silent, trying to remember Father Funk's big hands and the motel where we paid by the hour. It seemed so long ago. I was a different person then. What if Julie was right? People wanted me locked in a mental hospital. I could be wrong and everyone else could be right.

Julie's mouth set in a line that showed edge crinkles inside her cheeks. "You and I went out a few times, Kelly, a fact I deeply regret. That was all. Everything else is lies you invented to humiliate me."

"Went out?"

"That's it."

"What about our apartment in New Orleans? And the cats, the trailer with no door on the bathroom, the bug? What about the joint savings account and the family foodstamp card?"

"Never existed."

"I haven't even finished paying for your IUD."

"Don't have one."

"Oh." I tried to think of something in those six years with Julie that I could grasp and she couldn't deny.

She started to move off the porch. "I've got to be somewhere now, so you'll have to leave."

"Where you going?"

"None of your business."

I stepped aside to let her pass. What with the too-blond hair and the eye makeup and white slacks, Julie didn't much look like the girl in the tapestry-jeans skirt that I married.

"You're wearing eye makeup," I said.

Julie stopped. "So?"

"The Julie I lived with in New Orleans used to laugh at people like you."

She stared at me a moment. "I'm sure if we ever met, I would laugh at her."

September of 1977, Julie and I backpacked up Paintbrush Canyon to the divide between Holly and Solitude lakes. As we reached the top of the divide, a huge thunderhead blew in from the west and we found ourselves trapped in an electrical storm.

For outright fear, grizzly bears and raging rivers don't even compare to sizzling electrical death. A limber pine twenty-five feet below us blew up, showering Julie and me with coals. Lightning crackled off a peak to our left. My neck hairs bristled. The smell was awful. The whole sky lit like a strobe light.

We threw off the metal packs and flattened on our stomachs. "Are we going to die now?" she asked quietly. Julie always acts real calm when she panics.

"Probably."

"What do I do if it kills you instead of me?"

I gave her detailed instructions on wrapping my body in a sleeping bag and hiking back down to the ranger station for help. So much of my time is spent rehearsing tragedies that I always know just what to do.

When I finished, Julie said, "I don't want to be alone up here if it kills you. Don't leave me alone." Lightning exploded a rock above us.

"Maybe you'll get lucky and it'll kill you and leave me alone," I shouted over the roar of thunder and rain.

Julie started to cry. "Nobody should be left alone," she cried. "Come over here. If one of us dies, Kelly, we'll both die."

I scrambled the five feet to Julie and lay next to her with my arm across her back. We lay freezing in the driving rain, fully expecting to be killed together at any moment. I didn't mind because Julie needed me. Death isn't so bad if someone needs you.

That was the same woman who three years later told me we "went out" a few times and she deeply regretted it.

My earthly possessions filled three large garbage bags and six boxes—almost nothing, considering that Alice and I lived in that apartment for four years.

Cora Ann helped. We hauled the garbage bags, clothes mostly, also the great pile of dishes, pots, and pans, across the street to the thrift shop in the church annex. The boxes went upstairs, crammed between Cora Ann's kayaks, skis, ice axes, and the remains of the hang glider. They were packed with books—I never throw away a book—also a radio, some phonograph albums, the elk skull, my Scrabble game, things like that.

We carried the plants up two at a time. I left the furniture for Mr. Hiatt.

I could tell Cora Ann was thinking. Most of the time she's so comfortable and automatic in her little niche that Cora Ann doesn't have to think. All possible situations have happened before and all reactions are preplanned and rehearsed. My moving was an event she hadn't counted on.

I guess Cora Ann figured I'd always be there below her, crying and laughing and throwing rocks through her window whenever I got drunk.

"You don't really have to do this," she said, looking at me through the leaves of a wandering jew.

"Do what?"

"Leave. Hide out. Whatever it is you have in mind."

The wandering jew drooped. The move upstairs must have put it in shock because it hadn't wandered an inch in years. Things in my apartment tended to stay put. I once stumbled over a tennis shoe on the bathroom floor for six months before I realized it didn't go there and threw it in the closet. "What are the alternatives?" I asked.

"You could stay here. Sleep on the couch. I'll feed you until you find another job."

I thought about this as we carried an asparagus fern and a peperomia up the stairs to her place.

"It wouldn't work," I said. "I won't be able to find another job. Besides, as soon as someone told John Hart I was sleeping here, he'd have you thrown out too."

Cora Ann sat in the lone chair with the plant in her lap. "I'll take the chance. I'm not afraid of John Hart or anybody else."

She pouted. Looking like a blond, beautiful eight-year-old girl, Cora Ann stuck out her lower lip and pouted.

"I'll be all right," I said.

"You're the closest thing I've got to a family." Cora Ann gave me a weak smile. "If you stay, I won't eat your peanut butter anymore."

"I appreciate the offer, but I can't." I stood in the middle of the room with the peperomia in my hands, looking for a place to set it down. Every available spot seemed taken.

"Why are you screwing yourself up like this, Kelly?" Cora Ann asked.

I walked to the stove. "You'll think it's corny."

"Go ahead. I'm in a corny mood."

I opened the oven door and put in the plant. Then I walked back to Cora Ann, cleared a place in front of her chair, and sat on the floor.

"You really want to hear?"

"I'm your friend, Kelly. Of course I want to hear."

I took the loops on her shoelaces and twisted them around, then back. Keeping my eyes on Cora Ann's shoes, I said, "I love Colette."

"You don't even know her."

"That's not important. All my life I've bounced with whatever wave hit me, place to place, job to job, woman to woman, doing whatever I blundered into at the moment. I'm almost thirty and I've never made a decision."

"What's wrong with that?"

"It lacks something essential. If I go on like this until I die, the whole thing will have been a waste. I might as well have not lived." I looked up at Cora Ann's very young eyes. "It's take-a-stand time. I've chosen Jackson Hole as the place and Colette as the woman. I can't give up on either one without giving up on myself. If I give up, I'll be a drunken dishwasher until I die and then I'll be dead."

"Everyone's dead after they die."

I tied the loops of her right shoe into three knots. How could I explain to someone like Cora Ann what it's like to be under someone else's control all your life? She'd probably never made a move she didn't want to make.

"I'm committed," I said. "No matter how inconvenient it is, I've got to stick by Colette."

"You call what John's doing inconvenient?"

I shrugged. "It's a pain in the butt."

She sat, holding the fern and watching me. Finally Cora Ann said, "You're right. It is corny."

"Call me sentimental."

"All right, Sentimental, what's living like Tarzan of the Tetons going to prove?"

"Nothing. I just want to be near Colette. It makes me nervous knowing she's out on that ranch, alone amidst the enemy. She needs my support."

Cora Ann smiled. "Colette needs you like I need body lice."

• • •

Cora Ann came downstairs and sat on the couch while I loaded my backpack. Bare necessities—sleeping bag, tent, change of socks, binoculars, one pot and pan, Sierra Club cup, and my typewriter. No food would fit in the pack, so I took the type-writer out. It was a Royal portable in a case with a plastic han-dle. I could carry it. I only planned on walking a couple of miles.

The good-bye scene with Alice was touching. I sat on the porch in the old spot and held her in my lap, scratching behind both her ears while she purred quietly. Alice has a very quiet purr. Most people can't hear it.

It hurt to leave Alice behind. I knew Cora Ann would take care of her, but it was like a father leaving his virgin daughter at a coed summer camp. All the good intentions in the world can't protect the young like a righteous parent.

Another one of my flaws—some people call it a flaw—is that I don't differentiate between animals and people. I feel just as much companionship from a cat as I do from a person. The death of an animal friend tears me up as much as the death of a human friend.

All my Romantic Interests have been jealous of Alice, and Alice is jealous of them. She treats them like dead birds.

Julie was the only one who ever came right out and said something. About a week before she moved out, we were sitting on the couch, watching a Bob Newhart rerun, when Julie said, "No woman is ever going to love you for long, you know that, Kelly."

At that time I agreed with everything Julie said. I thought maybe if I was agreeable enough, she wouldn't go away. "You're right," I said.

A couple of jokes into the TV show later, I asked, "Why?"

Julie propped her feet up on the trunk and sipped on a Sugar-Free Dr Pepper. "It's that cat."

"Alice?"

"You love that cat more than you'll ever love a woman."
She took another sip. "And it's the same kind of love. A person
should have one love for pets, another for lovers, another for
friends. You only have one kind of love, Kelly, and no woman
wants to be second-class to a cat."

I thought about this a moment. "I suppose so."

"And if Alice dies, you still won't find a woman who loves
you because you'll moon over that cat until you get another
one."

"You're right."

For years, Julie had me convinced that no woman besides
her would lower herself to having anything to do with me. She
was only nice to me out of pity. She still believes that. I'm not
sure.

Anyhow, the fond farewell would have lasted a good deal
longer, but Alice got bored and jumped down and walked away.
Nobody ever cooperates when I try to pull off a sensitive moment.

On the way out of Jackson, Cora Ann and I stopped at the
grocery store for me to stock up on supplies before disappearing
into the mountains. Grocery shopping for a fugitive must be
very difficult. The outlaw housewife doesn't know whether to
buy on-the-run single servings, or giant economy holed-up-in-
one-spot-for-months bulk. Should I menu-plan for two days or
two years—or longer?

I ended up buying family-size flour, coffee, beans, brown
rice, and oatmeal, then small boxes of macaroni and cheese,
Rice-A-Roni, Cup-a-Soup, spaghetti, anything that could be
made into food with water and fire.

I just couldn't stand the thought of running off into the hills
without hearing Colette's beautiful voice again. I told Cora Ann
this.

"Stand the thought," she said.

"If I'm going to live weeks at a time without human contact, I need inspiration."

"I'll loan you my copy of *The Prophet*."

"Wait one minute while I call Colette."

"She won't talk to you."

"It'll just take a second," I said to Cora Ann. She was real patient—for Cora Ann.

I knew Colette wouldn't listen to me. She was distressed and couldn't think straight, but I didn't want to talk. I only wanted to hear her voice one last time.

Digging into the side pocket of my pack, I found a red bandanna. All backpacks have red bandannas in them somewhere. I crossed the street to a pay phone and dialed Colette's number. Before she could answer, I wrapped the bandanna around the mouthpiece.

An older tourist woman stopped to watch.

"Hello," Colette answered.

"Excuse me, please, Mrs. Hart," I said. "But do you think your husband would prefer stuffing or potatoes with his chicken tonight?"

"I told you not to call anymore," Colette said. She hung up.

I added up the words. Eight, if you count *hello*, which is a word and should count. Eight words total, they would have to nourish me in the months ahead.

Cora Ann drove to the jeep trail above the Broken Hart Ranch. I figured it would be too risky to drive on up to the creek where I'd parked the day of the ill-fated hang-gliding incident, so Cora Ann stopped on the main road.

We pulled the pack out and leaned it against the side of the Mustang. Then we stood around a minute, looking at the cottonwoods and the Tetons and feeling embarrassed about the whole thing.

Cora Ann crossed her arms and held her elbows like she was cold, which she couldn't have been. It was a beautiful, blue June

day. Grasshoppers flashed yellow in the sagebrush. Juncos and
sparrows flitted through the willow fronds. Sunlight glittered off
her Mustang, making it appear clean and new.

"Well, thanks for the ride out," I said.

Cora Ann leaned against the right front headlight and stared
off in the direction of Death Canyon. "You're just going to live
in the forest and eat bushes and wait for your true love to see
the light, huh?"

I kicked her tire. It was firm. "Yeah, I guess so."

"That's stupid."

"I know."

She looked at me. "How will you live?"

"I've got plenty of food."

"That's not what I mean. You'll die in a week up there,
Kelly."

"Maybe."

There wasn't much else to say. Then something kind of peculiar happened. Cora Ann walked over and hugged me—
hugged me tight. I'd known her two years, and she'd been my
best friend for one, but in all that time, Cora Ann had never
hugged me. In fact, except on the dance floor, I doubt she even
touched me more than twice.

It felt odd. I'm not used to touching anyone I'm not trying
to fuck. It felt very odd.

So—bright-blue overloaded pack on my back, Royal portable hanging from my right hand, I marched up the trail and
into the mountains.

9

My life has been full of periods. I wonder if other people know the moment that their lives go from flip to flop. I imagine some future biographer compiling a ten-volume study of Kelly Palamino. I know the date and hour that each volume ends. Each chapter in each volume. The nerd period. The hippie period. The mountain man period. Each period as different as winter and summer in Wyoming.

Wednesday morning I awakened in the same bed I had awakened in for the past four years. I had every intention of sleeping, waking, and, sixty years from now, dying in that bed. Wednesday afternoon I'm a man with no home, no cat, all his possessions on his back.

The same thing occurred when I left New Orleans. At noon I walked down Esplanade, confident my whole life would revolve around the Quarter. By two, we were gone.

Julie moved in with me the afternoon we met.

I dedicated my life to Colette five seconds after I first saw her.

God, or Whoever, doesn't nudge me toward my fate. She blows me out of a cannon.

This series of obsessions, if you want to call them that, has made me into what I consider a unique individual. Show me another man who can skin an elk, roll a joint with his eyes closed, knows every Dodger lineup from 1954 through '63, can recite the books of the Bible backward from Revelations, tear down and put together any dish machine made, and write a four-hundred-page novel on a typewriter without a space bar.

On the other hand, how many grownups can't check the oil on a car, tie a necktie, balance a checkbook, or remember the last time they changed underwear?

I set up camp along the creek about a mile and a half above the Broken Hart ranch. It was a nice, simple camp, the two-man tent and firepit hidden from the trail, yet close to water, a fine old aspen for hanging the food at night, plenty of dry firewood—ideal spot for a cigarette commercial.

Thursday dawn the birds threw a group tizzy that had me awake and blindly groping for my glasses hours earlier than what I'm accustomed to. I crawled from the tent barefoot, coughed, scratched, spit a bad taste, and pissed facing the rising sun. Indians always peed facing the sun. It has religious significance.

As the sagebrush turned from gray to pink and back to gray again, I slow-moseyed back and forth between the creek and the woods, gathering twigs, dipping water, stumbling over tent stakes. The creek played "March of the Cue Balls," by Henry Mancini. I take it as a good omen when the water sings something I know.

Dew had tightened up the knot on my bag, and I had a hell of a time getting the food out of the tree. I started a fire by spraying the kindling with lighter fluid and throwing in a match.

Four cups of boiled coffee and a bowl of oatmeal later, I brushed my teeth and wandered deeper into the woods to squat. Obeying the rule that one big pile is less likely to be stepped in by an innocent hiker than two little piles, I crapped on old coyote droppings. Then I wiped and burned the toilet paper.

After that, I collected the binoculars, a little bag of granola, and a packet of unsweetened Kool-Aid and went to work.

Work was easy. I lay on a flat rock next to a limber pine, with the binoculars pressed against my glasses, and waited for Colette.

The rock sat at the top of a steep hill above the ranch. Behind my spot was a flat, hidden meadow, then the forested ridge continued on up to camp. If I stayed in the trees coming down the ridge, crouched low in the meadow, and slid on my stomach across the flat rock, I was perfectly safe from being seen. I even made a cardboard shade for the binoculars so they wouldn't flash in the sun.

The view couldn't be beat. It covered the creek, the jeep trail, the sloping yard, and all one side and the back of the bunkhouse. While I couldn't see Danny and Colette's front door, most of the yard between their place and the big house was open, so it would be difficult for anyone to come and go from the bunkhouse without my knowing. The other side of John's big house was horse pasture and a barn, then the long driveway out to the arched gate. Beyond the gate stretched beautiful Jackson Hole, the Snake River, and the Gros Ventre Mountains.

With a good rifle, I could have pinned down a full platoon on the ranch grounds. Would have been a piece of cake to kill the whole Hart family. However, killing Harts was not my purpose. My purpose was to keep an eye on them.

I had no sooner found my position and settled in comfortably than Danny and Thor came out the front of the bunkhouse. Danny walked the hundred yards up a slight rise and went into his parents' house without knocking. The dog spotted a ground squirrel ducking down a hole and went after it, dirt flying.

Twenty minutes later, Danny and Mr. Hart came out the

back door, exchanged a few words, then each got into a look-alike Dodge four-wheel-drive Powerwagon and drove away.

Lying on my stomach, watching the Powerwagons turn right toward town and the bank, I developed a theory. I decided that Danny ate breakfast with his parents every day. I based this theory on my morning phone calls to Colette. Whenever I called before ten, I woke her up.

I made a mental note to correct this habit after we were married. Differing breakfast habits can ruin even the best of marriages.

For a while I watched Thor chase squirrels and pee on bushes, but he was boring, so I set down the binoculars and ate some granola.

Maybe an hour later, Mrs. Hart came around the front of the big house and began puttering in a little garden someone had staked out alongside the creek. If Mrs. Hart was weeding, she sure wasn't very systematic about it. She stood with one hand touching her chin and looked at the ground, then walked a couple of steps, bent over and pulled something up, then she stood straight with her hand under her chin and repeated the process. It looked more like picking lint off a large wool sweater than weeding a garden.

I could see Mrs. Hart clearly through the binoculars. She didn't seem alert—not dumb, necessarily, just gone to pasture. Her hair was short and brown. Her mouth neither smiled nor frowned. It just sat there above her one and a half chins as if it had nothing else to do. She wore cotton gardening gloves that hid her fingers, so I couldn't really judge her for quality. Fingers are the only way I have of judging a woman's quality—other than sleeping with her.

Colette has nice fingers.

Mrs. Hart didn't putter around the garden long, ten minutes tops, before she walked down to Colette's house and went in without knocking.

Mrs. Hart stayed in the bunkhouse a long time. I got hot and moved to the shade, then cool and moved back. A light spray of clouds drifted south from the Yellowstone Plateau, a sure sign that it would rain in a few days. A red-tailed hawk wheeled clockwise above me, checking to see if I was dead or deteriorating.

As it turned out, the unsweetened Kool-Aid proved useless because my lookout post was way above the creek. The creek bounced down from my camp and left the ridge a quarter-mile south of the ranch, where it curled along the base of the hill until, behind the bunkhouse, it cut east to the river.

I should have known about the curl from my hang-gliding adventure, but I wasn't thinking well. I hardly ever think well.

Around noon, I belly-slid off the rock to search for lunch. My living-off-the-land plant-identification menu is real limited. I can safely eat two things: berries—service, blue, and huckle—and the root of the Everts' thistle. Since June is a month early for berry season, I was stuck with roots. Everts' thistle tastes like a cross between a raw potato and cardboard. If I hadn't been so stubborn about the pure hermit-on-the-mountain ex-perience, I'd have stocked up on Twinkies and transcended bushes and berries.

Anyhow, after a hearty lunch of dirty roots, I crawled back onto the rock in time to see Colette bounce out of the house wearing nothing but a tube top and a pair of cut-off jeans. She looked beautiful—posture, hair, eyes, fingers, tattoo, the whole works. With the binoculars, I focused down close enough to eat her. Made me so hard I had trouble lying on my stomach.

Colette jogged across the lawn, climbed into an off-white Subaru, and drove away. I didn't see her again for six hours.

Every now and then, spread on that rock and watching an empty house, life seemed a bit monotonous. The clouds were great. Birds are always interesting, and I know just feeling the sun should be enough, but, much as I pretend I don't need them, I missed being near people. I mean, I'm used to spending most of my time alone, but I never completely removed myself from the human race before. In my most intense times of solitude, I could walk to the Cowboy and sit on a saddle and be surrounded by the smells and sounds of people.

Total withdrawal was odd. I lay with my cheek on the rock, studying the tree trunk next to me, and one stupid, meaningless phrase started up in my head and circled round and round, searching for a way out.

The phrase was "modicum of potatoes." Where did that come from, anyway? I must have thought "modicum of potatoes" a thousand times before Colette returned.

Several days later, after I caught flu and became feverish and my diet and sleeping habits slid, the phrases grew louder, lasted longer, made less sense. The last couple of days camping out, I felt like giant shells were Scotch-taped to my ears, but instead of the ocean, the shells roared "Smorgasbord slips by," over and over.

It was enough to drive me crazy.

The first day, though, "modicum of potatoes" felt kind of nice. A pleasant break from the water singing the blues, quoting *The Canterbury Tales*, and rerunning "Sergeant Bilko" TV shows.

The weather was perfect. The clouds drifted, the hawk drifted, I drifted. As I hugged the warm rock, all nature seemed about as stable and real as nondairy coffee creamer. Nothing mattered. I was happy again.

"Modicum of potatoes," I thought, staring at the rock.

I was almost disappointed when they returned home, first John, then, a couple of hours later, Danny followed Colette up the drive and into the family parking area. Danny got out first and walked over and opened Colette's door. When she stepped from the car, Colette was wearing sandals. She had been barefoot that afternoon, so I figured she either bought some sandals, borrowed them, or had them in the car all along. Or maybe she found them.

Arm in arm, Colette and Danny walked into the house. I waited until way after dark, but they never came back outside.

Back at the camp, I hauled water, built a fire, and cooked my macaroni and cheese, usual camp busywork. As I busied around the campfire, the creek bubbled and babbled, *"It is not worth the while to go around the world to count the cats in Zanzibar."*

"Thoreau," I said. "Conclusion of *Walden.*"

"Right," the creek answered.

The creek answered. In two years of listening to running water, the water had never listened to me. I had either dropped off the edge or made a major breakthrough in personified-object communication.

"Come again?" I said, but the creek went off on another train of thought.

"If a chicken is killed and it is not cooked properly, that chicken has died in vain."

"That one's easy," I said. "Lin Yutang by way of Alan Watts."

The creek wouldn't say whether I was right or not. It probably read the original and didn't realize Alan Watts used it later.

My camp was pitched just inside the border of Grand Teton National Park, which means I was highly illegal—federal-offense illegal. I had to keep the fire squaw-size so no one in the valley below would see it and come investigating. A ridge blocked direct view, and the spot was sheltered by Douglas fir on one side and *Mertensia* on the other, but I still wasn't taking any chances.

Even with this tiny fire, by the time the mac and cheese was cooked and eaten and the evening hot chocolate nice and hot, a fair mound of coals glowed pink and red against the dark circle of stones. I lay on my side next to the fire, watching the embers pulsate, thinking the same thoughts that men and women watching a dying fire have thought for centuries.

I thought about God and death and Colette and my books. The things I thought frightened me. Doubt crept in concerning all four. What if they weren't all they had been built up to be?

The inspired fanatic cannot afford doubt. The only possible way to continue an unrealistic life is to shut off all doubts, all qualms and compromises. Otherwise, you realize everything is a meaningless pile of shit and you kill yourself.

Wednesday and Thursday constituted the longest stretch I'd gone without alcohol abuse since Julie left, which may account for why I overslept Friday. Late that morning, sunlight on the nylon caused an oven effect in the tent, and I awoke in a puddle of sweat. Rolling over, I put on my glasses and stared at blue breeze ripples in the ceiling. Something was wrong. None of my joints ached. My stomach was nothing but a little hungry. I touched my head—no pain.

So this is what it's like not to have a hangover, I thought. To someone who's in pain most of the time, absence of pain is a creepy sensation. I felt guilty, like I was getting away with something nasty.

Saturday was the most exciting day of my time on the rock. They threw another cookout like the one on Memorial Day, and Colette stayed in sight all afternoon. She wore a dark pullover shirt, jeans, and Nike running shoes. She drank seven beers from the keg and played a mean game of volleyball. Her serves weren't worth much, but Colette's true talent was the desperate defensive save. Several times she set Danny up for killer spike shots.

After lunch, Danny and most of the men threw horseshoes while the women cleaned up the mess. Colette tried to relax in a lawn chair, but Mrs. Hart coerced her and one of the girls I recognized from the Cowboy into a round of croquet. I don't think Colette wanted to play. As Mrs. Hart dragged her by the hand toward the mallet rack, Colette kept glancing south. I think she was hoping me and my hang glider would swoop around the bend and save her from a game with Danny's mother. Before Mrs. Hart led off, Colette ran into the bunkhouse and came back with a bottle of Grand Marnier, which she held on to, tipping drinks as they circled the wickets.

The game progressed through the first five wickets without much fuss. The girl from the Cowboy was ahead, with Colette close on her heels. In front of the double wicket turnaround post, Mrs. Hart caught up and hit Colette's ball. Mrs. Hart put the balls together so they were touching, and with one foot on her ball, she walloped Colette's ball clear off the course and into a rut behind a lodgepole pine. I didn't see any way for Colette to get back in the game in less than two or three strokes.

But then Thor started a fight with a malamute, and Danny jumped in to break it up. People yelled and shouted, and while everyone but me was watching the action, Colette kicked her ball out of the rut, around the tree, and ten feet closer to the post.

I was shocked. Two rules are sacred to me: first, never cheat at games, and second, whenever a cashier gives you too much change, always give the extra money back. That's a simple code of ethics, if you ask me. I can live by it. Why couldn't Colette?

Setting the binoculars aside, I lay on my back and faced the clouds. Colette—the beautiful, the ideal, my chosen partner for life—was a cheater. A gyp. How could that be? Doubts swirled in the air over my lookout rock. Who was Colette, anyway? Why did I love her? She punted a football and looked at me with pitiful eyes, and instantly I knew her for the perfect woman.

Right now, that seemed like a rash assumption. Perfect

women don't cheat. She was playing against her own mother-in-law, for Chrissake.

Turning back over on my stomach, I searched the lawn with the binoculars until I found Colette sitting next to her bottle on the bunkhouse steps. Her posture wasn't as perfect as usual. Her eyes appeared kind of flat and glassy, nostalgic, maybe, or full of melancholy.

She looked like a lost little girl. I felt a moment of terrible sadness. She was probably thinking about her brother and how he was gone. And me, she must wonder where I am, why I left her alone.

For a moment, I almost walked down the hill to hold and comfort her, but Danny and John would have caused a scene—which was their right. Besides, Colette might not want comfort. Her body leaned at an odd angle. The melancholy face could have more to do with beer and Grand Marnier than any yearning for a fulfilling existence. Even so, I knew her thoughts and secrets were with me.

Sunday the weather turned cold, the wind blew, and the rain came down in sheets. I lay on my rock all day, exposed to rain, lightning, hail, and everything else imaginable. It's a wonder I didn't die. And not once, even for a second, did Colette or anyone related to her show themselves. All day I hunched up against the elements and watched the driveway fill with water. I would have thought they were all dead if somebody hadn't kicked Thor out and let him back in twice.

That night my wood was soaked and my fingers stiff, so I couldn't build a fire. I started shivering. I couldn't stop. In my wet clothes, I crawled into the sleeping bag and lay on my back and shook until morning.

After that, the days ran together. I know I was sick. I know I made it to the rock every day—I never missed a one—but other than that, it's hard to say what happened. I lost the ability to distinguish between being awake and being asleep. My clothes were dirty. I lost some weight and grew a spotty beard. I ate brown rice and Everts' thistle.

I talked to myself a lot.

Conversations with the water became very esoteric and filled with double meanings and extraneous verbs. I more or less blacked out for a couple of weeks.

10

Truman Everts was a man I can identify with. He should be enshrined somewhere in the Hall of Famous Losers.

In 1870, Truman came to the Yellowstone Plateau with one of the first parties of white men ever to explore the region. On the east side of Yellowstone Lake, he somehow lost track of his companions. His horse bucked him off and ran away. In the fall, Everts broke his spectacles.

I know the position. My glasses once sank in the Escatawpa River in southern Mississippi. The wilderness experience is not enjoyable for the newly blind.

Anyway, Everts stumbled around the forest, figuring he was dead or dying. Near starvation, he ate the root of a tall thistle with purple flowers. The root didn't kill him or make him sick, so he ate another the next day. Everts lived on the thistle root for over a month.

Some prospectors found old, blind Everts and stuck him on a horse and headed for civilization—in this case Gardiner, Montana. Indians attacked and Everts took a shot in the leg. The prospectors loaded him into a wagon and promptly rolled the wagon off a cliff. In Gardiner, they put him in a bed in a room above the doctor's office.

Just as the doctor arrived, the bed collapsed.

I don't know what happened to Truman Everts after that—whether he lived a wonderfully happy life or continued his string of bad luck—but the explorers were so moved by his story they named the thistle after him.

Fame has its price. I think I eat Everts' thistle more for Everts than the nutrition.

I take that other stuff back. It's an exaggeration for dramatic effect to say I blacked out for two weeks. I mean, I wasn't delirious or anything—at least not often. I was just confused. Thinking too many thoughts over and over, rehearsing tragedies, dwelling on the past, and living tiny details of the future. What would Colette and I name the kids? What albums would we buy? How would I behave when my dad died?

I developed the ability to watch scenes as graphically as if I was watching television. Sometimes I had lived the scenes or might live them someday. Other times I saw things I couldn't possibly have been involved in.

I saw Alice in a cat fight in which she was killed.

A girl I invented for my fourth novel came alive and crawled into my tent and stretched out on me.

Grandpa Hawken crowed like a rooster and held his great prick with both hands, spewing come at the sunrise.

Cora Ann shot down the Grey's River rapids in a silver kayak. She bounced over a boulder, took the bottom chute vertically, and landed right side up in a calm, willow-shaded pool.

They weren't dreams, I was awake. And they weren't visions, at least not the visions of religious fanatics who haven't eaten in a week. Psychologists say the most important thing about sleeping is the dreams. If a person doesn't sleep for a couple of days, he'll begin dreaming while he's awake.

I suggest that modern man is so dependent on television that if he doesn't see a TV show for a few days, a set will click on in his head. It's a theory, anyway.

One night I did go all-out, sweat-soaked, crazy-eyed delirious. Colette and Danny had been kissing in the backyard on the grass. It was nauseating. He put his hand on her stomach. At sunset, they stood up and went in the house, but no lights came on.

I crept down the hill. Thor was inside, so I figured it was safe to sneak up to the house and stand under their second-story window. I knew they were making love because I heard breathing and humping. I don't think Colette enjoyed it that much. Danny made a lot more noise than she did, but still, it didn't seem right. That loan officer was screwing my life mate. It made me feel strange.

I walked home and ate my brown rice, listening to the water replay the 1943 version of *The Phantom of the Opera*. I'll never know for certain, but the creek probably intended the movie as some kind of criticism on my life.

That night as I lay in my sleeping bag, the top of the tent turned into a movie screen. Like a dying person, I saw it all and understood nothing.

I saw Mom leaning over the desk and pointing at the check with her right hand, saying, "It's good. Call the bank. They'll tell you it's a good check."

And the abortionist's secretary, a young woman with short hair, saying, "I'm sorry, Mrs. Palamino. We cannot take personal checks."

Mom points again. "Why not?"

The girl is patient. "This is an illegal business, Mrs. Palamino. We can't leave records."

"It's a good check."

The doctor, overweight, no gray hair in his hair, comes into the waiting room. "What seems to be the trouble?"

"Mrs. Palamino wants to pay with a personal check."

"We can't accept checks."

"But it won't bounce. Would you like to see the deposit slip?"

Uncle Homer rocks back and forth, his left hand clutching at his right, his eyes focused on a gray spot on the baseboard. He's rocking and listening, listening for the citizen's-band signal that will kill him, the stray microwave floating through the atmosphere that will explode his heart.

I step over the body to pick up the derringer. I don't even check to see if he's dead. I step over the body, pick up the derringer, and put it in my pocket.

A highway patrolman in south Texas kicks a long-haired boy to his knees on the street and makes him bite the curb, then stomps the back of his head. I hold the boy's head while he vomits and spits out blood, teeth, and bits of jawbone.

Julie has her hands pressed against the small of my back. My face is burrowed in her shoulder while I grind myself into her. I look up and her eyes are wide open, staring at the ceiling, bored.

During the hippie period, I overdosed on codeine once. That night, lying stiff in my bag and staring at my past and future, I felt the same numbness and terror I had known on the codeine. I couldn't possibly move my head or arms. They were weighted down as if I was under a couple of feet of snow. I was very frightened someone might walk up to the tent and I'd have to talk or cope.

The night was not enjoyable. I saw—felt—family fights and picnics, meaningless conversations, meaningless days. I've heard the mind never releases anything. You just have to touch the right nerve end in the brain to remember the smell of the delivery-room nurse or the color of socks every kid in your first-grade class wore on opening day. Something must have scampered all over my nerve ends that night, because I remembered it all.

Meanwhile, between fits of relative insanity, I watched the Hart Ranch. I didn't miss a move down there. John Hart kicked Thor for no reason one day, just because he thought no one was looking. Colette scraped one of the Powerwagons with her Subaru and drove away without telling anybody. On a Monday when everyone else was gone, Mrs. Hart stood in the garden and cried.

I may have been a neurotic schizoid with tendencies toward psychotic paranoia and stage-four anxiety attacks, but I was observant. Nobody on that ranch could pick his nose without my knowing which finger he used and whether or not he came up dry.

There is a second abortion in my life. One I generally forget or choose not to remember. Three months before Julie left, I came home from work late one afternoon and found her lying on the couch, reading *The Bell Jar*.

"You look pale," I said.

Julie glanced up from the book. "I feel pale."

It was January and cold. I must have had on five layers of sweaters, vests, and coats. I asked, "What did you do today?"

She set the book in her lap and looked right at me. I stopped in the middle of pulling off my down vest. At that time, Julie didn't look at me very often, hardly ever, and I knew something had happened.

"I had an abortion this afternoon," she said.

"An abortion?"

"Yes."

I finished taking off the vest and dropped it onto a chair. "Are you pregnant?"

"Not anymore." That done, she picked up the book and started reading again.

I stood in the center of the room, watching her. Julie concentrated on the book. Her hair was kind of dirty and her eyes seemed tired. Other than that, she appeared the same as ever. "Why didn't you tell me?"

"You'd have made a big deal out of it," she said without glancing up.

"It was half my child. I deserved to know."

"See. I knew you'd whine and moan and make it into a moral crisis, and I would have ended up having the abortion anyway. I saved you all that poetic soul-wrenching. Be thankful."

"I'm not thankful. I deserve my poetic soul-wrenching." I sat in the chair and stared at her. She licked her thumb and turned the page. Nothing I said or felt could have affected Julie one way or another.

"How did you do it?" I asked.

"I went to the doctor's office and he took care of it right there. They gave me two shots that hurt like shit."

"How did you get home?"

"Rick drove me."

"You told Rick you were pregnant, but not me?"

She marked her place in the book with one finger and looked at me again. "Rick understands. You wouldn't have."

"Oh." We stared at each other for a while. I had lots of questions, but none of them mattered much. "Are you all right?"

"I'm fine, just a little tired. I'll be in top shape tomorrow."

"You want a pizza or something?"

"Sounds good to me. Italian sausage and mushroom?"

"Okay."

So I went out and bought a pizza and we sat on the couch, watching "M*A*S*H" and chewing.

The subject of the abortion never came up again. Like the marriage itself, I bet Julie's completely forgotten it by now.

We tried for two years to persuade Rick to move west. He was living a turbulent drugs-and-sex life with a fiery little woman in New Orleans. She left him every three months or so, and he would send us a letter saying it was all over and he had to leave New Orleans, would we put him up for a few days?

We'd write back and say, Come on, we'd love to have you. We'll feed you and keep you in alcohol through the crisis. He never answered, but three months later she would leave again and he would write another letter. This went on for two years. Once he even spent three hundred dollars on a tent so he could camp out with us, but he didn't have enough cash left for the trip, and by the time he made the money, she was back.

Then, one day in July, I walked into the Cowboy after work and there Rick was, sitting on a saddle, chugging an Oly, and looking pleased with himself. He jumped off the saddle and hugged me—the only time in my life a man has ever hugged me—and said he was so happy to see me he could shit.

We proceeded to drink ourselves near comatose and rolled home to Julie. I threw up in the sink while he threw up in the toilet. Julie wiped us both off with paper towels and carried me to bed and him to the couch.

When she left, I kind of figured Julie would drift over to Rick, but I didn't mind. He'd been nothing but honorable while she lived with me, and I didn't figure Julie could handle solitude any better than I could. Being from New Orleans, Rick was the logical choice in this town full of Californians and Yankees.

However, something happened along the way. After she left, we were all still friends. They got together, like I expected. I got drunk. I harbored no ill feelings, but I must have done something awful because soon people asked, "Why does Rick hate you so much?" and six months later it was, "Why does Julie hate you so much?"

I guess I miss him more than her. There's an old saying I read in the men's room under the rodeo stands in Pocatello, Idaho: *You can replace a lover, but you can't replace a friend.* I've had plenty of lovers since Julie, but I haven't had a friend since Rick.

A couple of mornings after my psychic flashback, I almost got myself killed. The hike down the ridge was the usual carnival of air, dirt, trees, and stones all vying for attention. As I walked, I worked on my gums and teeth with a blue spruce needle. Spruce needles are stiff like toothpicks, and fir needles are soft like floss, which is a problem because spruce needles don't slide into the spaces between the teeth, and if you force them in, they break off and stick straight out. On the other hand, fir needles fit the gaps, but they're too short to hold on to at both ends. You can solve both problems by going with blades of grass, but then your teeth turn green.

A baby moose trotted from a willow patch and stood in the trail, staring brown-eyed at me. She was young and cute in a lovable but ugly sort of way—all feet, joints, and skull. A frond hung out the right side of her chewing lips.

Like many people, I lower animals to my level by treating them as Peter Rabbit characters. "Good morning, Miss Moose," I said. "Fine day for eating weeds, isn't it?"

The baby bounce-loped into the woods and stopped again, this time staring past me into the trees.

A branch cracked and I looked back into the frontal view of a charging mother moose. I yelped and dived left into a choke-cherry thicket. She whirled and came on again. Hooves the size of MacIntosh speaker cabinets thundered by my ear.

I clawed upright and ran for the nearest tree, a lodgepole

pine without a branch below thirty feet. The mama wheeled and barreled back, head down.

Rangers claim that moose charge with their eyes closed, and to avoid them, all you do is step aside. Never believe a forest ranger. No animal with its eyes closed would chase me two full circles around the lodgepole before snorting and coming to a rest. I ran another ten feet, then turned around to face her.

She pawed the ground, eyeing me. The baby chewed a bush twenty yards down the hill. My legs shook and my chest hurt like shit. Lungs heaving, breath coming in choked sobs, I gasped, "This is bizarre."

She laid her ears back, flared her nostrils into huge black cavities, and charged again. I felt like a penny on a railroad track. I waited the way rodeo clowns and bullfighters wait for bulls, and at the last possible moment I cheated death by leaping into the dirt. Then I ran like hell.

This time I reached a climbable tree before she did. Bloodied my fingers, ripped my only shirt, and scraped my chest raw— but I made it.

Perched on a limb, hugging the trunk with both arms, I looked down at the mother moose and stuck out my tongue and sang, *"Nonnie-nonnie-pooh-pooh, you ugly bitch."*

It was an awful thing to say, childish and disrespectful, but I see it this way: Although her motives were instinctive and maternal, the moose tried to kill me. If others have the right to protect their security by harming me, I have the right to nonnie-nonnie-pooh-pooh a little when they don't succeed.

It took a while to notice, but as the days went by, my personal appearance began falling apart. I suppose the torn shirt tipped me off. Rags seem shabby even for me. I had jumped in the creek a few times, but that could hardly be called adequate hygiene for two weeks of camping. My clothes felt damp and moldy. My hair hadn't been anywhere near a brush or comb since I left Jackson.

Something had to happen soon or the Harts would smell me from the rock.

I lay in my little groove, watching the silent ranch and fingering my beard. I don't grow much of a beard. The right side comes out fine, black and bristly, but the left side grows in small Canadian-dime-size patches that never quite come together.

The food supply was running low and I was sick of Everts' thistle. My clothes and I stunk. I couldn't shake the fever, and the delusions or hallucinations or whatever they were were starting to frighten me. Hard as I tried not to notice, my present lifestyle couldn't last much longer.

Colette bounced out of the house and drove away. For three days, all I had seen were people walking from houses to cars and cars to houses. It wasn't nearly as interesting as I had hoped it might be.

After Colette left, I settled in to wait for the next Hart to drive in or away. As the phrase *smorgasbord slips by* rolled around my head, I faced the unpleasant situation.

Two facts could not be ignored. I could not continue in this fashion, and I would not leave Colette. These facts made all alternatives impossible.

I had vaguely figured on sneaking back to Cora Ann's every month or so for a bath and a change of clothes, but that plan only put off any decisions until winter, and winter would cut down my choices considerably. Besides, one more week on that mountain, eating roots and watching nightly mind movies, and I might lose touch forever—transmute into a mass murderer or public defecator or any number of antisocial things that don't even have names.

I set the binoculars on the rock and rolled over on my back to search the sky for solutions. My brain was in disarray. I knew if I could only think straight, the answer would be obvious. The answer is almost always obvious if you stop long enough to think.

Here was my list of choices: (1) Return to Jackson; (2) leave the area; (3) go higher into the mountains; (4) commit suicide; or (5) kidnap Colette.

What lousy choices. Every one was either awful or tedious. The first three were definitely out. They involved leaving Colette to the sharks. So did number four, but it appealed to my sense of drama and escapist attitude. However, I lacked the necessary energy for suicide. The effort would not be worth the result.

I didn't really want to kidnap Colette either. No woman is fun to live with if you have to hold a gun to her head.

What I wanted to do most was crawl under Lizbeth's desk and sleep for a week.

While I pondered the sky and my future, the Hart cars and trucks returned one at a time. I watched them upside down—first Mrs. Hart's Toyota, then Colette's Subaru, and later, both Powerwagons. Everyone went inside, leaving me with the sinking sun.

I slithered off the rock and trudged the trail back to camp. Life just wasn't fun anymore. At first, loving Colette was exciting. It gave me direction. Somehow, though, the perfect love hadn't lived up to my plans. I'd been watching for two weeks and, outwardly anyway, Colette gave no sign that she was miserable without me.

She was supposed to suddenly realize how useless life was alone and come walking up the hill crying and wailing, *"Oh, why did I ever let Kelly go. I'm such a fool. If only he would come back, I'd appreciate him and love him for all eternity,"* and I would jump out from behind a tree and yell *"Surprise!"* and she would run into my arms.

For some reason, things hadn't worked out right.

• • •

Toward the top of the hill, I smelled smoke. Between raving water and the television in my frontal lobe, I knew better than to trust my senses, but this definitely smelled like smoke, and my nose had never betrayed me before.

Dad knelt in front of the firepit, feeding sticks into a small blaze. "Didn't think you'd be here till dark," he said.

"I knocked off early."

"Knocked off what?"

I didn't answer. Stashing the binoculars in the tent, I walked to the water bucket and dipped the Sierra cup. Two large steaks covered in plastic sat on a rock next to the fire.

"Hungry?" Dad asked.

"Sure." I drank the water. It was fresh. He must have filled the bucket before I arrived. "Been here long?"

"Couple of hours."

I picked up the coffeepot and walked to the creek to fill it and clean myself the best I could. The creek sang a Willie Nelson song in which Willie alternately screams like a panther or cries like a baby throughout a tough night.

"You look a mess," Dad said.

"Had some trouble with a moose." I carried the pot back from the creek. Coffee was running short and I wasn't sure whether Dad was a hallucination or not, so I decided not to put in the grounds until the water boiled.

"How'd you find me?" I asked.

Dad glanced across the fire. "Little blond girl upstairs."

"The fink."

"Don't go blaming her, I'm your father. She hasn't told anyone else, and, Lord knows, there's enough people looking for you." He draped my grill over the coals and set the steaks on at about a thirty-degree angle. Juice ran off the bottom end and sputtered in the fire.

"How are Mom's dance lessons coming?"

"Aw, she looks kind of silly out there with those teenagers, but she's happy. I don't see as how she's hurting anybody."

"You still telling her she's talented?"

"She is talented."

The meat smelled too good to be a dream, so I dumped in a double load of coffee grounds. Dad watched the steaks and whistled. He never talks when he's upset. He just whistles—mostly old show tunes from *Oklahoma!* and *South Pacific*.

After we ate, I poured a cup of coffee and we passed it back and forth between us.

"Best food I've eaten in weeks," I said.

Dad held the metal cup with both hands, blowing softly through the steam. His eyes landed on me, then slid away. "What're you doing here, Kelly?"

"I'm in love."

Dad handed over the cup. "This is a curious way to show it."

Shrugging, I sipped the coffee. The grounds hadn't settled right. It was a bit chewy.

"You know a man named John Hart?" Dad asked.

I nodded. The sun was just going down and I couldn't see that Dad had a sleeping bag. I wondered if he meant to stay the night.

"This Mr. Hart has something against you."

"I don't know what."

"Well, it's something pretty strong. He and Julie have been around a good deal lately, talking to Mama and me about you."

"What about?"

Dad didn't answer the question. He sipped coffee awhile and stared at the fire. I reached over and refilled the cup. A night-hawk boomed overhead. Clouds above the Gros Ventres glowed a bottom-lit burgundy color.

Dad finally spoke. "Your mama thinks the first rainbow appeared when Julie was born, but honestly, Kelly, it's always been my opinion you picked the rottenest peach in the pile."

"Mom couldn't stand Julie before we split up."

"Why didn't you ever divorce her?"

After Julie left, I never thought much about the legal aspects. Maybe I was afraid to try for a divorce for fear I couldn't prove we'd been married in the first place. "Never had the money, I guess," I said.

Dad coughed, more of a disgusted snort than a cough. "Well, you screwed up royally. That Mr. Hart's hotshot lawyers have a decree signed by your legal wife and a judge, and if anyone ever finds you, you're committed to a mental institution until your wife lets you out."

I took the cup from his hand. "Did Mom and you sign the papers too?"

"Mama wanted to, but I wouldn't let her."

The coffee was cold, so I poured it back in the pot and set the pot on the hottest coals. With the firelight in my eyes, I could barely see Dad's outline on the other side of the pit. He seemed to be watching me.

Sighing, he sat up straight. "I love your mom, Kelly, and I'm tired of you breaking her heart. I won't put up with it anymore."

"What's that mean?"

"That means whatever you're doing now is bound to land you in prison or a mental institution or both. Don't look to us for help."

I nodded, staring at the coffeepot.

"You understand?" he asked.

I nodded again.

Dad stood up, looking down on me. "I'll be going now."

I looked at him. Dad is almost as skinny as me. "It's dark. Stay the night if you want."

He shook his head no. "I've got a flashlight." Dad stood

there for a long time. Maybe he wanted to say more or expected me to say more. I don't know. Finally he said, "Good-bye, Kelly."

I kind of waved with my right hand. "Thanks for the steaks." Dad walked away into the darkness.

Eating meat right before bed, especially if you haven't had any for some time, does odd things to the body and mind. That night I dreamed Julie and I were making love, and as I pulled down her pants, I realized she had hairy legs and a huge penis, big as Grandpa Hawken's.

I lay in the basic desert reconnaissance position—belly flat on the rock, elbows out front, feet slightly
spread with the toes pointing straight back—peering through
my cardboard-hooded binoculars. Colette rode Dixie in slow
figure-eights around the pasture.

At the crossover point of the 8, Dixie changed her lead foot,
always trotting with the outside foot in front. No matter how
fast Dixie trotted, Colette's right hand never touched the horn
or reins. I was reminded of Shirley, the kinky barrel racer.

It was a perfect day for spring. Chickadees chirped. The hill
bloomed red and blue from Indian paintbrush and lupines. Sunshine knifed through air so clean you could taste it at the back
of your throat. Jackson Hole in the summertime is the paradise
of the universe. God may live in Texas, but he vacations in
Jackson Hole.

Added to the glory of the day, my true love was all alone
on the ranch, riding a beautiful horse round and round.

It was sexually stimulating, in a relaxed sort of way. Each
time Dixie and Colette made the loop at the southeast corner
of the lot, I focused in for a perfect front view, her hair stream-

ing up and flowing down, her breasts bouncing lightly, the stretched crotch of her jeans banging against the saddle. Horse and woman seemed fastened together in one slow, steady sex act. Even the expression on Colette's face was sensual, a light smile, fixed concentration on herself.

I loved it. I loved her.

Colette broke the eight and rode Dixie to the woods next to the creek. Looping the reins over Dixie's head, she dismounted and stood watching the water while Dixie drank. Then she tossed the reins around a branch and disappeared.

The one drawback of my rock position was the blind spots. The front door of the big house, for instance. Or the woods along the base of the hill. What I needed—and what I'll have next time—was a series of closed-circuit television cameras. I figured I could cover the entire area with six. Then I could sit in my tent watching monitors and never miss a move.

Carefully, I scanned the edge of the woods, looking for a sign of Colette. All that bouncing up and down astride Dixie had probably excited her, and she was off masturbating in the shade of a pine tree. I didn't want to miss that. I wondered what Colette would do if I walked up on her while she was playing with herself. Would she want me to jump on?

"Hey." Someone kicked the sole of my boot. "Hey."

Boots, jeans, western shirt, brown eyes, Cinderella hair— Colette in the flesh stood on the rock, looking down on me.

I hissed, "Get down," and motioned with my hand.

"What?"

"Get down, they'll see us."

Colette looked over at the ranch. "There's no one to see us but me, and I'm here."

Which made sense, but I was still nervous. "Come on," I whispered, slithering back off the rock into the clearing. Colette followed like a kid watching a harmless snake.

When I had slithered safely out of sight of the ranch, I stood up, facing Colette, and smiled. "Gee, it's good to see you, Colette."

"Don't 'gee' me. You've seen me every day, schmuck." She talked angry, but her eyes sparkled as though I amused her in some way.

"Not in person, close up," I said.

I felt like we should have hugged or something. I mean, it had been at least two weeks, but Colette just stood with both hands on her hips, looking me up and down. "Jesus, Kelly, you look like shit."

"You look beautiful."

She dug into her pocket and pulled out an almost used-up bar of soap. "I brought you something."

When she handed me the soap, the tips of our fingers touched. "Thanks," I said. "That's really nice of you, Colette."

"I figured you didn't think to bring any. You never think."

I studied the soap closely. It was green. "How long have you known I was here?"

"I knew you were somewhere close ever since you disappeared. It took until a couple of days ago to figure out exactly where."

"How did you know I was somewhere close?"

Colette smiled, a beautiful, open smile. "I'm beginning to understand how that devious little mind of yours works."

"How does it work?"

"What?"

"How does my devious little mind work?"

"You always do the most immature and romantic thing possible. I searched the basement twice, thinking you'd probably hide down there."

The thought hadn't occurred to me. "I didn't know you had a basement." I put the soap in my pocket. Colette and I stood maybe a foot apart, not touching, looking at each other. I stared into her right eye, hoping to will her into my arms.

Quietly, I said, "I love you, Colette."

"I love you too, Kelly."

"You do?"

She broke the eye contact. "Yes, dammit. I've been miserable wondering where you were."

"Miserable?"

"I was so scared you'd given up and left."

Fantasies do come true after all. "Let me get this straight. You've been miserable without me?"

"Dammit all, yes."

"Isn't that nice."

Her eyes flashed, the first hint of building anger. "No, it's not nice. I can't stand being miserable."

I don't care for it much myself. Reaching across the gap, I took Colette's hands in mine. "Are you ready to go?"

"Go where?"

"Away. We'll live together and laugh and have babies and bake bread in the winter. You'll see. It'll be neat."

"You always say these ridiculous things, Kelly, and expect me to believe them. I can't run away with you."

"Why not?"

"I'm married."

"So am I."

"That's another thing I found out while you were up here enjoying yourself. You're still married."

"So are you." This flawless logic seemed to exasperate Colette. She looked at me and sighed. Then she looked away.

"John's after your ass," she said. "He won't tell me what he's got on you, but it must be awful. He says if you show your nose in Jackson, you'll never see sunshine again."

"To hell with John. I'm talking about us."

Colette threw my hands back at me. "What us?"

"You and me. Are we going to get married or not? I want to know, right now."

"Right now?"

"This minute."

Colette walked a few feet away. She picked a flower, a paint-brush, and twirled it slowly between her fingers. "I doubt it. I love you, Kelly, but I don't see how I could ever live with you."

"Why not?"

She looked at me. "You're too weird."

"Weird's better than mediocre."

"Is that a cut against Danny?"

"It's a cut against you. You don't want to be normal your whole life."

"What's wrong with normal?"

With each comeback, our voices rose higher and louder. The whole thing was stupid, two grown people standing in the mid-dle of a clearing in the Wyoming wilds, yelling at each other.

"Oh, hell, Colette," I shouted. "Do you want to be happy or not?"

"Fuck you, Kelly. What makes you think you know all the answers?"

"I know happy beats the holy hell out of unhappy. And you'll never be happy with him."

"What makes you think I'll be happy with you?"

"With me, there's a chance. No matter how slim it is, how can you pass up a chance?"

That did it. Colette's lower lip trembled. Her eyes got wet and shiny. She sat on the ground, picking leaves off the paint-brush and tearing them into green shreds.

I walked over and sat in front of her, picking leaves off my side of the plant. She wouldn't look at me.

"You confuse me," she said.

"You should be confused. It's much better than compla-cent."

Her voice shook like a scared little girl. "What's compla-cent?"

"Satisfied with shit when you could be eating prime."

"And you're prime?"

"You bet, honey. I'm the best you're ever going to see."

"Oh, fuck you." But this time when she said "fuck you," Colette smiled and sniffed. We sat a long time, ripping plants into tiny shreds. I threw my pieces up and let the breeze carry them off. Colette kept hers in a little pile.

She looked at me. "I'm comfortable with Danny. Because of him, I have a home and money and nice friends. He's given me everything."

"You won't have any of that stuff with me," I said. "I live in a tent and my only friend is Cora Ann and she doesn't like you."

"Why not?"

"She thinks I'm too good for you."

"Maybe you are."

"Horseshit." I doubled my fist and flattened a little green weed. Looking around at the trees and the sky and the Teton Mountains, my personal problems didn't seem worth all this horrible emotion. The whole thing was too much for one inept person to handle.

"Listen, Colette," I said. "I'm tired of this soap-opera jive. I'm ready to get on with my life." I touched her chin, making her look at me. "Do you love me, Colette?"

"Yes, Kelly, I love you." She didn't say it with any tenderness. More like grudging admission.

"Do you want to be with me?"

Colette tried to move her face, but I wouldn't let her. For a moment she looked at me, then she lowered her eyes. "Yes."

"Okay, let's cut the crap and do it."

"But the consequences—"

"Fuck the consequences."

"Danny—"

"Danny will be better off without you and you know it."

"My father—"

"Can get a real bank loan and pay off Hart."

"It's not that simple."

"It is that simple, Colette."

I released her chin. She twisted around to face the mountains on the other side of the valley. I couldn't see Colette's eyes, but her breathing came short, as if she was crying. Every now and then Colette mumbled, "Shit."

Finally she said, "Once when I was a sophomore and Dirk was a senior, he walked out of PE and came and got me out of Civics, told the teacher there was a family emergency. In the hall he said he was sick of school and he was going to hitchhike to Quebec."

"Why Quebec?"

"I don't know. Dirk read a book about it, I think. He asked me to go with him." Colette looked down at her hands. "I was afraid of what would happen to us. I said no."

"Did he leave without you?"

Colette nodded. "Dirk almost got run over, hitchhiking in Canada. Then when he came home, they kicked him out of school for a semester. Dad grounded him. Mom cried for weeks."

"You should have gone with him."

"I know." Colette looked back at the mountains. She pulled thick hair behind her ear. "Four years later Dirk died, and I'm still afraid."

I sat next to Colette, watching a raven soar in tight circles over the green band along the river. I wondered about Dirk who had been alive and important to Colette, but now was dead. I liked being alive. Life is interesting—sun, birds, love, food, television, sex—there's always something to think about. There's nothing to think about when you're dead.

Colette backhanded her pile of leaves, scattering green strips. "All right," she said.

"All right?"

She turned back toward me. "You win. I'll run away with you, but this new life you're promising better be pretty goddamn wonderful."

I couldn't believe it. The closest water was a quarter-mile away, though, so Colette must have said what I'd heard. I talked quickly, before she changed her mind. "We'll have a fantastic life. I promise. It'll be so wonderful. Rainbows for breakfast and orgasms for lunch. We'll name our firstborn Bliss and the second Honeysuckle."

"None of those weird hippie names for my kids. How many are you planning to have, anyway?"

Colette and I whiled away the afternoon in dreams and fantasies. How many children, and what sex? What kind of house? Who would make the coffee in the morning, and would our sandwiches be cut crosswise or diagonally? I promised I'd never trim my toenails in bed if she wouldn't eat a banana in front of me. I hate bananas.

We discussed preschool education, side-of-the-bed preferences, forms of birth control, favorites in cereal and country music—all things we should have talked about months earlier.

I confessed my awful habit of dribbling on the bathroom floor. She told me she liked to be on top. It was the happiest afternoon of my life. My loved one and I lay in the sun, planning our future together. What could be more satisfying?

I wanted to go that moment, hand in hand into the sunset, but Colette was too practical. "I can't leave my toothbrush. Or my nightie, my diary, my checkbook, the gold earrings, my pillow. I'm not like you. I have to have clean underwear or I won't get out of bed."

Colette didn't care how in love we were, she had to pack first. We decided on an elopement, a midnight rendezvous at her car.

"Lock Thor inside," I said.

"What if I chicken out?"

"I'll come in and get you."

Before Colette walked back to the ranch, I held her close and we kissed. The kiss was very nice, deep and meaningful.

At the University of Arkansas, I became the sociology department expert on suicide. The subject has always fascinated me—why do it, how to do it, do failures fail on purpose. Not that I want any firsthand experience at death, but if the urge should someday overpower the restraint, I'd like to know what I'm getting myself into.

Some facts: San Francisco, California, and Laramie, Wyoming, are the suicide capitals of America. Thursday is the most popular day to off oneself, and Christmas is actually a religious population-control device. The famous author Robert E. Howard wasted himself when his mother died. I find that interesting.

The most fascinating aspect of suicide is the children. Each year, between five and six hundred children under the age of seven kill themselves on purpose. At least ten times that number give it a try. Imagine that—being six years old and feeling the necessary grief to end yourself.

My idea is that the kid gets a glimpse of what the future is going to be like and decides it isn't worth the bother. Sometimes, parents overstress the religious heaven-is-wonderful, everyone-there-is-happy line, and the kid buys it like Santa Claus. "Okay, if heaven's so neat, I'm going there now instead of cleaning my room."

There's also the sour-grapes-against-mama theory. "I'll show that bitch," the little girl cried as she ran onto the Interstate.

Whatever the reason, the decisiveness of preschool suicide is remarkable.

My own attempts have been anything but decisive. Lizbeth says they were "half-assed." The only one that ended in positive action and the hospital was the tequila-up-the-veins trick I pulled in the Cowboy Bar, and to this moment I maintain all I wanted was a buzz before bed.

If only I hadn't left the note.

I always leave notes, though. There were two or three of them tucked in books around the apartment. Finger exercises just in case I pulled together enough nerve to do it—or in case I was ever run over by a truck.

One of the older jokes among us creative types is the one about the writer who wanted to kill himself but couldn't finish the fifth draft of the suicide note. I don't want to get caught too depressed at the end to write an original, witty, yet touching good-bye letter to the world. So I practice.

Julie came by to steal the Dutch oven. She had only been out of our apartment for a couple of months, and was just changing from the warm friendship of a former lover to the you're-an-asshole-and-I-wasted-my-life-with-you attitude.

She opened the door without knocking. "Hi," Julie said. "I didn't expect to find you home."

I lay on the couch, staring at a picture of a cat on a calendar on the wall. I hadn't moved in several hours. "I'm glad to see you, Julie," I said.

"I bet. I came to get the Dutch oven. It's shrimp creole night." She walked past the couch and into the kitchen. The dishes hadn't been washed in a month.

"I thought the Dutch oven was mine."

"I'm just borrowing it. You can't cook and I can. Why should it go to waste here?" Julie's finest point was her cooking. I would still give a year of my life for a plate of her shrimp creole.

Julie banged around the kitchen, digging through the dirty pots and pans. "This place is a pit," she said. "Why don't you pull yourself together, for Christ's sake? No wonder you don't have any friends, Kelly. All you do is lie around feeling sorry for yourself."

I said, "Okay."

She came out of the kitchen, carrying the Dutch oven and the lid. Standing next to the trunk, Julie looked down on me. "Don't be so pitiful, Kelly. Thousands of people break up and you don't see them whining around, behaving like babies."

"Who's the creole for?" I asked.

"None of your business."

"Okay."

Julie left. I sat up and wrote a twelve-page suicide letter, explaining how I had done everything I cared to do—loved, watched some sunsets, screwed to my heart's content, seen Willie Nelson live—and there wasn't any more reason to put up with all the bad for the little bit of good I might blunder into later.

The letter rambled. I read it years afterward, and I'm glad I didn't die because it was a sorry piece of writing to leave for a legacy.

I decided to go to the Cowboy and drink myself to death, but I only had five dollars, and getting drunk—much less dying—on five dollars in the Cowboy went out with nickel Cokes.

Deep in the middle cushion of my couch lay a barely used, 28-gauge, half-inch insulin syringe left there by a traveling diabetic junkie from Oklahoma. It stayed in the cushion, dormant yet capped, for two years. I was always scared to death a passing parent might find the syringe, but I never had the courage to throw it away.

I dug the needle out of the couch, stuck it in my back pocket, walked to the Cowboy Bar, and ordered a shot of tequila, straight. I told the bartender not to bother with the lemon and salt.

I carried my tequila to a stall in the bathroom and sat on the toilet with my pants up and the shot glass on the floor between my feet. The floor was filthy. Bending way over, I drew in a barrel full of tequila. Then I leaned back and held the needle straight up, tapping it with my fingers to clear the air bubbles.

Holding the needle in my left hand, I rolled my left shirt-sleeve just above the elbow, then twisted the material around to form a tourniquet on my arm. I held the tourniquet in place with my teeth and felt for the vein with my fingertip. It swelled up, round and blue.

The shot was easy. The needle popped into the vein, I drew back the plunger, and blood popped into the barrel. I released my shirt with my teeth and drove home the tequila.

It felt like somebody hit me hard in the forehead. My stomach wrenched. I could taste the tequila in my salivary glands.

Staggering some, I made it to the sink and cleaned out my needle. There was still plenty of tequila left in the shot glass, so I figured if I was going to die, I might as well do a good job of it.

After that, I blacked out. Pam told me later that she poured me another shot of tequila that night, but I picked it up and walked away without paying. I guess they found me with the syringe hanging out of my arm and a good deal of blood on the stall floor. I don't remember.

I woke up with a much bigger syringe taped to my arm, a tube down my throat, and two sets of electrodes clamped to my chest. My wrists were tied to the sides of the bed. I didn't know why all these things were attached to me. So far as I could remember, one moment I was lying on my couch, looking at a cat calendar, and the next moment I was in a hard bed with a tube down my throat.

"Number two is awake," someone said.

A girl in a white uniform came up beside me and pulled the thing out of my throat. "You won't need this anymore," she said. A name tag above her breast said NAN. She had a voice like a cartoon mouse.

Nan held my head up and gave me a sip of water. "You can't have much," she said.

"My tongue," I croaked.

"You swallowed it last night," Nan said. "It hurts to swallow your tongue, doesn't it?"

"Where am I?"

"Intensive care."

"Where?"

"The hospital."

I closed my eyes and tried to remember. Something had gone wrong.

"Good morning," a voice said next to me.

Opening my eyes, I saw a short, slightly overweight woman, smiling at me. "Who are you?" I asked.

"I'm Lizbeth Morley. I'm with the Jackson Hole Mental Health Association. I understand you had some trouble last night."

"What happened?"

Lizbeth sketched in the details of how I was found. She held my farewell letter in her right hand. "Your landlord picked this up in your apartment," she said. "That's why they called me."

"I didn't try to kill myself."

"Oh?"

"I just wanted to get drunk and go to sleep."

"You almost got drunk and went to sleep forever." I closed my eyes and groaned. "Why did you write this letter?" she asked.

Purple splotches floated on the insides of my eyelids. "I was sad."

"What seemed to be the problem?"

I thought about the problem. "Julie made shrimp creole and didn't invite me."

"That's why you tried to kill yourself?"

"That's why I wrote the letter. I didn't try to kill myself."

"This is a lot of trouble to go to because you didn't get invited to dinner."

"You don't know Julie's shrimp creole." I looked at Lizbeth. She seemed kind. "How much does this room cost?" I asked.

"Two hundred forty dollars a day."

"I should have killed myself."

"Don't think about the money now. Tell me more about Julie's shrimp creole."

That's how it began. I talked to Lizbeth at least once a week for two years. In fact, that first Wednesday on the mountain was the only appointment I ever missed. I knew Lizbeth would be mad about the missed appointment. That's one of the reasons I wanted to run away with Colette right then. I was more afraid of Lizbeth catching me than John Hart.

Why, poised on the brink of the greatest victory in my life, was I sitting next to my tent and typewriter, reliving old suicide attempts? Why can't I ever relax and enjoy good fortune?

The one thing I've learned since high school: If times are good, they're bound to get worse; if times are bad, they're bound to get better. This makes me optimistic when I'm down and pessimistic when I'm up—unhappy when I'm happy and happy when I'm not.

Lizbeth says I'm not relaxed unless I'm tragic. Breaking down the tent, stuffing my sleeping bag in the backpack, hiding all traces of the campfire, I was in nervous ecstasy. Suddenly there was something, and when you get something, you get something to lose.

But Colette was worth the trouble. I might hold her for a day or six years—I can't comprehend longer than that. However long Colette stayed, having her would be worth losing her.

And I might not ever lose her. The romance had already soared beyond my wildest dreams. Maybe Colette and I would own land, raise a family, find financial security, reach orgasms every single day until we died together on the dance floor seventy years from now. Lord knows, it was worth a try.

All packed and ready to go, I pulled off my clothes and jumped in the creek for a bath. The water was repulsed. *"Is that soap biodegradable?"* It used the Kurt Gowdy voice.

"Nope," I said. "It's Irish Spring."

"You're polluting me."

"Sorry."

After that, the water refused to speak anymore. I climbed out of the creek and sat on the bank watching another in a series of beautiful Wyoming sunsets. This one had no clouds to reflect orange and purple, but it was nice anyway.

The sun dipped behind Rendezvous Mountain, the temperature dropped, and I started to shiver. Not waiting for my body to dry out, I hurried back to camp and dressed wet. Those weeks of sitting in dirt and sleeping in sweat had taken their toll on my boxer shorts. I couldn't bear to put them on my clean crotch, so I buried them respectfully and went without.

Because it was dark, I hiked down the jeep trail to the main road, then backtracked along the road to the Broken Hart gate. Stashing my pack and the Royal portable behind the buck-and-rail fence, I settled in to wait for midnight.

Of course, I had no watch and no idea how long it was to midnight. Up on the mountain, I'd pretty well transcended the theory of time. When the sun rose, I woke up. When I felt hungry, I ate. I tried to reach the rock before Danny and his dad left for work, but it meant nothing if I missed them. This midnight assignation was my first appointment since the Wednesday visit with Lizbeth over two weeks before.

I hid in the dark a long time, wondering if it was midnight or not. Every now and then a car came along, shining its lights on the fence and my pack, but none stopped.

Finally I got desperate. The next car that drove by, I walked onto the road and stuck out my thumb. It didn't stop. Because of talking with Colette and packing and bathing, I hadn't watched the ranch all afternoon or evening. I had no idea who was home or who might drive in. Wouldn't John Hart be surprised to find me hitchhiking in front of his house?

The next car didn't stop either.

Timing was important. If I wasn't there at midnight, Colette might go back inside to bed. It would be just like her. So, the next lights I saw coming, I stood in the middle of the road, waving my arms.

The car hesitated, sped up, then stopped right in front of me. It was a Grand Prix with California plates. A man and a woman sat in the front seat, looking rich and nervous.

The man rolled down his window a full half-inch. "What's the matter?" he asked. "Some kind of an emergency?"

"Excuse me," I said. "Do you know the time?"

"The what?"

"The time. What time is it?"

He looked at his wife, who said, "It's a trick, Lawrence."

"It's no trick. It's very important that I know what time it is."

The man looked at his wrist. "Eleven-fifteen."

I thought of something. "Is that California time or Wyoming time?"

"Wyoming time."

Backing away from the car, I said, "Thanks a lot. You've been a big help."

The man looked at his wife. She shrugged. As they drove away, I stood in the road, watching their taillights.

I sat next to my pack, cleaning my glasses with what was left of my shirt for what seemed like forty-five minutes. Then I walked through the gate under the broken heart and up the long drive.

The moon was up, which made it nice. I could see the form of the big house off to my left, and beyond that the barn and bunkhouse. An owl flew by, silent as the owl that took my Snoofy.

The cars were parked in a row across the drive from John Hart's house. Colette's Subaru sat second from the left, between the Toyota and Danny's Powerwagon. I hoped she had remembered to gas it up. This elopement might turn into an anticlimax if we ran out of gas ten minutes down the road.

Colette wasn't there. Thinking maybe she'd gotten cold, I looked in the window of the Subaru, but no Colette.

Both houses were dark. It wasn't like Danny hadn't gone to bed yet so she couldn't leave. Maybe she was fooling around with him one last time, for nostalgia's sake. Maybe she'd fallen asleep in front of Johnny Carson. Maybe she'd backed out.

I wasn't about to let Colette change her mind. She promised we would run away and be happy, and we were going to run away and be happy if I had to drag her out of the house by her hair.

Feeling like a comic-book commando, I crouched next to the cars, watching the bunkhouse door. No sound, no movement, nothing. It was stupid.

I waited a half hour before going in after her.

The front door was unlocked. Quietly, I walked into the dark room. I mean, that place was dark. Right off, I banged my shin on a chair.

"Colette," I whispered. "Colette, where the hell are you?"

From outside, I knew which bedroom was hers, but I didn't know how to get there from inside. I had no idea how to find Colette without finding Danny.

The problem didn't last long. I took two more steps forward and the lights came on. Blinded for a moment, I shielded my eyes with both hands.

"Colette?"

"Get him!" John Hart shouted. John and a policeman blocked the door. On the other side, next to the stairs, stood Danny Hart and another policeman.

I ran for the window and dived. The glass must have been made of space-age plastic because I bounced like a Ping-Pong ball off a cement floor.

John Hart jumped on me, holding down my face with his knee. The cops each held a shoulder. Kicking and screaming, I managed to shake one arm free long enough to poke John in the side. It didn't have much effect.

"Bring Colette," John ordered.

"Dad."

"Danny, bring Colette."

I stopped writhing and tried to bite his knees. John slapped me on the ear.

Colette stood above me, wearing a blue bathrobe. She looked pale and shaky. I could tell she had been crying.

John removed his knee from my face.

"Why didn't you meet me?" I asked.

"Oh, Kelly." Colette stopped. She held her hands together in front of her chest. Danny stood behind her.

John growled, "Tell him."

"Dad," Danny said.

"It's time to get this over with forever. Tell him what you did, Colette."

Colette started to cry.

"Not only did she decide not to meet you," John continued, "but she told Danny you were coming."

Colette looked so unhappy. "Did you do that?" I asked. Colette nodded, tears flowing from her eyes.

"She turned you in," John shouted. *"Do you understand? She betrayed you."*

On the word *betrayed*, Colette's chest heaved and she moaned. I tried to reach out for her, but they held my arms.

I said, "Colette, I understand."

12

They charged me with trespassing, breaking and entering, attempted kidnapping, assault (the poke at John), resisting arrest, and voyeurism (Colette told where I'd been for two weeks).

Between 1969 and 1973, I figure I committed an average of seven felonies a day, but, strange as it sounds, I had never been in jail before. I'd come close twice.

One Christmas Eve, I flew a trunkful of marijuana—forty-two pounds wrapped in garbage bags—from Tucson, Arizona, to Boise, Idaho. Some fool teenager waving a snub-nosed .38 hijacked the plane and ordered the pilot to fly to Cuba. How trite can you get? "Turn this plane around, capitalist pig, and take me to Havana." This was at least three years after everyone else hijacked planes to Cuba. And the pilot was no capitalist, much less a pig. He belonged to a union. I was probably the only true capitalist on the airplane.

I sat in the first row of first class, watching in amazement. The kid was a clown. He couldn't have been over sixteen, had a big red zit on the back of his neck. He was so excited his voice squeaked like Alfalfa's in the "Our Gang" TV reruns. The whole thing would have been pitiful if I didn't have a trunkload of pot in the baggage compartment.

I could just picture the Cuban army or whoever handles these things opening my trunk. Each pound was wrapped in six plastic bags, with talcum powder and ammonia in every other bag to fool the dope-sniffing German shepherds in the Tucson airport. The Cubans would sing with glee and dance in the plaza. They'd make an example of me: DECADENT AMERICAN DOPE PUSHER CAPTURED AT AIRPORT. My picture would be in *Newsweek*, Mom and Dad would be disillusioned, and I'd spend the rest of my short life hacking sugarcane with a machete.

If the Cubans didn't open the trunk, American customs would for sure find the marijuana on the way back into the States. Any way the deal came down, I wouldn't be in Idaho for Christmas.

Luckily for me and unluckily for the poor hijacker, when we stopped in Houston to refuel, an FBI sharpshooter blew the kid's brains all over my brand-new Levi Saddleman Boot-Cut jeans. I had some trouble explaining the blood to Mom.

Years after my outlaw period, after Julie left and I no longer broke any laws that I knew about—I was actually arrested for anal entry. It was her idea. She said she liked it that way. Hell, if a woman says she likes something I generally do it. The purpose of sex is to please someone else while she pleases you. Isn't it?

What happened was this Evanston, Wyoming, oil baron discovered a tube of Preparation H in his daughter's underwear drawer. She could have claimed Act of God or lack of roughage or plain ignorance, but *no*, she had to tell the truth and point me out as the cause.

Personally, I'd like to know why the oil baron was playing around in his daughter's underwear drawer in the first place.

Perhaps kinkiness is hereditary. His daughter sure was an odd one.

Anyway, two hours later I'm handcuffed in the backseat of a police car that stinks—they must never clean up after drunks in Evanston—and this pudgy, red-faced, righteous father is screaming at a cop to shoot me and throw my body in the river.

I didn't even know anal entry was illegal in Wyoming. I've always done pretty much anything a woman told me to do. It never occurred to me that I might be breaking a law—although to be fair here, I doubt if legality would have been a factor at the time.

"Please, Kelly, give it to me my way."

"I can't, dear, it's against the law."

The cop refused to shoot me until we talked to his cousin who was a judge, so the three of us drove over to the judge's ranch house on the north end of town. The judge listened to the facts, nodded a couple of times, then pointed out to the oil baron that my crime was unprovable unless his daughter testified in court, in front of a jury, that she had been butt-fucked by a transient derelict.

I was given an escort to the Uinta County line and told never to return.

The oil baron's daughter wasn't the only strange woman I met after Julie left. I was twenty-seven years old then and I had never been on a date, flirted, courted, or pursued a woman. I had never played the field. I didn't even know there was a field. Puberty and Julie had come into my life simultaneously—like white men and hookers to a third-world paradise.

With some fury, I set about making up for lost time. I wanted to fuck every woman I came in contact with. I set quotas and kept score. My first goal was to ball my way, in order, around the zodiac. I never made it—got stuck on Sagittarius—though God only knows I tried.

Andy was the first. I chased her a couple of weeks before tricking her into the sack one night. The next day she quit her job and moved to New Mexico. I figure I was either very good or very bad. Whatever, Andy saw something in me that scared her clean out of the state.

Then came Ginnie, the runaway, the most enthusiastic lover in the Rocky Mountain West. She wanted me to meet her parents. One morning I woke up and Ginnie and two hundred dollars were gone.

There was an older woman, forty or so. Her brother caught us in bed and beat me up.

Another girl, I swear I thought she was twenty, stayed a weekend. On Monday she asked if I would give her a lift to school.

"School?"

"Yeah, Jackson Hole Junior High."

I met and seduced the visually most beautiful woman on earth—Lacy Rasher from Mobile, Alabama. Lacy was a botanist for the Park. She's the one who taught me the Latin names for all the flowers I like.

The day Lacy moved in, she contracted an unbelievable case of diarrhea. She took it a week, then said, "Kelly, I love you, but I'll die if I stay another night." She left and the diarrhea cleared up.

The strangest one, Missy Black, was a waitress who must have hung around microwave ovens too much, because her IUD picked up a country-western station from Fort Worth, Texas. The first time I slithered on down there the Oak Ridge Boys' version of "Will the Circle Be Unbroken" came piping out the slit. I accused Missy of unnatural acts with a transistor radio and she flew off the handle. We ended up with nobody getting off and her leaving in a bad mood.

I talked to a doctor about it later and he said this sort of thing had happened before. Honest.

Would I make that up?

Every single one of them bruised or broke my poor heart. When they left, I'd go tragic as hell for a day, then rush off to find a replacement. I loved anyone who liked me. Or acted like she liked me.

For two years, I drank a lot, danced a lot, threw out hundreds of lines and caught a few lightweights, but the whole ordeal was a bother. I should have stayed home, reading and waiting for Colette to drop into my life.

I used to hate being a skinny, assless wimp. In high school it mattered. For any kid under, say, twenty-five, a bad body is a detriment to simple seduction, but once over twenty-five, the pinhead is in.

You look at the major sex symbols of the seventies. Not those flash-in-the-pan lust objects that lasted a year or two and faded to the stud farm, but the men looked at with more open mouths and wet cervixes than all others.

The way I figure, the three men who could have gotten laid most often by the most women the decade of the seventies were Willie Nelson, Woody Allen, and Mick Jagger.

Average height—five feet six inches. Average weight—137.

So there.

Jail, in Jackson Hole, in the summertime, is cruel and unusual punishment and should be unconstitutional. I sat on my bunk, staring out the window at the fresh air and sunshine and the mountains in the distance. I hadn't slept indoors in weeks and now I was confined in a green room, five paces by eight paces, with a line of bars a foot or so in front of the windows, four monastery-hard bunk beds, two toilet-sink combinations, a shower, a portable black-and-white TV, and a huge pile of ancient magazines.

They stuck me in orange coveralls and cotton slippers. Orange coveralls. Jesus.

Cell One goes to juveniles and women. Cell Two is for dangerous criminals, murderers, rapists, bad people. Cell Three is the drunk tank, and Cell Four holds up to sixteen of the endless chain of small-timers who come through Jackson. They steal towels from a motel, or drink a beer on the street, or take an unpaid-for shower in a private campground, and end up in Cell Four.

I was thrown into Cell Two with a murderer and an environmentalist.

The murderer was okay. His name was Luke and he smoked Larks all day and watched soap operas on the TV. Luke didn't mind jail at all because he knew he would be out soon. The odds of a man being convicted for murder in Wyoming are about fifty to one. Some counties have never had a single conviction.

But the environmentalist was in big trouble. All coarse black hair and muscles, Jimmy looked like a gentle bear. Jimmy had shot down a seismograph helicopter. He'd done it nicely, so no one got hurt. He thought he was saving the wilderness, but instead he gave himself ten years of living indoors.

The only thing I didn't like about Jimmy was that he paced up and down all day, hogging the floor space for himself.

I didn't know it at the time, but they arrested me on a Friday night—June 25, to be exact. I slept most of Saturday and Sunday. After three weeks of insanity on the mountain, it was almost a relief to be around people again, piss in a flush toilet, hear feminine hygiene commercials on the portable TV. Wouldn't have been that awful if I hadn't been in jail.

On Monday a court-appointed lawyer came to see me. He had pink cheeks, very long earlobes, and a brown three-piece suit.

"The judge is making me handle this case," he said miserably. "John Hart owns the house we're renting, and my wife is pregnant. I don't know what we'll do if I win."

"Thanks for your help," I said.

The lawyer looked very unhappy. "You don't understand. I just passed the bar exams in May and this is my first case. In law school I swore never to compromise my values or do less than my best for a client." He looked away and exhaled deeply. "How will I face my new baby if I sell myself out on the first case? What do I say to my wife?"

"You're idealistic?"

He nodded. "It was easy being idealistic in college. I didn't expect a test so soon."

He told me his name was Robin. His wife's name was Sybil and they were from Colorado Springs. If the baby was a boy they would name him Ralph, after Ralph Nader.

"All through law school we dreamed of living in Jackson Hole and raising a family."

"That's my dream also," I said.

Robin looked back at me and kind of smiled—like a sick person assuring a loved one that he doesn't really feel bad.

"I'll do what I can," he said.

"That's all I deserve."

"We can beat most of the charges by putting Colette on the stand and hoping she admits you were invited into the house. Where they've got you against the wall is that mental incompetency complaint your wife signed. John Hart's lawyers worked it up. Must have cost him ten thousand dollars."

"Have you seen it?"

He nodded. "Looks convincing to me."

"You think I'm insane and dangerous?"

His eyes traveled down my orange coveralls, then back up. "I don't see how you could be that dangerous."

"Thanks."

Robin may have been idealistic, but he dressed like one of

Danny's fraternity brothers. Maybe all the idealistic people wear three-piece suits and wide ties these days.

"How much is bail?" I asked.

"Eighty-five thousand dollars, but they won't let you pay it until after the sanity hearing Friday."

"Eighty-five thousand. I can't be that dangerous."

"At the sanity hearing, the judge will probably send you to the State Mental Institution in Evanston for thirty days' observation. If the shrinks say you're psychiatrically fit, they'll haul you back here, lower the bail to around fifty thousand, and try you on the kidnapping charge. It's all pretty much routine."

"Where am I going to come up with fifty thousand dollars?"

"Don't worry about it," Robin said. "With Hart's team of lawyers against you, you don't stand a chance in hell of coming back from Evanston."

"But I'm sane."

"Convince your wife and the judge of that."

I didn't know about the judge, but Julie wasn't about to admit to my sanity. "Maybe I can help with your problem," I said.

"How's that?"

"You won't win even if you try, so I come out the same either way. I'll release and absolve you of any responsibility for my fate if you'll do me one favor."

"I'm not certain a client can absolve a lawyer of his responsibilities."

"If you make my wife admit she is my wife, I won't ask you to go up against John Hart."

Robin stared at me and nodded a couple of times. "Is it ethical to sell a client down the river even if he gives his blessing?"

"How should I know, you're the lawyer. I'm the guy in jail."

Robin stood up and smiled. "Right."

· · ·

When I talked to the lawyer we both sat on stools and faced each other through a double-paned window, but later in the day, when Lizbeth came, they put us in a room about the size of a two-hole outhouse.

It was real nice to see Lizbeth again, but I was kind of nervous. Landing in jail is not a sign of psychological progress.

She sat in one of the two chairs. I stood, leaning against the wall.

"How are you, Kelly?" Lizbeth asked.

"Fine."

"They treating you well?"

"Good as can be expected."

Except for the time in the hospital, I always saw Lizbeth in her office with the comfortable chairs and the pile carpet. She seemed smaller in jail.

Lizbeth crossed her legs at the ankles, right over left. "What happened, Kelly?"

I coughed. "Colette said she'd run away with me, then she changed her mind."

"Why did she change her mind?"

"Hell if I know." I coughed again. I didn't know what to say. I felt embarrassed, standing in front of Lizbeth in cotton slippers and orange coveralls.

"Are you suicidal?"

I thought. "No. I haven't wanted to kill myself since I met Colette. How about that?"

"How about it?"

"Guess I have a reason to live."

"Do you still want Colette, in spite of what she did?"

"You don't stop loving someone because she lets you down. I'll always want Colette."

Lizbeth stared at me and I stared at the floor. She waited. I waited. The little room grew hot.

"So what's going to happen at this sanity hearing Friday?" I asked.

"Julie will bring forth evidence to show you are mentally incompetent and dangerous to yourself or others. Your lawyer will show evidence that you aren't. The judge can commit you permanently, throw the whole thing out, or send you to Evanston for thirty days' observation. The third is most likely."

I looked at Lizbeth. It seemed like a long time since I'd talked to her the day I walked up on the mountain. I felt like a different person, but she looked the same.

"Which side will you be on?" I asked.

"What?"

"Will you testify for Julie or me?"

"I'll tell the truth."

"Which is?"

Lizbeth made eye contact. "That you suffer from depressive neurosis and that you're a passive dependent, which accounts for the obsession with Colette, but you are no danger to yourself or anyone else."

"Thanks. I guess."

"It's my job."

I pulled the other chair over and straddled it backward with my arms across the back. "I tried to kill John Hart once. If Colette hadn't promised to run away with me, I thought I might kidnap her. Doesn't that make me dangerous?"

"You didn't, though."

"Didn't what?"

"Didn't kill John or kidnap Colette. Face it, Kelly. You're sane."

"Thanks. I was beginning to wonder."

Luke turned out to be an intellectual murderer. When I returned to Cell Two, he was sitting in his chair in front of the TV, explaining situation ethics to a pacing Jimmy.

"It's like this." Luke inhaled his Lark as if it was a joint. "Bishop Pike says that any single act is justified and right if the conditions deem it justified and right. There is no absolute right and wrong. No *thou shalts* or *thou shalt nots*."

Jimmy growled, "Shooting down oil company helicopters is absolutely right. Not shooting down oil company helicopters is absolutely wrong."

My one romantic preconception about jail—besides busting out in a hail of dynamite—was that I would be able to walk up and down nervously like a caged coyote. Jimmy made this impossible and I resented him for it.

"Some people don't think it's right to shoot down helicopters or you wouldn't be here," I said.

"Some people are fucked," Jimmy answered, turning at the south wall.

Luke leaned forward and tapped his Lark against the window bars. "Take killing in self-defense," he said, "or stealing bread because your sister is starving. Or lying to protect a friend's feelings."

"How about adultery?" I asked.

Luke closed his eyes, thinking. "No, there's no situation in which adultery isn't a sin."

Jimmy stopped in front of Luke. "Why did you kill?"

"Someone paid me to."

"Is killing for money ethical?" I asked.

"Depends on how much money."

Jimmy showed me pictures of his wife and kids. The wife stood in front of a cabin, not smiling. She was kind of skinny—looked like a city hippie who'd tried acid and Jesus, then ended up living off the land with a treadle sewing machine, a nine-volume diary, and a tattered copy of *The Compleat Midwife*. The boys both had blond hair and short noses. Jimmy told me his wife wouldn't let him see them.

"I got this letter back yesterday," he said, holding up a soiled envelope covered with stamps and cancellations. "Fourth time. She won't open it."

"Your wife's angry because you shot down the helicopter?"

"She's mad 'cause I'm in jail and not at work."

"That's fair."

Jimmy stalked to the window and held the bars with both hands. "If she'd read my letter she'd understand why I had to do it. Some things matter more than a family."

I couldn't think of anything that mattered more, but then I didn't have a family and Jimmy did. What you don't have always matters more than what you do have. I said, "Most women with kids, and a husband in jail, don't see it that way."

Jimmy punched one of the bars. "My woman should."

Had I met Danny Hart anywhere in America, I would have recognized him for what he was: a former high-school football captain who went to a good college, then returned home to a secure job with his father or father-in-law's company.

There's a whole cult of them—at least two or three in every town. They are all nice enough fellows. Nice men leading nice lives with nice wives. Their only problem is that they face no challenges. They are born into a slot, a preplanned existence.

They're boring.

Danny came to see me during visiting hours Tuesday. Like honest rivals, we faced each other through the glass partition, he in his chamois shirt, Haggar slacks, and Tony Lama boots, me in orange coveralls.

"Can I get you anything?" he asked.

"Out."

Danny laughed. He thought I was kidding.

"Why did you come?" I asked.

Danny rested his hands on the counter in front of him. The fingernails gleamed, they were so clean. Each one was the same length and shape. "I don't understand how any woman who likes me could like you," he said, "or how any woman who likes you could like me."

I thought about this. "Did you ever notice that Colette is kind of peculiar?"

Danny nodded his head. "Yeah."

"How is she doing?"

"She's worried about her father. We had to sell our bonds to pay off some debt he owed Dad."

"Those bonds were for you to have babies and land."

Danny kind of snorted. "Thanks to you, babies and land will have to wait a few years. We are moving, though. She and Dad can't stand each other and she told me about turning the ranch into condominiums. I gave notice at the bank."

"Where?"

"What?"

"Where are you moving to?"

Danny looked at me strangely. "You honestly think I would tell you, even if I knew?"

"I guess not."

"Maybe we'll leave town."

"You can't take Colette out of Jackson Hole."

Danny's face turned red, dark red. "I can do anything I damn well want. You've screwed up our lives enough."

"Let her go."

"I came here to look at you, to try and understand how Colette fell for your line of crap, but you aren't human. How could she possibly feel anything for you?"

"I understand your point of view, Danny. It hurts to lose a wife, but you must face the truth. Colette doesn't love you. She loves me."

"Fuck you," Danny shouted.

• • •

Julie was waiting to see me next. She slid quickly into the chair just vacated by Danny. "You have a real knack for winning people," she said, nodding at his back.

I looked at her through the double pane of glass. Julie seemed a lot older than me. Her blond beauty was tamed, paid for. She still looked tough, but in New Orleans it was a fuck-with-me-and-I'll-split-your-skull tough. Now it was fuck-with-me-and-I'll-slap-you-with-a-lawsuit.

But the dyed hair, nail polish, and Calvin Kleins didn't change the way I felt. As disappointing as Julie turned out, she was still the person I'd woken up with for six years. We had adventures together. We'd eaten breakfast and played with our cats and done the laundry together. Julie may deny it, but I'd married her and that alone was cause for some loyalty. Maybe even a few kind urges.

"It sure is nice of you to come see me," I said.

Her eyes flashed with scorn. "I didn't come to be nice."

"I'm glad you're here anyway."

Julie reached into her leather daypack and fished out a pair of Vuarnet sunglasses. It was as if two layers of dirty glass weren't enough. She could only stand looking at me through polarized lenses.

"I came to tell you something," she said.

I looked at two fuzzy versions of me. Even in the reflection of her Vuarnets, I could see that my glasses were smudged.

"What did you come to tell me?"

She crossed her hands. "I'm going to take the stand Friday, and I'm going to testify as your wife, but I don't want you getting any ideas that we were ever married. I'm just doing this to make sure you're locked away for good."

"Why are you so angry with me?"

One of her hands closed into a fist. "You use people, Kelly. You lie about them, manipulate them, make them feel guilty for doing things they should have done years ago. You waste lives everywhere you go. I don't like you. You cling to the past and the past is dead."

I took off my glasses and tried to clean them on the front of my coveralls. "You remember that afternoon the lightning storm caught us up on the divide between Paintbrush Canyon and Lake Solitude?" I put on my glasses and looked through the window at Julie. Her face appeared to be set in wax. "Remember after the storm, we started over the ridge and saw a perfect double rainbow across the gorge north of the trail? Three coyote pups played on the rocks. The rainwater flowed through a pool and over that little waterfall, you remember?"

"Sounds like a Disney movie to me."

"You and I are probably the only people on earth who have seen those things all at once, Julie. We thought we were going to die, and when we didn't, God or nature or somebody showed us wonderful things we'll never see again."

I looked into her sunglasses and saw myself. "Julie, you have control over my freedom. John Hart can't hold me here, at least not for long. Doesn't six years of seeing and doing things together count for anything? Was I that awful to you?"

Julie didn't move for a long time. Her tongue pushed a bump into her lower lip. The index finger of her right hand moved up, then down. I wish I could have seen her eyes. I'd like to know if she was affected.

"I can't," Julie said.

"I wish you could."

"You're too dangerous to me, Kelly. I can't afford your freedom."

"What's that mean?"

Julie stood up. "It means I'll do whatever it takes to get you put where you can never spread vicious lies about me again."

"Even admit the lies are true?"

"You got it."

• • •

The day Julie moved out, she was very kind to me. It was a Friday in late March, a cloudy, windy day. Julie told me she wanted to leave, but if I was going to fall apart and die without her, she would stay. She said she was horribly lonely living with me.

I told her I wouldn't die. I said I wished her only happiness and good fortune. We swore a pact of eternal friendship, then she left and I was alone.

Wednesday morning they threw me back in the little room with a psychiatrist. Not Lizbeth, but a male psychiatrist—a court-appointed, John Hart–owned psychiatrist.

He was an older man, at least fifty, with shiny silver hair, a white turtleneck sweater, and a red blazer. He looked like a host at a golf tournament.

"Call me Gene," he said, indicating I should sit in the chair opposite his.

"Morning, Gene." He sat too close. I hate it when anyone, especially a man, gets too close to my body. He leaned forward when he spoke, and blinked quickly, like a small animal.

"Let's talk." Gene smiled. "Try and get to know each other."

"So talk." He smelled like Brut and Listerine. I felt reasonably negative about the whole thing.

"What's your name?" he asked.

"Kelly Palamino."

"Do you know where you are?"

"Jail."

"What day is this?"

"Wednesday."

He asked me all the stock questions, testing me for orientation and awareness. Name the first five Presidents of the United States. What's six times thirteen? Giving me an awareness test is like giving an eye test to a man who has the chart memorized. My awareness has been under question for so long, and I've taken the test so often, I could name the first five Presidents if I was comatose. Couldn't name the sixth for a million bucks.

After Gene established that I knew what was going on, he touched me on the knee with his fingertips. The man had perfect teeth. "Do you know what you did to get here?" he asked.

"I crossed John Hart."

"Are you sorry you tried to kidnap the girl?"

"No." I pulled my knee away from his fingers. "I didn't try to kidnap her."

"What were you doing in the house?"

"She invited me in. We were going to run away together."

"You know better than that, Kelly." He looked at my knee for a moment. "Tell me about your parents and early life."

"Oh, horseshit. You know I'm not insane."

"I don't know any such thing. Do you like your parents?"

"Are you going to tell the truth or suck ass to John Hart and obey orders?"

"You sound paranoid. Do you think John Hart is out to get you?"

"Yes."

"Do you think he controls everyone around you?"

"Yes."

The psychiatrist and I stared at each other. My nose itched badly, but I didn't scratch. He blinked quickly, constantly. "Have you ever been in a mental institution?" he asked.

"No."

"It's much worse than jail. Everyone treats you as if you're crazy, even though you know it's a mistake that you're there. And all the other patients tell you that they were committed by mistake, only one look at them and you know they're all total macadamias."

"Macadamias?"

"Pretty soon you don't know if it's a mistake or not. You start thinking maybe you are crazy. Then, after a while, you are."

"Yeah?"

"Oh, it's much worse than jail. Mental institutions are nightmares."

Gene let me ponder this a moment. I pondered while he blinked. He asked, "Do you believe I have the power to send you to a mental institution or save you from one?"

"I'd rather not think along those lines."

"I control your life right now, Kelly." Gene stared deep in my eyes. I thought he was trying to hypnotize me.

"John Hart wants you put away." He blinked. "But I have the power. You might persuade me to use that power to save you."

"How?"

Gene shifted his weight forward, grasping me around the wrist. "By cooperating with me."

"I've always been cooperative."

He squeezed my wrist. "You know what I mean by being cooperative, don't you, Kelly?"

"I suppose so."

He smiled, flashing his perfect teeth like pearls. "I knew I could count on you." Gene let go of my wrist, unzipped his pants, and pulled out his stiff tool.

I stared. It was shaped like an old-fashioned, six-ounce 7-Up bottle. "God," I gasped.

Gene smiled. "Suck this and you're free."

Suddenly I realized what he wanted. *"I'm no fucking queer."*

His face flushed red as his blazer. "You suck this or spend thirty years in a straitjacket."

"Ish. Jesus. Put that thing away."

"Suck it," he ordered.

"Suck it yourself." I jumped up and started banging on the door. *"Help, rape! Rape! Get me out of here."*

I screamed and yelled until a deputy came to unlock the door. By then the psychiatrist was tucked back in.

"What's the problem?" the deputy asked.

"He tried to make me bite his dick. It was awful. Awful."

"The patient became hysterical," Gene said. "He's hypohallucinative. Latent homosexuality and mother guilts."

"Oh," the deputy grunted. "Come on, Kelly."

"He *exposed* himself to me. Isn't that illegal?"

"Tell the judge. Time for you to go back in your cage."

I've never understood the homosexual inclination. I know it's legitimate. Be happy any way you can without bothering anyone, I always say. But to kiss a man on the lips? That's beyond my scope.

My freshman year at the University of Arkansas, I lived in the dorms next to two gay guys named Marc and Reed. They had been going steady or whatever the word is since they played together on an eighth-grade basketball team.

Marc and Reed were noisy. Every night around eleven, Marc started moaning and Reed started grunting. For several hours my roommate, Carl, and I sat on our beds, pretending to ignore the thrashing sounds from next door. Sometimes it went on all night.

Reed was a sadist. Marc was a screamer. He'd moan, "Reed, Reed, don't don't," or "Do, do." He cried a lot. I lay with my head under my pillow, trying to imagine exactly what was going on over there. It was sickening, yet kind of interesting. What positions were they in? How did this fit in that?

After a while, Carl lost patience. He banged on the wall with his fist. "Quiet, perverts! No fucking in the dorms!" Carl was a big, not-so-very-smart boy from West Memphis. I think he had less experience with gayety than I did. It scared him. Carl and I were very careful never to stand or sit close to each other.

Once Reed stopped me in the hall and asked, "Have you ever had a homosexual experience?"

"Not that I know of."

"Would you care to?"

"Not now."

"You shouldn't condemn things you haven't tried. It might be fun. I've got some cocaine."

"None for me, thanks."

"I've got pictures of things I bet you've never seen."

"I'd like to see them sometime, Reed, but I'm late to class."

Reed shrugged. "Give me a chance, I'll turn your life around."

"I don't want to be turned around."

Reed had white-blond hair and a pale face. I don't know what Marc saw in him.

Carl and I would have flunked out from lack of sleep, but right before Thanksgiving, Reed found an upperclassman who was even more sadistic than he was. We heard Marc's crying sessions for a week, the accusations, lamentations, pleas for one more chance—the routine of heartbreak is the same, no matter how deviant the love.

Marc dropped out of school and joined the army. Reed later said he was shipped to Vietnam.

Thank God Jimmy dozed off or I would have knocked him out with the toilet lid. The time had come to think, and no one— no one in jail, anyway—thinks well sitting down.

First I took a hot shower. Then I paced. The open part of the cell made a dogleg north around a pair of bunks, so I got eight steps west to east, then left for five steps, about face, clockwise, and back again. My hands alternated from stuffed in the coverall pockets to clasped behind my back.

Evanston was out of the question, of course. I couldn't even consider traveling so far from Colette and the Tetons. And the things Gene had said about the mental institution scared me. Besides, I still had an outstanding anal charge in that county.

However, there didn't appear to be much choice in the matter. I was incarcerated—in jail. Where my body went and didn't go seemed fairly out of my control.

Who had control? Julie, John Hart, and a judge. Julie and John wouldn't help. They hated me. That left the judge, and I don't like putting my fate in the hands of strangers, even judges.

The only alternative was escape. I stopped at the door and felt the lock. Fat chance of picking it, even with a bobby pin. All prisoners think up escape plans—it's an interesting way to pass the day—but without tools and time, what could I do? Desperate escapes are out of my league.

Luke was in a real tizzy. The actor playing his character on "All My Children" had changed. Luke lived in the soaps and an actor change, especially *his* character, created a tremendous identity crisis. It was as if I walked over to the apartment and found that the person playing Cora Ann was suddenly five years older, had black hair, and couldn't dance.

I felt sorry for the poor murderer.

He turned off the TV and lay on his bunk, flipping through one of the two thousand magazines stashed around the cell. Every now and then he gazed out the window and sighed.

"You ever thought of breaking out?" I asked.

Luke's eyes weren't focused. "What's that?"

"Busting out, cutting loose. I have some appointments and can't stay here much longer."

"You can't escape."

"I've got to. I can't stay."

Luke pointed at the door. "Three locks between here and the sheriff's department, then down through the courthouse and on the street. How long would you last in orange coveralls and slippers? It's impossible. Read magazines and watch television. You aren't leaving."

I was leaving, I just didn't know how. There's never been a problem yet that I couldn't solve by thinking. I just don't usually choose to think.

Hands in pockets, I propped my forehead against the north wall and willed the left side of my cerebrum into action. There had to be a way. Brain particles clattered. Nerve ends tingled. Nothing happened.

Escape. How to do it? How to proceed after I did it? How to contact Colette and persuade her to cooperate? None of the questions had answers. The only thing I knew for certain was that I couldn't allow myself to be shipped off to any mental institution three hundred miles from Colette. She'd be in big trouble without me.

More from boredom than any real need, I took a leak in the northeast corner toilet.

My piss said, *"Only Lizbeth can get you out of this."*
"What?"
Luke grunted, "Huh?"
"Did you hear anything?" I asked.
"I heard you say 'What?' "
"Lizbeth can do it," the piss said, then dribbled into silence.

Flushing toilets speak to me. And showers and rivers and perking coffeepots, even a waterbed if I rock it hard enough.

But never my own body fluids. At first I thought it might have been the still water in the toilet bowl, but no, it was unmistakable. My own urine had said, *"Only Lizbeth can get you out of this."*

I drank two quarts of water in the next ten minutes.

• • •

Not thinking anymore, I sat on the edge of the bunk with both hands folded in my lap, waiting for the water to work its way down the system and into the bladder. Everything was okay now. My pee had it figured out. In no time at all I would receive a urine analysis of the situation.

Maybe it wanted Lizbeth to smuggle in a pistol or a file. She could see me privately and no one else could, though that seemed a lot to ask of a therapist. She might lose her license. Maybe the piss wanted us to switch clothes. I didn't know. I'd just have to build up a good load and see what it had to say.

"Garbage." Luke threw his magazine on the floor. "That was the stupidest story I ever read."

"What's this?" I looked down at the magazine. It was a *Real Life Romance*. A girl on the cover was cowering in front of a greasy biker with a knife. She looked scared.

"What kind of sick person writes crap like that?" Luke said. "I've got enough problems without warped people laying their perversities on me. First 'All My Children,' now this."

I picked up the magazine. It was dated August 1970. "Which story?"

"The first one. Hell. My day's been ruined twice."

The first story was titled "Is My Daughter a Cow Mutilator?"

"My mother wrote this," I said.

Luke rolled over on his bunk to face me. "You're kidding."

"No. I saw it on her desk once. I wasn't allowed to read it, though."

"I don't believe you."

I shrugged. "Believe what you want. Mom wrote this story."

"No wonder you're crazy."

The title was in large black letters under a picture of a woman confronting her daughter with a swollen cow udder. "Cattle mutilations were real big back then," I said. "Most people thought the UFOs did it because no one ever found any tracks around the cow. Mom followed the Satan-worshiper theory."

Luke rolled back over in disgust. "I don't believe you. Nobody's mother is that twisted."

It was quite a long story. I read it while waiting for the water buildup. It started with a mother finding a cow udder under the daughter's bed. In the final climax, the girl is staked out on a flat rock and branded with the Satan sign. The mom fights off the cultists with a big cross while the Romantic Interest of a boyfriend hurls himself between the girl and a rattlesnake. He lives, she repents, and, like all true-confession stories from that time, the mother thanks God in the final paragraph.

"I think the story is kind of exciting," I said.

Luke growled, "You have no values."

"Look who's talking."

He turned over quickly. "What the hell does that mean?"

"Nothing." Luke was overly serious about his job. I never knew if he free-lance killed people or not, but I decided early to stay on Luke's good side.

Sometimes I wonder if Mom's short-story period had anything to do with my desire to become a writer. Wouldn't that be a kick? I never read any of her confessions, but I remember thinking how neat it was to get paid for doing something all by yourself.

I never told Mom that I write books. I was afraid she might want to read one. She might decide I'm a bad writer and try making me face reality. She's always after me to face reality, but I don't see how it's possible to do that and write a novel at the same time.

Not that launching a modern dance career at fifty-two is facing reality.

I let Julie read the first three westerns, but she thought they were low quality. She refused to read the fourth book—the one I wrote the last months before she left. Julie said my writing was shallow and horrible. She said I was going to be a drunk and a dishwasher all my life, and the novelist act was just pretension. She said I was a failure and I should accept it gracefully.

The fourth book isn't very good. An agent told me my westerns were not commercial enough, so, in a huff, I wrote the most commercial outline in history. A Mafia bagman returns home one night and finds his girlfriend in bed with another man. He kills the other man, but when they turn on the light, the bagman discovers he has murdered the President of the United States.

The book has a presidential assassination, a Mafia ripoff, two sex scenes, a professional football player, and a thinly disguised Kennedy character, all in the first four pages.

The agent loved it. At his insistence, I finished the book. Somewhere in there, the President's head explodes in a Litton microwave oven. It climaxes at the Super Bowl at halftime, when the Secret Service pulls a fake assassination.

The flaw was that I don't know anything about presidents, mafiosi, Washington, D.C., or anything else in the book. The Vice-President talks like an Idaho potato farmer and the First Lady comes off like a bartender at the Cowboy. It is a terrible book, worthy of Julie's scorn.

I only keep it around to impress waitresses with what a deep, sensitive young novelist I am. Us tortured souls need comfort.

My career goal isn't the Nobel Prize or Pulitzer Prize or any other Prize. It isn't even being the last guest with only three minutes until we have to leave on "The Tonight Show," on a night when Johnny Carson is host. What I'd really like is to write a book that matters so much that someday Willie Nelson shows up at the door and asks me to sign his guitar.

The key, I decided, in the message from my bladder, was the wording. Throughout the long night I drank and dribbled, but all the piss ever said was, *"Only Lizbeth can get you out of this,"* and occasionally, *"Lizbeth can do it."*

Get you out seemed important. She didn't necessarily have to help me escape. All I needed was assistance in getting out of the jail. Around dawn, the master plan took shape. It was daring and gutsy. It required timing and self-inflicted pain. The plan was riddled with holes, and only a lovesick genius fool would attempt such a death scheme. I had two of the important traits and they were strong enough to make up for the third.

One of the major holes filled itself the next day during visiting hours. Cora Ann appeared.

After all those years around the apartments, I guess we'd gotten used to seeing each other every day, because when the deputy led me to the glass partition and I looked through at Cora Ann, I was so happy I nearly cried. I felt tremendous relief, as if my lost family had come to take away the solitude.

All I could say was, "Hi."

Cora Ann half-smiled. "Well, you finally made it."

"You always said this would happen someday." Cora Ann appeared perkier than I recalled, tanner. Our split-up certainly hadn't affected her health.

"How did you find out where I was?" I asked.

She stared at me intently, as if she could tell more by how I looked than what I said. "You made this week's paper. I saw the story at breakfast."

"Was there a picture?"

"No, just the story. Did you really try to kidnap her, Kelly?"

"Of course not." Quickly I sketched out the details of my bust.

"She turned you in," Cora Ann said.

"She didn't mean to."

"How could she have not meant to?"

That was an interesting question. I hadn't quite worked out

an answer yet, so I didn't care to get into it with Cora Ann. "You look healthy," I said.

"I've been in the sun a lot—kayaking, climbing. I'm taking up windsurfing."

"How's Alice?"

"Mean, spoiled, and crabby as ever. I don't understand what you see in that cat, Kelly."

"She's family." We sat still, not looking in each other's eyes. Cora Ann wore a blue T-shirt that said CLIMB A ROCK across the front. She had dangly silver earrings.

Cora Ann sighed. "I'm sorry this happened, Kelly."

"It's okay."

"It is not okay. Every time I think about that rich bitch I get so mad I could spit."

"She's not so bad."

"She is too."

"It wasn't her fault."

Cora Ann's hands doubled into fists. "Look what she's done to you. She encourages you just enough and strings you along to stroke her injured ego. She uses you, Kelly. Don't you hate her?"

"I can't hate Colette."

"If you won't, I'll hate her enough for both of us." Cora Ann's mouth drew into a line.

It was my turn to sigh. "I wish you liked her more, Cora Ann. Maybe after you get to know her better."

"You're hopeless, Kelly. I can't even feel sorry for you anymore."

This surprised me. "Why would you feel sorry for me?"

Cora Ann didn't answer the question. "Are they treating you okay?" she asked.

"Fine, except they won't let me leave."

"Is there anything I can do for you?"

"As a matter of fact, there is."

For the first time, Cora Ann smiled. I don't know why. "Shoot," she smiled.

"You can take a message to Colette."

The smile evaporated. "No."

"What?"

"No, Kelly. I won't do it."

I went ahead on faith. "Tell Colette to saddle two horses and meet me at the cottonwood behind her house at one o'clock tomorrow afternoon."

"Kelly."

"Tell her timing is important, and she should bring her toothbrush. She'll know what that means."

"Kelly, she betrayed you. Nothing's changed."

"Just give her the message, Cora Ann."

"No."

Through the glass, I stared at her hard. "Please. As a friend. Trust me, Cora Ann. I know what I'm doing."

"How could you?"

"I'm a realist. It's a long shot, but if I don't try once more I'll be locked away for life and never know if she cares. I need one last chance, Cora Ann."

"No."

I was silent.

"Just how do you plan to arrive at the Hart Ranch tomorrow at one?" she asked.

"I'll be there. Give Colette the message."

"No, I won't do it."

That night I watched an Atlanta Braves baseball game with Luke and Jimmy. The Dodgers beat them 8-2 on a six-hitter by a Mexican rookie named Valenzuela. Taggart Creek would be pleased.

"Give me that letter to your wife," I said to Jimmy.

"Why?" He was cross because he'd rooted for Atlanta. Nothing was going right in Jimmy's life.

"What's the address?"

"Idaho Falls, she's staying there with her darling sister who's a bitch."

I felt generous since I was going to escape and he had to stay. "I'll deliver the letter by hand and tell her I'm not leaving until she reads it. Maybe she'll forgive you."

Luke leered at me through Lark smoke. "You planning to be in Idaho Falls soon?"

"I might stop by." I wasn't feeling generous toward Luke. He'd said my mother was warped.

Jimmy fished around under the bed and handed me the letter without a question. "Tell her I love her or something," he said.

"Or something." I put the letter in my front coverall pocket and leaned back to stare at the ceiling. It was the same dull green as the walls.

The beauty of my plan, the only thing about it that made me dream it might work, was that everyone involved had to act completely out of character. Cora Ann had to give a message to Colette—a thing she had sworn she would never do; Lizbeth had to help me bust out of jail—ethically an outrageous favor to ask of a psychiatrist; and Colette had to meet me and run away with me—a task she'd failed once before.

There's a law of nature, Darwin's Black Hole Theory, I believe, that states that the impossible is much more likely to happen than the highly improbable. God's way of keeping us on our toes.

14

The sanity hearing was as stiff and choreographed as a Lawrence Welk dance routine. I had no more chance than a black rapist with an all-white jury.

My lawyer and I sat on the right. Julie, John Hart, and three big-city, snappy-dresser lawyers sat on the left. Lizbeth and Gene were behind me, and the deputy with the sideburns stood back by the door.

They hadn't let me change out of the coveralls. It was embarrassing being the only one dressed down for the occasion. Julie wouldn't look at me, but John Hart stared and growled—growled like a damn bear. I couldn't believe it.

The judge walked in and we all stood up. I'd expected an old man—gray hair, strong chin, will of iron. This judge wasn't even forty years old. He could have been my brother. Tanned, blond, he looked like a fucking surfer.

The kid judge slapped a gavel, announced what was going on—mental incompetency complaint against Kelly Palamino—and the preplanned show rolled on. Those city lawyers knew their stuff. Right from the opening statement they made me out as a dangerously twisted deviate, baby snatcher, and political assassin—a Rocky Mountain Jack the Ripper, Lee Harvey Oswald, and Charles Manson packed into one vicious little body.

They put Lizbeth on first to get her out of the way. She brushed close to me as she walked to the stand. Then, as she talked, Lizbeth looked at me kindly. She knew I was screwed.

Her testimony went about the way I expected: depressive neurosis, addictive personality; the suicide attempt two years ago was an isolated incident, not likely to be repeated.

The hotshot city-slicker lawyer leaned against the stand and leered at me. "Are you aware that Mr. Palamino talks to water?"

Lizbeth shifted in her seat. "Kelly listens to the water talk. He doesn't talk to it."

"*Listens* is different from *talks to*?"

"I suppose."

"But he does hear words. He receives messages from the water."

"Yes."

"Would you describe this as a psychotic episode?"

"Yes."

"But you do not diagnose Mr. Palamino as psychotic?"

"No."

"He has psychotic episodes, but he is not psychotic."

"That is correct."

"Miss Morley, if you treated a patient for several years and grew too close, became too involved with that patient to be objective, would you admit it to this court?"

"Yes."

"No further questions."

Julie must have been wearing a lot of makeup because she glowed nicely, almost primly. Her blond hair was piled on top of her head, which made her seem taller than ever. With her hair up, Julie's long neck and high cheekbones gave her a fancy woman look, the exact opposite of me in wrinkled orange coveralls that hung down in the butt. It was hard to conceive of a lie coming out of that sweet mouth.

"How long were you with Mr. Palamino?" the lawyer asked.

"Six years that we lived together, plus two since we separated."

I blew her a kiss.

"You mean you never divorced?"

"No."

"During your time with Mr. Palamino, did he ever exhibit any signs of antisocial or paranoid behavior?"

"He thought the phone was bugged." It was. "He thought his mother spied on us through a telescope." She did. "At one time he claimed the editors of *Rolling Stone* magazine were out to get him. He sent them a number of threatening letters." That was an exaggeration. I sent one letter.

"Did Mr. Palamino ever threaten anyone else?"

"Himself. He wrote hundreds of suicide notes. They were all over the house. And one period when we were traveling he decided the Kentucky Fried Chicken had saltpeter in it. He burned down all the Kentucky Fried Chicken billboards in South Texas."

I jumped up. "That's a lie. Two. I burned down two billboards, and according to *Esquire*, one of the secret ingredients is saltpeter."

The judge banged his gavel and shouted, "Sit down."

Robin pulled at my arm. "Shut up, Kelly. You'll only make it worse."

"But it's a lie. *Esquire* knows."

Julie kept going. "I was terrified. I tried to stick by Kelly, but his paranoia and senseless rages got so bad I couldn't stand it anymore. I had to leave."

I swear to God, tears formed in Julie's eyes. She had makeup, a long neck, and tears. Even I believed her. It's a wonder the judge didn't have me hanged on the spot.

Robin turned to me. "I decided to take you up on your offer."

"Go for it."

I don't know why I call John Hart's lawyers city slickers just because they were dressed for the cover of *GQ*. Robin wore the same three-piece costume—only he came off more like a teenager pretending to be legitimate. He must have been nervous about his first cross-examination. His voice quavered as he spoke.

"Mrs. Palamino—your name is Mrs. Palamino, isn't it?"

"I've kept my maiden name, Julie Deere."

"You married Mr. Palamino, but kept the name Deere?"

"Lots of women do that now."

"In your testimony, Mrs. Palamino, you said that you and Kelly never obtained a divorce."

"That's right."

"You didn't say the two of you ever married each other."

Julie stared at Robin, then at me.

"Are you married to Kelly Palamino?"

Julie gave me a look of intense hatred.

"I asked, are you married to Kelly Palamino?"

Julie nodded.

"I didn't hear you, Mrs. Palamino, or is it Miss Deere?"

"Yes."

"Yes, what?"

"Yes, I'm married to Kelly Palamino."

I applauded. The judge banged his gavel. One of Hart's lawyers leaped to his feet and objected. He called Robin's questions "immaterial."

Robin spoke to the surfer. "These questions are quite material, Your Honor. This woman signed a complaint claiming she is my client's legal wife. I have a right to establish whether or not she is indeed his legal wife."

I liked the way he emphasized *indeed*. Sounded like a pubescent Perry Mason. The surfer overruled the objection. Julie tossed back her head and gave Robin a look of superior contempt—the nasty kind of contempt that can only be pulled off by a tall, severe blond with her hair in a bun.

"Of course I'm Kelly's legal wife."

"Where were the two of you married?"

"Victoria, Texas."

I hooted.

"On what date?"

"June 16, 1972."

I laughed aloud. John Hart growled at me again.

Robin leaned an immaculate hand on the witness stand. "Can you prove that you and Kelly are married?"

Julie turned her ice-cold eyes from Robin to me. I gave her my cutest smile.

"Yes," she said.

"How?"

Julie signaled one of Hart's lawyers, who brought her a stiff sheet of paper. "Here." Julie handed the paper to the judge, who read it and handed it to Robin.

Robin grinned, brought it over to me, and said, "I can look my new baby in the eye."

It was a marriage license, dated June 16, 1972, Victoria County, Texas, issued to Kelly Palamino and Julie Deere. It was stamped with the seal of Texas.

She'd carried it around all these years. I looked at her, glaring down from the stand. This Julie really was the same woman who married me and laughed and rolled with me in a Houston motel room on our honeymoon.

"I'm not crazy after all," I said to her.

"Yes, you are."

I can't be certain, but I'm almost sure, that the last time Julie and I made love, the day before she left me, we both simultaneously faked orgasms. I know I did.

• • •

The rest of the testimony was just dirt on the grave. John Hart told about my hang-gliding escapade and breaking into his son's house. He claimed I threatened him in the bank that day. He said he had received several abusive anonymous phone calls that he was sure were from me, and he accused me of throwing a chunk of concrete through the bank door. John said he was afraid to go out at night for fear I might "try something."

Gene came up next. Silently I asked God to give Gene a dose of colon cancer. After listing an armload of qualifications, the gay shrink called me a "paranoid schizophrenic, a second-degree psychotic, a latent homosexual, and an obsessive violent." He said I was just the type to "climb a tower with a rifle and start plugging strangers."

The judge seemed spellbound by every word. I imagined that Gene and the surfer were lovers who would slip off to a small café during the lunch break and hold hands under the table while staring into each other's eyes and sipping zinfandel wine. It made a nauseating fantasy.

Robin didn't cross-examine either witness. He sat next to me, giving no indication that he heard what was being said. Leaning his chin on one hand, he drew several models of what appeared to be a crib on a yellow lined notebook.

When it came time for our defense, I leaned over and whispered, "Put me on the stand."

He looked up from his drawing. "I've already done what you asked. I'm absolved, remember."

"Just get me up there. You don't have to say a word."

Robin's eyebrows drew together, forming a little lump at the top of his nose. "I don't want John Hart mad at me."

"John Hart won't get mad at you."

He studied me a moment, then stood up. "I call Kelly Palamino to the stand."

• • • •

Left hand on the King James [v S m i l]
modified Heil Hitler, I repeated
wooden chair, facing everyone but the judge. ...athing deeply,
I gazed out at my gathered enemies.

Julie had the tan kid-judge convinced I was a mass murderer
searching for a mass. Nothing I said would make any difference,
so I had nothing to lose. A man with nothing to lose is a dangerous man.

Turning to the judge, I said, "I watched the Broken Hart
Ranch for over two weeks, and on three separate occasions I
saw John Hart have sex with a hog."

In unison, practically in harmony, the three lawyers shouted,
"I object." John Hart was up, screaming, "I'll kill you, you
punk."

I pointed a finger at him. "Deny it, pigfucker."

I turned back to the judge. "You want paranoid psychosis,
I'll give you paranoid psychosis. John Hart wants to crucify me.
He owns those lawyers, he owns that psychiatrist, he owns that
deputy sheriff back there, and he owns you."

As I said "he owns you," I stood up, reached across the rail,
and thumped the judge on the chest. *Thump.*

The judge would have been less surprised had I pulled a knife
and slit his throat. Prisoners don't thump judges, at least not in
Wyoming.

Many hands grabbed me and pulled me out of the witness
stand. John Hart was bitter—vicious. Robin, my own lawyer,
struck me in the back of the head. The surfer judge banged his
gavel and shouted and generally tried to reassert his authority,
but once a man has been thumped, there isn't much he can do
to reclaim his dignity.

"Court is adjourned for lunch," he shouted. "I will dispose
of the prisoner at two o'clock. Take him back to his cell."

I didn't like the way he said *dispose.*

• • •

The deputy treated me roughly on the way back to Cell Two. He opened the door, shoved me in, and slammed the door behind me.

"What happened?" Luke asked.

I ran across the cell, climbed on the bars in front of the window, and screamed—I mean I really screamed.

"*I want my psychiatrist.*"

Then I smashed my head against the bars. There is a spot just above the hairline that I found accidentally one summer when I dived into an air conditioner. If you hit that spot, cut it, the head will gush blood like a stuck pig. It's not too painful. When I hit the air conditioner, I didn't even know I was hurt until the blood covered my glasses and I couldn't see.

The first smash on the bars wasn't hard enough—not convincing. The second smash, I almost knocked myself out.

"*Lizbeth,*" I howled. *Bang*, I hit the spot. Blood sprayed out onto the bars and the window beyond.

Luke ran to the door and pounded with his fist. Jimmy didn't move.

"*Lizbeth!*" I smashed myself again, then fell back onto the floor, streaming blood.

The cell door swung open and people crowded in. First the deputy. He pushed past Luke and knelt over me. "Oh my God."

"*Where's my psychiatrist?*" I shouted, kicking the deputy in the face. He fell back. I writhed around, wishing I had some Alka-Seltzers in my mouth to make foam.

Lizbeth shoved her way through the crowd, manhandling the deputy out of the way. Leaning over, she held my face firmly between her hands. Lizbeth bent low and said quietly, "You're faking, Kelly."

I flailed around and screamed.

"You didn't even break your glasses," she whispered. "Suicidal face-smashers break their glasses."

"Get me out of here," I mumbled. No one heard except maybe Jimmy. I yelled, *"Mama, let me die."*

"I don't know what you're up to," Lizbeth said quietly. She turned to the deputy. "Call an ambulance." She swung back to me. "It's all right, Kelly," she said for all to hear. "We'll take care of you."

"Let me die, I want to die."

Lizbeth held my head in her lap and we waited. Someone handed her a bandanna which she pressed against my spurting gash.

By then, a good-sized crowd had formed at the cell door—secretaries, receptionists, off-duty cops. I heard Julie's voice asking, "What happened?"

"He tried to kill himself," a secretary answered.

"What, again?"

In the confusion, Luke tried to sneak out and got caught.

The ambulance finally arrived and two orderlies loaded me onto a stretcher. I moaned and groaned and bled and begged for morphine.

Jimmy's face appeared before me. He smiled for the first time since I'd come to the cell. "Tell her I love her," he said.

"What's that mean?" Lizbeth asked.

I screamed and writhed.

They carried me out of the jail and down the stairs. People lined both sides of the halls, peering at me as we passed. I was a bloody float in a narrow parade.

The orderlies threw me in the back of the ambulance. As one of them ran around to the driver's door, Lizbeth and the deputy jumped in after me. Lights flashing, siren howling, we took off for the hospital.

Moaning and mumbling, I opened my eyes to assess the situation. It was one of those big van ambulances where the stretcher is strapped to the wall directly behind the driver and everyone can stand up or sit down or whatever they want. Lizbeth sat next to my head, then the deputy, then the orderly down at my feet. The driver couldn't see me.

Raising one slippered foot, I kicked the orderly in the stomach. I screamed. I wailed and hollered. My feet kicked like a two-year-old having a tantrum. Only my hands didn't move.

The deputy lunged for my legs, holding them down with both arms. "Hold the cocksucker still!" he shouted at the orderly.

The next step was simple. Anyone could have done it. I reached up and slipped the deputy's revolver out of its holster. Pointing it at his left ear, I said, "Stick 'em up, honky."

He stuck 'em up.

The orderly and Lizbeth froze.

"Stop this ambulance," I shouted, but because of the siren or his concentration on traffic, the driver didn't hear me. I fired a bullet through the windshield.

"Stop this fucking ambulance."

He pulled over to the curb and stopped. The revolver made a lot of noise going off. I think it scared us all, because no one moved for a moment.

"Cut the siren."

The driver cut the siren.

"Now turn around and head back the way we came."

"They're going to wonder what happened if we don't get to the hospital soon," the orderly said. He looked real pale. The deputy didn't appear to be breathing.

"It'll take a few minutes for anyone to get suspicious," I said. "Turn this thing around and drive to the Broken Hart Ranch."

Lizbeth chose that moment to turn brave on me. Holding out her right hand, she said, "Give me the gun, Kelly."

I looked at her hand. This was an unexpected twist. "I'll shoot you."

"Kelly, I've listened to you for hundreds of hours of therapy.

I've seen your Rorschach, MMPI, thematic apperception profile, and house-tree-person results. You are incapable of killing anyone."

"Want to bet?"

"Besides, you'd collapse if you had to go three weeks without seeing me."

"You also know I don't plan that far ahead."

She hesitated a second, then moved her hand closer to the revolver. "Give me the gun, Kelly. You're not going to shoot anybody."

"Would you stake your professional reputation on that?"

"Yes."

Firmly, with my left hand, I cocked the hammer, CLICK-CLICK. "Would you stake your life?"

Lizbeth faltered. She looked down at the revolver, then back at me. "No, I guess not."

All together, the driver, the orderly, and the deputy exhaled. Some people will bluff an open gun barrel, but no one can stand up to a firm cock.

"Let's go," I said.

Fourth of July weekend in Jackson Hole is like a Rocky Mountain Mardi Gras. Three-fourths of Utah invades the valley to drink themselves sloppy. Motorcycle gangs hold conventions. Cowboys vomit and pass out on the streets. Two hundred thousand tourists pass through the center of town.

Everyone in the ambulance was tense, and creeping through the throngs at four miles an hour did not help.

"Hell," I said. "Turn on the siren and blast through the crowd."

We blasted—almost ran down a few slow ones—but we made it past the town square and onto the highway toward the Broken Hart. Once in the clear, I had him leave the lights and siren on. That risked picking up a police escort, but I was in a hurry and someone at the sheriff's office or the hospital would figure things out soon anyway.

The deputy seemed to be coming back to life. I half expected him to try something. I mean, he didn't have a lot to lose himself. Disarmament by a delirious prisoner would not sit well on his record.

Risking a look out the window, I saw the Tetons standing off in the north. It would be nice to get back in them. Jail was no place for a free spirit like me. So far, everything had worked. Lizbeth had come through. Now, if Cora Ann delivered the message and if Colette bought it . . . a lot of ifs for a guy in a funny orange suit with blood-matted hair and a loaded revolver.

Nothing to do but relax and see who was waiting at the Broken Hart. My three hostages watched me closely, not talking, but paying strict attention to every move. The power was neat. Testing the weight of the revolver in my hand, I decided to get one of my own.

Lights flashing, siren screaming, we wailed under the front gate of the ranch and up the drive past the big house, grinding to a halt in front of the bunkhouse.

Colette stood next to the cottonwood tree, holding the reins of two saddled horses.

Danny stood beside her.

I jerked open the back doors of the ambulance and sprinted across the lawn to Colette. "Let's go," I said.

Danny held one of Colette's hands. He was pleading. "I love you, Colette. I can't live without you. Please don't leave me."

Colette looked at him sadly. "I don't know."

I took the reins of one horse—not Dixie, the other one—and sprang on his back. Far down the road, toward town, I heard approaching sirens.

"Let's go," I said.

Colette looked from Danny to me and back to Danny. I pulled the reins tight, backing the horse up two steps.

"Colette," I said, "choose your life."

Colette lifted her hand and touched Danny's cheek. "I'm sorry." With a single flowing motion, she mounted Dixie.

We whirled the horses and galloped up the jeep trail next to the creek. Behind us, the sirens pulled into the ranch drive.

I glanced at Colette beside me. Her beautiful hair bounced and floated. Her eyes shone with excitement and life as she concentrated on running Dixie up the hill.

On my other side, the creek broke into the "Hallelujah Chorus" from Handel's *Messiah*. "*Hallelujah! Hallelujah!*"

"Do you hear that?" I shouted at Colette.

She leaned toward me and shouted back, "The creek is singing the 'Hallelujah Chorus' from Handel's *Messiah*."

Raising my right fist high, I stood in the stirrups and howled, "*Yee-haw.*"

I had my soulmate at last.

About the Author

Tim Sandlin is the author of *Sex and Sunsets,*
Western Swing, and the GroVont trilogy—*Skipped Parts, Sor-*
row Floats, and *Social Blunders*—as well as a book of columns
entitled *The Pyms: Unauthorized Tales of Jackson Hole.* Mr.
Sandlin has worked as an elk skinner, dishwasher, neighborhood ice cream man, and cook in the Lame Duck Chinese
restaurant. He continues to live with his family in Jackson Hole,
Wyoming.